# PREDATOR
## And
### PREY

## THE DESERT SAGA

### By Donna Krutka

**Illustrations by Andrew Ellingson**

Donna Krutka

## PROLOGUE

The blowing wind ripped across the face of the granite boulder, carving fine markings onto the surface. Despite the wind's intensity, the sun's heat beat down on the parched land. The coyotes stood together, low growls emerging in a symphony of opposition.

The bobcat stared back, and his eyes looked away to find the escape path. The prairie dog dove into his burrow to thwart the claws of the diving red-tailed hawk. The mountain lion ignored them. Instead, he marked the western rattler coiled under the prickly pear cacti. He looked up in time to see the young girl pass by with a basket of corn tightly held at her waist.

The land's harshness confronts survival. Predators search for prey. Prey must outsmart predators. Finally, to ensure species' survival, pairs must mate. All of this defines the desert, and these are its stories.

The Desert Saga

# THE BOSS

# Part One

## Chapter One

The midday sun made the air hot and dusty. Little wind was causing stuffiness to hang over the three as they trekked along their carefully picked pathway. Rafe grabbed Cache by the neck and threw him onto the ground. Cache winced and jumped back up, looking comically fierce for the smaller brother. He got down on all fours in an attack stance while Rafe again grabbed Cache's hindquarters and spun him around.

"Rafe," Jet called out sternly. "You must be careful playing with your smaller brother. You and Cache are just playing now, but there will come a time when the play turns violent, and you could hurt your brother!"

Rafe began licking his little brother all over his matted fur. Then he nudged him from the side.

"I could never hurt Cache, Mom. He is my best friend." Again, Rafe bit down teasingly on Cache's ear. "You don't let us be around other coyotes, so I only have my little brother to pick on. But I would never hurt him."

Rafe trotted along and turned to look at his brother. His yellow eyes squinted as he remembered when he grabbed Cache's ear a few days ago.

"Ouch, that hurts, Rafe. You are going to rip my ear off." Cache had cried.

Rafe had jumped back away from Cache and gasped in horror. His heart pounded, and his mouth became dry.

"Gosh, Cache, I'm sorry." Rafe had said, rubbing and licking Cache's ear. "I didn't mean to hurt you." Cache rubbed his ear on the ground, trying to stop the sting. Rafe shook his head, unsure where the instinct to hurt Cache came from.

Cache brought Rafe's attention back to the present as he body-slammed Rafe in triumph, catching his brother off guard. Rafe's unsettled feeling washed away, and the two tumbled down the side of a hill howling uncontrollably.

Jet called to the two pups, and they jumped up the hill to follow behind their mom. The air was warm, yet Jet's fur shivered in the sunlight. Her pace slowed, then she hesitated, deciding to continue her discourse.

"It is part of your nature to fight violently among yourselves," she began slowly. "The Coyotes of the East, where I come from, start playfully fighting among themselves. Later the conflicts become real, and the weaker of the clan is cast out or relegated to a lesser position." Jet's pace picked up as she continued.

"What's cast out mean, Mother?" Cache asked, his paws crunching rocks on the ground as he tried to catch up to his mother.

"It means sent away," answered Rafe, leaping over a bush filled with sharp spiky branches. "Come on, Cache, follow me and jump. Bet you can't bet you can't!" sneering as he watched Cache pass far away from the bush.

"All the males want to be the number one Coyote," Jet continued.

"Like me," Rafe quickly blurted out, this time vaulting high onto a rounded boulder. He cocked his head into the air and howled. Cache looked up at his brother. Rafe's formidable body cast a large shadow onto the ground, resembling a blackened Live Oak Tree. The dark shadow dissipated as Rafe slid down the side of the granite outcropping and pranced alongside his mother, occasionally resting his oversized head on hers, sniffing the air with his prominent snout.

"Yes, Rafe, like you." She resumed trotting at the normal pace. "The western coyote does not have playful behavior. When they start to brawl with other family members, they sometimes fight to the death."

# The Desert Saga

Cache gasped and suddenly halted. He could feel his breathing quicken and his eyes squinting. "I'm not like Rafe, mother. I can't fight. What am I going to do?" Cache dropped his head and looked straight down to the ground.

"I'll make sure you are not kicked out, Cache." Rafe pushed Cache forward with his snout making him lose his balance. "I will protect you, won't I, Mom? I will protect him!"

Jet licked the black stripe on her smallest son's reddish-brown coat. The stripe coursed from his head to his tail, as hers did. She lifted his downcast eyes and spoke with authority.

"You're very clever, Cache. You'll use your wits which will get you much farther than just using your muscles. Rafe will be able to fight his way out of anything. But you, my little pup, will think your way out of everything. Now straighten your back, look straight ahead, and follow your brother's strong muscular body. He will be by your side, leading you on this journey."

The three trotted through soft wilderness grasses that opened into vast plains of purple and yellow-blossomed plants. Cache bounded over hills and canyons, never needing to stop. Rafe sprinted ahead of the other two, then fell into a heap of bushes gasping for breath and unable to get his body to move any further. He loved running fast, but his body could not match Cache's endurance. Jet remained steady in her pace, lifting her head to smell the air for danger. She abruptly stopped if she perceived a predator, and so did her pups. If she traveled as usual, the pups naively played with each other as if the three were invincible.

They had passed under two moon cycles when Jet peered upward at the overhead sun. She scanned the surrounding terrain to see short stubby trees with black bark and spiky green leaves. The predominant plants in the area appeared hostile and non-protective. She slowed her pace and brought her pups closer to her.

"We have crossed into what is known as the desert. Can you see that shade is sparse? The days will be hotter, and we must find good shelter to keep cool."

Rafe ran ahead, and Jet chased after him, forcefully pulling on Rafe's tail and growled. He yelped as he skidded to a stop. "Stop jumping over the cholla cactus, Rafe. If you land in one, it will take us hours to get the stickers out of your thick gray fur coat."

"Oh, Mom," he fired back at her. "I got this!" he said, springing over a sizeable prickly pear cactus barely missing the top of it by inches.

"Rafe, did you hear what Mom said," Cache yelled at his brother, tripping over a rock that blazed the trail where he was trotting.

"You howl like a ferret!" Rafe taunted back at Cache as he ran off, trying to grab a yellow butterfly in his snapping jaw.

The sun settled, layering a brilliant orange glow on the horizon, as the rush of cold air precipitated a drop in temperature. Jet herded her two pups toward a bushy alcove. Cache plopped onto the ground, and Rafe moved as close as possible to blanket his brother's shivering body.

"We must eat. I will be back soon," billows of steam came from Jet's mouth as she spoke.

The two pups peered out from under thick bushy brambles. A dried prairie bush crunched under Jet's paws as she quickened away to look for prey. Both Rafe and Cache began to drift off to sleep when a scent of dried animal blood and sweaty animal fur filtered into the small coyotes' nostrils. Rafe's eyes widened as he stared at Cache, both hearing sounds of multiple footfalls surrounding them. Their eyes squinted, and a noisy pack of coyotes came into view. The animal at the front of the group trotted with his head high, looking from side to side. A female, next in line, also held her head high, sniffing the air. The coyotes that followed cackled and growled, hurrying to stay up with their leader. There were eight in total, Cache counted. He saw that the female was smaller than his mother. The coloring of the group was gray and black, much like Rafe's fur color. Rafe crept ahead of Cache and spat on the ground.

"That's the alpha and his mate in the front," Rafe snarled. "Jet could overpower them both, I am certain. I would never follow those two the way the others are following." Rafe spat on the ground again.

The group passed. An owl hooted, causing both pups to startle in unison. Cache moved closer to Rafe. A foul smell hit their nose.

"What is that smell?" Cache asked Rafe.

"Ugh, I don't know!" He took his paw and tried to block the smell from his nostril.

A medium-sized pig-like hoofed squadron of animals began to forage close by. Large straight tusks emerged from the jaw and gnawed on the top of a collection of prickly pear cacti right in front of Rafe and Cache.

"They are looking right at us," Cache whispered to Rafe. "How come they are not running away or charging? It's like they can't see us."

"I know," mumbled Rafe. He stared into the eyes of one of the animals who kept eating. The smaller pups rubbed against each other as if polishing the other's thick, greasy outside lining. The foul smell again permeated the air, and the coyotes gasped. The larger animal moved closer to the pups and stopped chewing abruptly. His pointed muzzle turned in their direction. Thick hair immediately puffed up from his body, and he turned and ran as fast as possible, the others following close behind.

"I think they were a skunk pig. Mom told us about them. She called them a Javelina." Again, they both rubbed their snouts into the ground to offset the horrible smell.

At first light, the brittlebush crunched, and the brambles parted. A freshly killed piece of meat plopped on the ground before the pups. Jet moved slowly into the protected space and settled next to the pups, her eyes unable to stay open as she breathed slow and deep, draping her head over her muddied paws.

"Today we talk about hunting pack rats," she said and fell asleep in front of her pups.

Rested, Jet was eager to teach her pups more about different prey and led her two offspring out to a desert wash. She smelled the recent droppings that lay in their pathway. She nudged the two pups forward and indicated for them to do likewise. Cache scrunched his nose to get the scent and raised his head triumphantly.

"I recognize that scent. I've smelled it before." He stuck out his chest, prancing about, eyes glued on his mother's.

Rafe smashed a spider with his paw. He yawned and rolled over on his back.

"Rafe, do you recognize the scent?"

"Yes, of course, Mother. I chased the little, long-tailed furry creatures into the desert and found their collection of sticks and dried cacti. I know their scent."

"Now, you must show your brother how to chase and capture the pack rat. You work together. We never kill just to kill. And we never kill more than we can eat. That is the law of the Coyote. But we must eat." Her voice was soft and assertive.

Warm, cloudless days followed, with lessons of hunting rabbits, prairie dogs, and snakes. Rafe smelled a scent and took off, Cache breathing hard to keep up. The two watched as their mother often looked behind her, her eyes wary. She might grimace a warning to be silent or lower onto her belly to creep along the desert floor. Cache and Rafe followed, trying to mimic her movements. Their eyes met, on one occasion, blinking and widening. They both smelled a familiar scent of sweaty, dank fur and heard multiple footfalls. It was another pack of coyotes. Cache stiffened, and Rafe hissed. Jet again hurled them a warning of silence through her stern countenance. The three crouched motionless until Jet finally rose from the ground, moved out into the open, and continued on her way. Rafe and Cache bolted forward to catch up.

"Coyotes," she said to her pups. "We hide from coyotes until we are in the West."

The brothers glanced at each other, puzzling over her words.

"We will stay in this area for a few days to hunt and rest." Her eyes spotted a large outcropping further to the West.

"Up ahead," Jet declared, scanning in the distance, "a cluster of large boulders may provide a good shelter. We can check up ahead."

When she declared what Rafe decided was a mission, he took off, playfully jumping over thick low-lying bushes, exhibiting his athletic prowess. Cache followed in quick pursuit, both animals howling. They had been frightfully tethered to their mother's side, and for some reason, they took their mother's announcement to mean they oversaw finding shelter. They ran with reckless abandon, not paying any attention to the smells or sights surrounding them. Reaching the boulders first, Rafe leaped over the top of the outcropping and disappeared from Cache's site.

"Wait, Rafe. Wait for me.!" Cache yelled at Rafe.

A terrorizing howl reached Cache's ears. He momentarily paused, then flung his body toward the top of the rocks to peer down. His brother was lying on his side, a large group of nesting pit vipers slithering over his thick fur. Rafe whimpered and moaned in agony as the snakes hissed and rattled, weaving their way around his neck and body. There must have been ten vipers, all sinking fangs into Rafe's limp body.

Jet shot to the pinnacle of the outcropping to stand next to Cache. A terrified howl released from her throat as she walked back and forth on top of the outcropping, assessing what she could do. She called to Rafe, and as he answered, his voice was weak and muted. She saw one of the snakes starting to move away from Rafe, and she instinctively jumped down and stomped on his head with both forepaws, issuing a mighty blow, momentarily impeding the predator's senses. The commotion distracted the other snakes, so they, too, began to move away from the wounded Coyote. Cache stood on the edge of the outcropping, motionless.

His mother moved carefully to Rafe's side, licking his nostrils clear of the mud and blood that were present. His eyes were shut but slowly opened as he sensed the presence of his mother.

"I feel cold, Mother," he whispered.

"Shh, don't talk, Rafe. You must save your strength." Tears were forming in her eyes.

"I can't see you very well," he said. "Why can't I see you, Mother?" His breath was shallow. Reddish purple discoloration formed around his neck and paws. His coat was matted with goo and dirt.

"What's happening to me?" He called out.

Cache picked up one paw to move it forward, but it stuck to the top of the outcropping as if buried in sap pouring from an injured tree, preventing him from jumping to where Rafe lay.

"What's happening, Mother?" Cache called out from above. "Is he going to be all right? What is happening?"

Jet sat silently next to her son. She nudged him gently to see if he could get up. There was no response. Rafe closed his eyes. His breathing slowly receded, and he lay motionless. The adrenaline began to retreat from

Cache's body, and he vaulted to where Rafe lay. He moved close to his mother, his eyes filled with panic and horror. The three lay together for a long time as the sun set and the cool night breeze floated over the stillness surrounding the desecrated coyote family.

## Chapter Two

The large-winged bird flew above Cache and his mom as they lay sleepless next to Rafe. In time, there were two more circling overhead. Jet looked up and calculated her options. She could not permit Rafe to remain unattended in this crevice of the boulders allowing birds of prey, other coyotes, or bobcats to feast upon his fallen body that seemed so small and vulnerable in death. Her upward glance spied smaller boulders hovering overhead at the cliff's edge. She firmly but gently nudged Cache's trembling body to begin moving, knowing that he, too, would have a heavy heart.

"Those birds will pick apart your brother in hours. We cannot let that happen. We need to find a way to bury him with those rocks overhead. Do you think that you can help me?" Her voice was steady and directive.

"How are we going to do that? How can we move rocks?" Cache looked up to survey what his mother was instructing them to do.

"There must be a way, but we must act quickly. The raptors will move in as soon as we leave Rafe's side. Are you ready?"

Cache stood up, his legs wobbly with devastation as well as from the long period of immobility.

"I'm ready," he answered.

Jet led Cache swiftly up and over the outcropping. She saw a fallen tree precariously teetering above the edge of the cliff.

"If we roll this log down toward the cliff's edge, it may take the looser boulders with it as it falls off the edge. But, it is worth a try." Jet nudged Cache to approach the tree trunk from opposite ends.

"Remember how you used to body slam your brother?" she asked, her voice breaking slightly as she said this, "We need to do that to the log. We will back up and run at it as fast as we can. We must hit the log at the same time so watch me closely. You can do this, Cache." her voice steadied as she looked at Cache.

"I can do this, "Cache replied, uncertain in his response.

Jet nodded, and they took their approach from twenty yards away.

"On my count. One, two, three."

They sprinted toward the loose log with rapacious speed. They hurled their bodies into the log with a revengeful force. The log responded with a jerking motion, then quickly picking up momentum; it hit the smaller boulders with a force that defied gravity. The boulders fell over the cliff along with the log. A large amount of dirt and dried plants catapulted over the side along with the displaced boulders.

Both coyotes hurdled toward the edge due to the speed they had generated hitting the log, but both used their athletic agility to fling their bodies to the side, avoiding a freefall. Jet was on her feet faster than Cache, streaming back down to where they had left Rafe unattended with lightning speed. She stopped at the top of the outcropping. Rafe's body was nowhere in sight. The rocks, the log, the bushes, and the dirt had covered his body completely. Cache caught up to her side and peered down over the edge. He slowly looked up and saw the tears in his mother's eyes as she reverently bowed her head at the hidden grave of her precious Rafe. She glared up at the sky and no longer saw the predatory birds. She glanced down at her remaining pup. He was all she had now. Her life had been shattered in too many ways. She had failed to tell her two pups why they needed to go to the West. She had been silent and protective, and now she could never explain to Rafe who she was and whom she hoped he and Cache would become. She needed to be honest, now, with Cache.

"We must be on our way," she said quietly to Cache. "I need to tell you about your family. I must tell you who you are and where you come from." She picked up her speed, and the two coyotes moved away from the East toward the destination Jet sought: the West.

# Part Two

## Chapter One

There were six coyotes in the group, each watching for the sign to attack from the alpha. The alpha, the one they called "The Boss," surveyed the surroundings carefully. The mule deer was grazing on a patch of grass, apparently unaware of the presence of the pack. The deer was paying attention to the terrain behind him; he knew wolves attacked from his back. But it was from the front that the coyote attacked. The deer wasn't worried about the coyote. He felt like his size would protect him.

The Boss bowed his head, and the group attacked. Their speed was extraordinary; they bore down on the unsuspecting deer in unison. The Boss grabbed the deer's neck and slung it around with tremendous force while the other five sunk their teeth into his thigh, abdomen, and hindquarters. The deer's effort to fight was thwarted quickly as the coyotes worked in synchronized efficiency to best their prey. The deer lay motionless within minutes, and the pack went to work feeding on the prey with a howling frenzy.

The coyotes huddled in their den, feeling drugged from the feed of the deer. The den was large and spacious and comfortably handled the expanding number of animals. It was situated in a valley carefully protected by numerous shrubs and trees. The air around the den was still, and the heat from the sun made it difficult for the den to feel comfortable with the Boss during the day. He liked cooler temperatures. This was one of many differences between himself and his pack. They relished the hot sun and needed a lot less water daily than did The Boss. He had thicker fur, a sable coat with cinnamon-striped flanks, and a white facial mask. A black stripe adorned his back from his head to his bushy tail. He was taller than the other coyotes, with a lean muscular body. Deep scars laced his long narrow snout, along with others found at various parts of his trunk. His eyes were yellow, peering out from a virulent countenance. He was the oldest of the group and felt to be the wisest in the territory. But no one disrespected The Boss. He had earned his alpha position by his ruthless nature, and it was perilous to cross him. There was no alpha female. No one knew the tale as to why and no one dared to ask. It was understood that he ruled alone and was never to mate again.

Every group member placed pieces of deer meat at his feet, a custom to ensure the alpha was well-fed. This was somewhat amusing to The Boss because he always led the attack on larger prey, the coyote that got the preferential first feed at the kill site. He was the first to attack and last to leave, not leaving any coyote behind during a hunt, especially if the hunt had not been successful.

The slice over his right eye and left shoulder had come from the bobcat, who was stronger and smarter than the group of coyotes had calculated. The two battled until the bobcat decided to retreat, the remaining clan hiding in the nearby bushes, unable or too frightened to intervene. The slice from his forepaw to his hindquarters and over his abdomen had come from the black bear who had happened upon the distracted pack scavenging for prey late one summer evening. This time the fight was near death for the coyote, who refused to run away. The bear, too, had been sufficiently injured so left the fight before killing his prey. The clan dragged the coyote back to the den, where he lay delirious for prolonged sunsets, many feeling he would die. When he did recover, myths that he was indestructible traveled across the clan's territory.

On a particular day, the clan fed comfortably on their prey as the sunset. The air was warm, and the smells of the desert were intoxicating. But then, a clan member boldly asked the aloof alpha a question no one had dared ask before...

"Was your name always "The Boss?" Where do you come from? Why don't you have a mate?"

The alpha turned his face toward the asking member of his clan. His eyes shone with a penetrating, yellow glare.

"That is a fair question. We have been a pack for a long enough time for me to answer your question. My name was not always The Boss. It was Kiya, and I came from the East. I did at one time have a mate. Her name was Aloma."

Emboldened by his alpha's answer, another clan member quickly asked for more.

"Can you tell us your story?" The members of the group hushed to listen for his reply.

"My story?" The Boss' voice cracked, and glistening drops of moisture appeared in his eyes. "Yes, it is time I remember my own story."

He furrowed his forehead, focused straight ahead, and began to tell the others.

# The Desert Saga

## Chapter Two

"Aloma, are you there?" Kiya called affectionately to his mate. "Where are the pups? I need to show them something important." Jet was the first to appear, eager to listen to what her father would tell them. She was the favorite of his pups, she self-proclaimed. She had a black streak down her back, just like her father, making her proud and preferential.

"I love him more than they do by far," she told herself, fueling her claim that she was the most cherished.

Cinder and Cinnamon soon appeared. The three female coyotes jumped onto their father, receiving scolds from Aloma for being boisterous.

"Come," their father said, and the four female coyotes followed.

Outside of the den, Kiya pointed to the sky where a semicircle spectrum of light shone in the sky. Their eyes had trouble seeing colors other than gray and different shades of blue, but for a time they could see the beautiful colors of red, yellow, purple, and orange. The family stood transfixed looking at the rainbow. Never in the small pups' lives had they seen anything so spectacular. Aloma had only seen a rainbow once, on the actual day of her mating with Kiya. She, too, stood spellbound, finding herself uncharacteristically speechless.

"What do you think this means?" She finally asked Kiya.

"Seeing the colors can mean safety and prosperity, as it did for us when we mated, or it can imply danger and destruction. We must figure out which one it means for us because it may mean the difference between life and death." Kiya's voice trailed off as the colors slowly faded, leaving a clear sky.

The evening grew cold as the sun set. The pups snuggled together in a tight netting easily going to sleep.

"You are troubled," Kiya said to Aloma. "Do you want to talk about it?"

Aloma looked away. Her eyes scanned the enclosure surrounding her family, then returned to their pups. "Three females. Do you sometimes regret not having a male pup?" Aloma's voice was soft, almost a whisper.

"They are part you! They will someday be mated to a strong alpha coyote and lead a pack." Kiya smiled and watched as Aloma looked back at him.

"It is hard to forget. I sometimes feel frightened and uncertain." She rested her head on her outstretched paws.

"We have talked about this many times before. If a situation arises, I will deal with it. I will protect you and our pups with my life." Kiya's response was reassuring. He nuzzled up to his mate, burying his large snout in her furry neck. "We are strong together, Aloma. We can manage any confrontation".

Aloma settled down into Kiya's strong, powerful body. His strength and certainty gave her courage. But the sighting of the colors in the sky unsettled her. She fell asleep dreaming of wolves invading their den, tearing into Kiya, and stealing her precious pups. She awoke with a startle, trembling and sweating with panic, shaking her head forcefully to repress the frightening images. Her thoughts were flooded with the time she was the mate of Big Grey.

## Chapter Three

The wolf pack circled the bobcat. They were accustomed to taking down any large prey they hunted. But this was an especially large bobcat. It would take wit and speed to capture him. The bobcat peaked one of his ears, hearing a snap in the bushes. He bolted away so fast that it flustered Big Grey. He signaled to the others to begin the chase. They chased the animal through brush and branches. The bobcat was clever and took a convoluted course, making it difficult for the wolves to gain distance. The wolves were exhausted, weakened by their empty bellies. They needed to feed. After a long chase, Big Grey gave the signal to relent, and pulled back his pack. The other wolves knew the alpha would be in a foul mood because they had been thwarted. He would blame someone for the failed hunt, and, one by one, they sulked into the den, staying out of Big Grey's way. Big Grey's mate looked up at him with expectant eyes. She had not gone on the hunt with the pack. Her body was still healing the assorted fractures she had sustained from a fall. The alpha wolf scowled at her and growled, predictably blaming his bad luck on her.

"What happened? "The female meekly asked. Black eyes stared back at her, his scowl intolerant, stopping any more questions.

"We'll go again tomorrow," he grumbled, turning his back on the female. He laid his head down on his paws and became silent.

The next day, the pack again went out in search of food. Again, big Grey pushed the female out of the den. She winced, but quickly caught herself from making any other sounds of injury, not allowing him smug satisfaction.

"You are coming with us on the hunt. Your excuse of injury is no longer tolerable. Get out of the den and help the pack." His voice was threatening and unsympathetic.

She dared not meet his gaze. Bile erupted into her throat, and she swallowed with revulsion. She left the den, head high, staring back at the others in the pack. She smirked, lowered her eyebrows, and quickened her pace. She resolved to get away from this wolf and his pack. Her next move was uncertain, but she'd make it happen.

The pack roamed the countryside, unable to spot large prey, such as deer, that would supply food for days. Moreover, the weather was turning cold, and the game they hunted would soon be pushed up to a higher elevation. Big Grey refused to hunt smaller prey. Rabbits and prairie dogs were dismissed as incidental prey, and he preferred the hoofed grazing animal and the black bear. Once, the pack had taken a black bear at Big Grey's command. This had made him revered, and it was then he had chosen his alpha mate. She was a smaller wolf, and her size pleased him. He would never have tolerated a mate larger than him.

Shortly after they had mated, his violent temperament surfaced. Displeased with any of her actions, or that of any pack member, he might bite and tear into flesh. He would humiliate any that displeased him by making them eat last at the pack's catch. This had happened to the female mate more than once. On one occasion she had gone days without food, because no more scraps were left when it was her time to eat. Other females in the pack would tell her she was fortunate to have been chosen by Big Grey as a mate and that she should work hard to please him. When a wolf alpha mated, if he didn't like his chosen mate, he could discard her and choose another. Mating for life was not instinctive in the wolf world. The discarded mate would sometimes be beaten, killed, or even worse, cast out of the pack, never allowed to belong to another pack while she was alive.

As they now hunted, Big Grey was the first to spot the deer. It was grazing in an open field, aloof to its surroundings. The alpha snorted pompously, confident of success. He signaled for the others to get into position. Wolves were known to attack their prey from behind and Grey sent a group of wolves up toward the front to confuse and cut the deer off when it tried to bolt. Grey would lead the attack and lowered his head toward the ground, slowly creeping toward the prey. His lightning speed always amazed the pack, and they struggled to stay on his heels. The deer stood stunned as if frozen in time and was subdued with barely a fight. Its legs flew up in the air and the body fell harshly onto the ground. The whole pack was swiftly upon it. All except one.

The alpha female remained low and crept on all fours away from the feeding frenzy. She moved toward the surrounding bushes and glanced at the pack one last time, ensuring none followed. She bolted into the trees and brush ahead, running at her top gallop, ignoring the screaming of pain from her injured ribs and damaged muscles. Her stride improved as adrenaline lessened her pain and her breathing became regular. She had no idea the direction she was headed. Glancing quickly at the sun, she surmised she was running toward the West. It didn't matter. She would not stop until she could run no more.

## Chapter Four

Every member of the pack felt his fury. He made the pack circle for days in his territory, trying to find any scent that would give him clues to where his mate had disappeared. He felt stupid and humiliated that he had taken so long to discern that she was missing. At first, he was alarmed that something had happened to her during the hunt. She had been acting severely hurt after he had pushed her over a high boulder when she had angered him on one of their hunts. After her fall, he had told her that an intelligent wolf would have safely landed on all fours, dismissing her complaints to be caused by her own foolery. After several days of worry, it became apparent that she had run. His alarm turned to annoyance. His annoyance turned to livid wrath.

The deer meat the pack had procured lasted for well over a week. Then, he decided to hunt her down, no matter how long it took him. He informed the pack they would leave their territory to help search for her. The whole pack of 12 wolves would come, including the new pups in the den. The other members of the wolf pack growled amongst each other. If they left their own territory, they would be entering another wolf-pack's land, which meant they could experience a fatal confrontation with neighboring packs.

A Group of four wolves came to Big Grey, approaching him warily. Howler was the oldest of the four and began the confrontation.

"The search for your mate will take us beyond our territory," Howler said, calm but wary.

"Some members of our pack have just had a litter of pups and do not want to leave the den or the territory. They feel you should choose another mate and forget searching for the missing alpha female."

Big Grey approached Howler, his sharp-smelling breath filtering into the confronting wolf's nostrils. His eyes were squinting and penetrating.

"Well, this is a first, Howler. Do you dare to challenge me?" He circled the group of wolves, snorting with fury.

"You are my brother, Howler, and second in command. Do you want to engage in a fight to the death? If you lose and I don't kill you, I will ban you from our pack forever."

The silence amongst the group of wolves was deafening.

"Are these your feelings too?" Big Grey demanded of his brother, staring at the other wolves and releasing a low rumbling growl.

Howler was slow to answer. He peered at the members of the pack that were plotting a confrontation with his brother. Such action could end in death to Big Grey or to another wolf. His loyalty was to Grey, but he didn't want a split in the pack to happen.

"I will go with you to find your mate. Together we'll have a better chance with only the two of us to get through the other pack's lands. Then, when we return, the pack will have remained intact, and you will resume as alpha." Howler watched his brother, uncertain of his reply.

Big Grey was silent for a long time. His wrath was focused on his mate. The chances of a pack of 12 wolves getting through the many territories they might have to cross would be more complicated than with just two. Wolf packs never mingled. They were mortal enemies. If they all came with him, his pack would have to feed, shelter, and care for their pups. This confrontation threatened his power and authority, but he realized his brother was right. He would agree, not because of the confrontation, but because of the practicality.

"All right. I will take you, Howler, and leave the others here. But when we return, I will fight to death any wolf that questions my authority." He looked at the other three wolves.

"Is that understood?"

The other wolves nodded and backed away from Big Grey with their heads down, slowly retreating from his presence. Howler turned to him.

"A wise decision, Grey," said Howler. Grey growled and curled his upper lips at his brother, showing his large canines. He nodded in acceptance.

"We must prepare." Big Grey snorted and turned away from his brother.

Donna Krutka

## Chapter Five

She had no idea how far she had run. Her injured but exhilarated body finally shut down, and she fell onto the ground, exhausted and breathless. She clawed her way to shelter under a thick bush and fell asleep, unable to be sure she was not being pursued. When she awoke, her eyes were matted, and her throat extremely parched. She was unable to move her hind front or forelegs. The pain in her ribs and legs felt excruciating. She fell back to sleep uncontrollably, melting into fitful nightmares dreaming of being chased by an enraged monster wolf.

She awoke with a start. Large gentle eyes were staring at her. His body was motionless, and his breathing was controlled. She was too tired to be frightened or to move. He looked like a wolf, and yet, he didn't. Her eyes focused on him, and she attempted a moan, a sigh, or some communication sound. He still did not move, and she became somewhat annoyed.

"Are you alright?" He finally inquired. His voice was reassuring and empathetic.

"How long have you been there?" She retorted, trying to sound sassy and in charge.

"A while." Again, he watched her with interest. "You are a wolf," he followed.

"Yes, I am a wolf. What are you?" Her thinking became clearer, and he was being bothersome.

"I am a coyote. You don't know what a coyote is?" he asked patiently.

"Of course, I know what a coyote is. Do you know what a wolf is?" Her voice is curt and confident.

"What are you doing here alone?" he asked. "Where is your pack? Wolves travel in packs." He looked around to see if there were any other animals.

The wolf turned her head sharply to look for any following wolf. She remained silent, scowling, not answering.

"My name is Kiya," the coyote said.

"The Trickster, "she finally replied. "I grew up being told you can never trust a coyote. Tales were told to me that the coyote is a deceptive creature, using humor to tell lies." Kiya continued to look at the wolf with a quiet stare. He nodded, then added,

"But have you also heard that the coyote is extremely intelligent and adaptable? You are here, wolf, in the wilderness alone, helpless, and probably hungry and thirsty. Maybe you should trust me."

The wolf tried to swallow but couldn't find moisture in her mouth. She snorted and slowly bowed her head.

"My name is Aloma. I am from the East. I am being hunted."

# The Desert Saga

## Chapter Six

Kiya continued to monitor the petite female wolf. It became apparent that she was injured. Her paws were bloody from the long travels across various terrain. Her coat was matted and smudged with mud and burrs. She moved cautiously as if other parts of her body were in pain. Holding her eyes open seemed to take great effort for her. Her breathing was forced with a slight catch during its rhythm. Not knowing if she would be receptive to his offer, Kiya told her he would stay close in case she needed him, watching for danger if she wanted to sleep. Almost in relief, without replying, she fell into a deep state of oblivion.

Aloma awoke with a start. Her senses had alerted her to something, but her mind was still foggy. In front of her was raw meat, already stripped of its fur. She gulped down the meat, choking from swallowing so fast. It had been days since she had eaten, yet she was dismayed that she had thrown all caution to the wind. Her eyes widened in panic, and she tried to focus and remember where she was. Then, remembering the coyote, her breathing calmed, and she looked around for evidence of the coyote.

"What was that coyote's name?" she whispered.

"Kiya!" came a deep voice from behind. "Kiya, from the West. And you are Aloma from the East." Kiya lounged on the ground to her right, choosing a better placement this morning so she wouldn't notice him staring at her.

"Thank you." She said slowly. "Thank you for the food. I was hungry." She felt her lips trying to make a slight smile, but then checked herself, preferring a blank expression.

"You were hungry. How far have you traveled?" His questions were simple, without trying to pry, although he had much he wanted to ask.

"Far, I think, although I am not sure." She shook her head and looked away.

"I think I need to drink. Is there water close by?" She was suddenly aware of her dry throat and difficulty swallowing.

"Unfortunately, not. It is about half a day's walk. I can take you there," he hesitated, "If you would like."

Aloma nodded and tried to get to her feet. She wobbled and groaned, pain ripping through every part of her body. Kiya jumped up instinctively to try to help. She flinched at his approach but felt herself falling before she could object. Kiya slid his muscular body under her to catch her before she slammed into the ground. He propped her legs up under her weakened body and helped her stabilize. As soon as he felt confident, she would not fall, he moved out from under her and watched as she tried to take some steps. He stood alongside her as she attempted to balance. She slowly moved forward, each step with more confidence and resolve. Even in her state of injury, Kiya felt like she was one of the most beautiful animals he had ever seen. Her fur was reddish blond with blackish cinnamon streaks over her chest and flank. Her limbs were long and slender. She had tawny to white fur surrounding her mouth with dark eyes melting into a tightened jaw. Her ears were more prominent than his, giving her an appearance of constant alertness.

She stepped gingerly on her paws, at first very lightly trying to manage the rawness and tenderness. Finally, her initial wince and rapid breathing were replaced with a more controlled gait, and she moved toward Kiya.

"I think I can make it. I may have to go slowly. I would like you to take me to the water." Her voice sounded stronger to her as well as to Kiya.

"I will walk alongside you for a while, and when you feel ready, you can follow me," Kiya slowly edged her toward the open prairie, and the two began walking to find a stream close by,

It was not long before Aloma began to trot. Her head lifted, and her muscles elongated as she picked up her pace. She had been one of the fastest females in her territory. Before she had been mated to Big Grey, she hunted with the best of the males. She was quick and perceptive, and her wits had often saved the clan. She scowled in disgust, not sure what had happened to change her life so drastically.

"Is this your territory?" she finally said to Kiya, feeling like she needed to try to be friendly.

"I am from the prairie. But I am heading to the West," he replied, happy she was talking to him. "The West?" she said expectantly. "I want to go to the West. Tell me about the West."

"I've never been there, but my father was from the West, and he always told me and my brothers that he wanted us someday to get back to the West. He said it was a place that had wide-open skies, and warm, sunny weather, with abundant wildlife that meant we would never go hungry. He said there were no bears or wolves in the West." He gave her a tentative look before continuing, "But there were so many rabbits and prairie dogs to feast on that life was good. He also said the territory was fair game, meaning there is enough room for many coyote clans with little need to fight for space." Aloma noticed his voice trail off with sadness.

"Did you say there were no wolves?" She shifted her gaze toward Kiya optimistically.

"I can't say for sure, but that's what my father told us."

"Where are your father and mother now? Did they go back to the West?" she asked.

There was a long pause, and Aloma immediately regretted her question.

"I'm sorry. I don't mean to pry," she quickly said.

"It's ok, "he said with a sigh. He hesitated, then he spoke abruptly.

"My father adored my mother. He followed her from the West to the prairie, as I told you. They had three litters. My brother Scout and I were from the third litter. My father had talked so much about the West that all their other offspring had taken off for the West. Scout and I had decided to stay with our parents. My father was an impressive alpha, as was my mother. I don't think wolves are like this, but coyotes mate for life." He paused momentarily, then began again. "One day, we were hunting a large animal. It was larger than any other we had hunted. I later found out it was called a sheep. We were fast and furious." A slight smile came over his face. Then it quickly faded.

"We launched a surprise attack and forced the prey into a blind corner surrounded by rocks. We were about to land a decisive blow when we heard a loud, piercing noise. It came from behind us, and another similar noise rang out. I heard my father yell at me to run. I followed his order, and when I looked back, none of my family had followed. My father was standing motionless in the middle of the field. Another loud noise bellowed through the valley. And then I could not see him anymore. I could not see my mother or Scout. I had made it to the bushes by this time, hidden out of sight. I turned and saw it all happen...."

His voice trailed off, filled with horror and guilt. He began again.

"Two larger creatures on two legs moved toward where my father had been standing. They each began pulling something along the floor of the field. The sheep we were chasing had run off. I saw... I saw... it was my father, mother, and Scout they were dragging. They put them into something I did not recognize. It was square and heavy, but you could see my family through the walls. They loaded it onto something else I didn't recognize, and then they were gone. They moved out of my site. I later discovered that if an animal is loaded into one of those square enclosures, the animal never comes back.

The wolf and the coyote didn't speak for a long time. Aloma was sure she saw moisture falling from the coyote's eyes and felt her eyes responding similarly. They eventually made it to the stream, and Aloma drank, thankfully. For the first time in a long

The Desert Saga

while, her heart was heavy for another animal other than herself.

## Chapter Seven

As days went by, Aloma felt her strength return. Her broken ribs and tattered feet healed. She began hunting with Kiya. He appeared surprised and delighted with her tracking skills. She was proficient in her ability to sense their prey, and her masterful speed almost matched Kiya's. He seemed to enjoy her trying to outsmart him or best him in his stealth approach to trap an animal. He sometimes let her feel like she had done so for fun. But he felt pride in how comfortable she was in the open prairie using her sense of smell, astute hearing, and visual cues. They hunted well together. Their ability to work as a unit improved. Both began to feel a sense of companionship. Aloma soon began to appreciate Kiya's gregarious nature and found herself telling him more about her past than she thought she ever would.

Kiya seemed to listen intensely, rarely interrupting or forcing her to tell him more. He had funny stories that he told her, and he loved it when she laughed. She eventually told him the story of Big Grey and how he had beaten her and pushed her off a cliff causing multiple injuries that her mate repeatedly ignored. Kiya visibly became silently enraged about her treatment. He found himself wishing he could one day encounter Big Grey to match off against him with all his fury.

The two continued their journey to the West. They traveled over the plains, eventually reaching high mountains. Finding a passageway through the mountains took cunning and skill. There were larger animals in the forest that the two needed to avoid. Water was abundant after the winter snow. They initially encountered lush, fragrant pine trees until the high terrain changed to rocky, boulder-filled mounds devoid of many trees but thick thorny brush.

Aloma began to feel her body cycling in a female way about her. She noticed that Kiya was watching her with a curious eye. He became more outwardly attentive, moving closer to her in the nighttime, often brushing his snout against hers in a moment of intimacy. She also noticed feelings she had toward him that were unexpected. She had never wanted Big Grey close to her. With Kiya, it was different. When he brushed up against her, a tingly sensation pulsed through. She wanted him to come close to her. Strange urges surfaced inside her, and she wondered if Kiya felt the same. She began to watch him more closely. He, too, seemed unsettled.

In the middle of a warm afternoon, the two were tucked inside a secluded temporary den Kiya had secured the night before after sufficiently feeding. A surprise rainstorm suddenly erupted and passed just as quickly as it had come. The sun began to shine through the parting clouds, and Kiya suddenly jumped up from the ground and peered out from under the rain-washed brush.

"Aloma, look. Quickly. It's the colors!" His voice was urgent and exhilarated.

Outside the den, the sky was transformed into a brilliant arc of colors. Blue, red, indigo, green, violet, orange, and yellow. Aloma had never seen anything like this.

"What is it?" she exclaimed.

"It's called 'the colors.' It can be a once-in-a-lifetime experience." His voice was deep and soft. Aloma was standing next to him. Her closeness swirled all around him. He turned to her. She smelled of desert mixed with rain-soaked fur. He felt his heart racing and his breathing quicken. Unexpectedly, moisture beaded up in his eyes, partially blurring his vision. He blinked several times to refocus. His mouth suddenly was dry, and he swallowed, struggling to make words come out.

"Aloma, will you be my mate?" His voice sounded foreign to him. It cracked and was high-pitched.

"It has been done before," he continued quickly, his eyes showing worry that Aloma would not understand.

"The coyote and the wolf, I mean. Will you be my mate? I want to be your mate, forever,"

Aloma shivered. She sighed deeply and noted that her head felt clear and her senses heightened. The air around smelled of blossoms and nectar. She took a step toward Kiya, overpowered by an urge for closeness. She buried her head into his trembling, muscular body and whispered.

"I accept."

"Forever."

## Chapter Eight

The days went by quickly, and the two hunted, frolicked, and traveled toward the West. Soon, Aloma strolled up to a lounging Kiya, sat beside him, and laid her head next to his warm, soft chest.

"There is something I need to tell you." Kiya turned his head slowly to look at Aloma, his eyes curious and eager to hear more.

"We are going to have a litter of pups." Aloma hesitated as she saw Kiya's eyebrows raise and his ears peak upright.

"Well, what do you think?" She queried, alarmed at his hesitant reaction to her announcement.

"What does that mean? When will it happen? Is it soon? What should we do?" His words flowed from him like a cascading waterfall with so many questions she wouldn't begin to know how to answer him. Aloma snorted in amusement. This large, confident alpha male knew nothing of female things or about starting a family. She nuzzled up next to him and affectionately bit his ear.

"It takes about two moon rises to have pups. So, we have plenty of time to prepare."

"What do we have to do to prepare? I know nothing about what we should do. I know how to find prey and hunt them down, but having pups," his voice was shaky, "I have no knowledge." Kiya's eyes were wide with near panic.

"You will do fine when it happens." Aloma let out a low cry and snuggled closer. "We need to prepare our den. It must be safe and secure from other predators.

The pups will be small when born with tightly closed tiny eyes." She watched as Kiya seemed to relax. "They will suckle milk for ten sunsets. Then, the eyes open, and the pups will be on the move. That's when we must watch them closely because they can get into all kinds of trouble. After about twenty sunsets, they will have most of their teeth, so we can feed them bits of food to chew. It will not be until about one- and one-half full moons that they can eat the food we do."

Kiya's ears stood erect, and he lifted his head higher. Pride and protection welled up inside of him. His eyes darted to the brush and trees around them, choosing the best material to make a den. He and Aloma had become an effective team in hunting and roaming the territory looking for safety. Their companionship had blossomed beyond his wildest dreams. She was everything to him. Would having pups change any of this, he wondered? Finally, he calmed his thoughts and turned to reply to his mate.

"I slightly remember my father telling me that a coyote alpha male plays an active role in feeding, grooming, and guarding the pups," Kiya said.

"He also told me that wolves weren't like coyotes. The wolf alpha rarely gets involved." He glanced over at Aloma, wary of her reaction. "Now I wish I had paid better attention to my father when he had talked about family."

"When can they run about on our territory, and when can I teach them to hunt?" He felt something like bubbles in his stomach. A gust of wind blew the leaves in the den, and he lifted his nozzle, the scents of the surrounding bushes bursting into his nostrils as if it was the dawn of his senses. Aloma's countenance sparkled with animation as she sensed her mate was getting excited about the news.

"A little before two moons, they can go with you to follow you on a hunt. By three moons, they should be able to hunt with you. They will grow fast, and before we know it, we will be able to get on our way again to travel to the West, all together."

" How do you know all of this?" Kiya asked, regarding her in awe.

"A female knows." she answered, nudged his snout, and ran off.

Kiya spotted and chose an area high in a canyon surrounded by multilayered boulders where it would be difficult for predators to attack. The two began to build their den. He remained vigilant to his surroundings, watching for signs of wolves. It was indisputable. Despite how he treated her, big Grey would not allow Aloma to slip away and would eventually find her. There would be a confrontation, and Kiya would be ready when he showed up.

Aloma pranced around their chosen spot, continuously digging and cleaning the hideout. Kiya hauled branches and brush to fortify the walls of the den. He devised several entrances from the main chamber to allow them to quickly come and go from all directions. He knew he would have to stockpile food for the time Aloma would be unable to hunt. She would need abundant food, the sole source of nourishment for the pups.

Aloma had never provided Big Grey with pups. Her mind drifted back, and she shuttered at his anger when she had not given him any offspring. Perhaps, she wondered, his beatings had made her unable to have pups. And yet, here she was with Kiya fulfilling her female role.

The time came quickly. Kiya surveyed their den, nodding in readiness. He stayed close by her side as her pains came and soothed her sweating brow as the birthing took its course. Then, late into the hour, she gave Kiya three young pups, all alive and spontaneously moving. They were all female. She watched Kiya carefully as he inspected the litter. She sighed in relief when he finally spoke.

"I guess I will have to be looking for strong male coyotes to mate with what I would predict would be rather feisty females!" He nuzzled her closely, and she let out a soft, high-pitched howl as she lay her paw over his and her head into his muscular torso. Kiya licked away the sticky residue coating the tiny creatures' hairless bodies, and together Kia and Aloma snuggled the pups, keeping them warm and dry throughout the night.

The pups fed well. Aloma's depleted strength began to recover as she gobbled down the meat Kiya carefully lay in front of her. As Aloma had predicted, on the 10th sunset, the pups' eyelids popped open, and they began to squirm with quick unpredictable movements. They were growing fast. Kiya would spend hours watching them, directing their paths so they would head back toward their mother if they wriggled away.

As they grew, their fur emerged. To Kiya's delight, one of the pup's fur coat had a dark black streak down her spine from the top of her head to her fluffy tail.

Her coloring was reddish blonde with streaks of black interspersed throughout her trunk. Her father began calling her Jet due to her coloring. The other two were predominantly gray, taking after their mother's coloring, with black and white streaks visibly present throughout their fur. Aloma would refer to them as Cinder and Cinnamon. And so, the pups were named.

## Chapter Nine

The days were balmy, and stifling air made it hard to breathe. The nights were cool and pleasant, prompting Kiya to hunt at night and sleep with Aloma and the pups during the day. One day, he decided to hunt early in the morning, just as the sun was rising. He peered through the thick brush of the den and sensed the day getting warmer. He hesitated to leave the coziness of his family, but they needed food. It had been hard to keep up the demand for fresh meat his mate craved, and the pups were now starting to consume bits of the meat. Kiya got up on all fours, rubbed his snout into Aloma's warm, furry body, and quietly left the den. Aloma lifted one eyelid to say goodbye, then dozed off again, the day's heat making her less alert. She failed to detect the small pit viper slither through the den's opening toward her pups. The snake slowly edged toward Cinnamon, who was awake and fidgety. The tiny pup's instincts were still developing, and she had no sense of danger. When the small snake approached, Cinnamon moved closer to investigate the visitor. Cinnamon outstretched her tongue to lick the snake when it struck the pup, biting her tongue.

A loud, high-frequency yelp came from the pup as Aloma turned to see the snake slither out of the den. Cinnamon thrashed and choked, moving toward her mother's side in desperation. Aloma's panic erupted, and she released a loud, piercing howl, immediately alarming Kiya that something was wrong.

By the time Kia arrived at the den, Cinnamon's mouth was purplish red, and her tongue was swollen, making it difficult for her to breathe. She attempted gasps of air, her eyes speechlessly locked onto Kiya's for help. Aloma tried to steady her thrashing pup as Kiya quickly moved from the den. He returned soon with a flattened piece of wood the size of his paw.

"There is only one thing I can do to save Cinnamon," he said to Aloma, breathing slowly and decisively. He looked into Aloma's eyes, tears forming. "The tongue will continue to swell, taking days to return to normal size. She has to be able to breathe." He paused, time standing still, until he finally said to Aloma, "I must bite off her tongue. I must do it now. If I wait to do this, she will die."

Aloma howled in horror and then looked back at her pup. She slowly nodded, eyes pouring water, unable to think of any other option.

She gently angled tiny Cinnamon toward her mate. She trembled and almost dropped the little pup. Cinnamon's breathing was shallow and slight.

"You must take this stick between your teeth," Kiya instructed. "As soon as I bite off the tongue, you must plunge the stick into her mouth and hold it down over the back of the stub. It will allow the blood to stop flowing, and maybe she has a chance to not drown from her blood. You can do this, Aloma. It's her only chance."

Kiya's confidence gave her hope. Again, she slowly nodded, wanting to close her eyes and wish all this would disappear.

Cinnamon's breathing continued to be labored, and her body movements became still. Kiya worked fast, and within seconds, the swollen tongue was removed. Thick red fluid gushed from the back of Cinnamon's mouth, and she went from gasping to choking profusely. Aloma forced the flattened stick into the weakened pup's mouth. The gagging and choking slowly quieted, and Cinnamon's breathing became easier. The coloring of her lips gradually changed from blue to pink. Aloma dared not move the stick until the oozing blood in the back of her mouth steadily lessened.

The following hours were critical for little Cinnamon. She lay in Aloma's outstretched paws, almost lifeless but still breathing and heart beating. Kiya tended to all the needs of the other two pups while he watched the tiny body of Cinnamon fight for survival.

His head fell to the earthen floor, and a slow, despairing growl came from his vanquished body. Then, exhausted with emotion, he closed his eyes and fell into a tormented sleep.

## Chapter Ten

Jet snuck around Cinder and "hip-slammed" her. Cinder, taken by surprise, was knocked off her feet and rolled into the dirt. She jumped back up and began chasing Jet. Cinder was fast, but she couldn't match Jet's agility. She grabbed Jet's tail between her solid jaws and slowed Jet momentarily before Jet twirled around and grabbed Cinder's ear. Cinder let go of Jet's tail and yelped angrily. Once again, Jet's body slammed into her sister, and Cinder found herself on the ground again with blood oozing from her ear.

Kiya watched the whole interaction with his silent daughter beside him. Cinnamon snorted in glee, looking up at her father, requesting permission to join in. "Go ahead, little silent one. But remember, your sisters can get mean. So, if that happens, get mean back. Now go on." He smiled as she took off with enough speed to hip-slam the other two before they realized she was coming.

"It is so hard to see them go through the phase of serious fighting," Aloma retorted to Kiya. "I can't wait until they are just playing with each other. Wolves have the opposite behavior. As pups, we were first playful in our encounters, and then later, we began to engage in serious fighting. It is hard to see this happening in reverse with our pups."

"First, the coyote pups establish the pecking order and dominance. After that is established, they can become friends," Kiya explained. "I think it looks like Jet will be the alpha among the three, although if she had her voice, Cinnamon sometimes looks the strongest."

"When will you begin teaching them about our prey?" Aloma asked Kiya.

"We need to talk about the predators first," he said, looking cautiously at his mate. "We must begin that now. It is time."

Aloma gave a slow nod. The pups had to learn about their heritage. She knew it would be difficult to explain how one of their most dangerous predators was part of who they were. How would they teach both acceptance and caution? And what if one of her pups someday chose a wolf to mate? It all seemed very complicated.

Aloma called the pups, and they obediently ran back to her. She headed toward the den, the three trotting behind her, grabbing or tripping their sister, and trying to howl like a grown animal. Kiya waited for them with fresh meat hanging from his jaw. Each attempted to outrun the other to get home faster when they saw their next meal. They feasted on the meat, and then Aloma told them to sleep for the rest of the day.

"Tell us the story about how you escaped from the East," Jet pleaded to Aloma, "and first met our father, Kiya, on your way to the West."

"Again?" said Aloma, gently rounding her upper lip. "Then, after the story, will you sleep?"

The three pups nodded, their eyes twinkling, and their ears stretched upright, showing no apparent signs of sleepiness.

## Chapter Eleven

"So, are we a wolf or a coyote?" Jet asked her parents, feeling a little exasperated.

"Well, you are half wolf and half coyote," Kia answered. Aloma glanced at the three in agreement.

"So, are we not supposed to be friends with the wolf or not with the coyote?" Cinder asked.

"Well, that is a tricky question. You must be aware that wolves do not like coyotes and want to eliminate them from their territory. They may do that by taking all our prey so there is no food left or killing us off."

Kiya wanted to be as honest as possible with his pups. The questions were good, and he wanted to have all the answers.

"But they won't want to kill us, will they? We are part wolf." Jet's eyes were concerned and a little frightened.

"We need to be truthful," he said to his offspring. "We are not sure what could happen. This is new ground for us, too. But for now, please forget about the wolf and be aware of the other animals we are cautious about. Our other most serious threat is the cougar, which is a large cat. They are often bigger than us, and we eat the same prey. They are sneaky and know how to stay hidden."

"Are they as fast as we are, papa? We're fast!" said Jet, looking at Cinnamon, her eyes wide and proud.

"Almost," quipped Kiya. "So, we must constantly be checking our surroundings. We have a profound sense of smell, but our vision is superb. We hunt mostly by seeing what is around us. The cat's sense of smell may be better than ours."

"I heard Mom talk about a bear. Are they around where we are?" asked Jet.

"They are always around, but never in the numbers of the wolf and the cougar. But we must always stay alert for bigger animals that could overpower us. We work well as a team and can be cunning and quick. That is our strength."

The talk continued for hours, the pups asking about every animal they had heard about. Kiya then talked about all the animals they could hunt, including deer, rabbits, mice, and prairie dogs. He told them they would love to eat blackberries, blueberries, and even prickly pears if they could not find meat. The pups had heard about the desert plants and snorted at the sound of cacti, hearing they had sharp stickers that sometimes stung if many were embedded into their snout. They preferred that not to happen.

After a long talk about predators and prey, while munching on the meat their father had collected for them, they fell asleep dreaming about chasing rabbits and foxes and huge black bears chasing them. But they slept well; all the while, Aloma and Kiya were vexed about what would happen when they met another coyote or a wolf.

## Chapter Twelve

Jet was emerging as the alpha of the three half-wolf half-coyote pups. She became masterful in sensing prey. She watched her father closely when they hunted and learned to anticipate his every move. She loved the chase more than the kill. At times she became sad and conflicted about the animal they were chasing, even if she realized that it was part of the process of life and death. She also loved hunting alongside Cinder and Cinnamon. They were skillful trackers and gave Jet confidence that they had her back. Sometimes she had made a wrong turn or bad decision, and they were there to catch her mistake. When the family hunted together, they always got their prey.

On one humid morning, at the break of dawn, she became restless and wanted to go for a stroll. She nudged her father and told him she would stay close to their den. She wanted to watch the sunrise. Watching the sun come over the horizon had always been the grandest part of the day to Jet. Since the clan usually hunted in the night and early dawn, she reveled in watching the brightly glowing ball come over the horizon. Tiny sparkles of light would splatter the hillside, and a flushed feeling of warmth would bathe her body. However, she would have to shield her eyes from the brightness or become momentarily blinded, unable to see around her.

She meandered along her favorite path, looking for insects or fresh sprouts of grass to munch on for a morning snack. She turned toward the thick tall, bramble bush to her right, hearing a low growl. She stopped and crouched on high alert. A pair of yellow eyes peered out from underneath the brush. The eyes bore no malice nor threat, but Jet prepared her body for an attack. The animal did not come forward but released a low growl again.

"Who are you?" Jet shouted, using all the menace she could produce in her voice.

There was no reply, and again Jet called out, "Who are you? What are you doing here?"

Only a disquieting yelp emerged from the bushes. Jet stepped closer.

"Come forward. Show yourself." There was no answer, and Jet lifted her ears and snout and moved ahead.

The animal's scent hit her nostrils, smelling familiar yet different.

As she approached, she saw ears different from hers, a broader snout and fur coloring like Cinders and Cinnamon- gray with dark black streaks. She sensed the animal was a male, larger than she was, but he made no effort to get up or act aggressively. She moved closer, and the smell of blood immediately met her nostrils, causing her to wince.

"You're injured!" she said. There was still no reply. The animal put his head down on his paws and closed his eyes. When Jet got closer, she saw his left hind leg was mangled and bleeding, caught in some entrapment. He was not moving.

"What happened? What is on your leg?" The animal again did not reply, but this time opened his eyes and snorted. Jet turned to get her father, uncertain about what this animal was and what to do.

She approached the den and let out a howl of warning, beckoning Kiya to follow. He sprinted from the den, followed by the others. Kiya and Aloma reached the site first and signaled for the rest to hold back. The two moved forward with caution.

"It's a wolf," Aloma whispered. "He's injured."

"His leg is trapped. I have seen this before. The traps were put there by the two legs."

"What is your name?" Kiya asked gruffly." What are you doing here?"

The animal did not reply. His breathing was shallow, and his eyes remained closed.

"He is going to die. Leave him alone. We can do nothing." Kiya's voice was absolute.

"No, Papa," Jet yelled. "We can't do that. We must help him." Jet ran to the animal and blocked her father's approach.

"Jet, Get back! We cannot help him. He is a wolf!" Kiya retorted.

"Mother is a wolf!" she exclaimed. "We are part wolf! We must help him."

Kiya looked down at the wounded animal. He surveyed his injuries and what must be done to save him.

"I don't know how to help him. His leg is trapped. All I know to do is to cut off his leg."

Jet looked at her father in horror. She had heard the tale of how he had saved Cinnamon. He knew how to save animals this way.

"Do it!" She growled. His father had never heard Jet be so forceful. Then, her voice became low and angry, "Or I will do it instead!"

Jet glared into her father's eyes with the look of an alpha. She had made up her mind, and there was no turning back. Kiya turned back to the injured wolf and saw him lift his head, open his eyes, and nod. His head then fell back onto his paws, and he remained motionless.

Kiya and Jet crept toward the animal and together began the process of gnawing off the lower half of the wolf's leg. The muscle and bone tasted bitter on Jet's tongue. Jet pulled off to the side twice and retched while her father continued. Kiya dipped his head in acknowledgment when she returned, admitting her strength. Aloma gathered mud and leaves and packed the stump to halt the bleeding. She watched the wolf for signs of life during the ordeal and reported that he was breathing but lay unmoving on the hard-packed dirt floor.

After he was removed from the trap, the rest of the clan returned to the den, and Jet remained, observing for any signs of movement and life. She stayed by his side for hours. Eventually, Cinnamon and Cinder hunted and brought fresh meat to their sister and indicated that they would stay alert to allow Jet to sleep.

Sunrises and sunsets came and went before the wolf began to recover. First, he became alert enough to smell the meat set before him. Little by little, he nibbled at small pulled-apart pieces that Jet had laid before him. He lifted his head upward and started looking around. Slowly, he began to move his extremities. His eyes cleared from this mindless stare, and he gazed at the female animal before him.

"You!" He seemed weak and yet alert." You have helped me. Who are you? Why have you done this?"

"You were gravely injured." Jet then whispered slowly." Your leg was trapped, and you were going to die. We had to gnaw off your back leg to save you."

The animal swung his head around to look at his hind leg. It was gone. He let out an agonizing howl and continued until his strength gave out. Jet sat beside him and watched until the wolf began to whimper and then became silent.

"I've watched you." she finally said." You will recover. You'll learn to use your three good legs and be as strong as ever."

"What is your name?" the wolf asked, his eyes still moist with distress.

"I am Jet. Yours?" Jet felt a strange tingle inside her chest.

"My name is Cutter."

"I'll help you, Cutter. We can do this."

The wolf began to move around and soon was easily getting up on all three of his legs. Jet remained by his side, despite her father's reproach and admonishment. Kiya began to sulk and show anger at his alpha daughter as she bonded with the wolf. Aloma would try to remind Kiya of how she inescapably fell in love with a Coyote, no different from their offspring bonding to a wolf. However, Kiya's actions did not soften, and when Jet came to him to tell him she wanted to choose the wolf as her mate, Kiya exploded with Fury.

"If you do this," he howled at Jet, "you will have no place in our family."

Jet growled and lowered her head as she stared at her father. Finally, her deep penetrating eyes made it clear she would leave. She left the den, and Kiya turned away, head high and ears laid back.

Aloma followed Jet and caught up alongside her alpha offspring. Jet's nature was obstinate and decisive. She was not known to back down.

"Jet, stop," Aloma said, blocking the way forward." Your father is wrong, and I will help show him that he is. But it would be best if you gave me a little time. His love for you is fierce. Are you sure about your choice? It will not be easy. Your offspring will be more part wolf and less Coyote. This could eventually come back to haunt you."

Jet hesitated, clearly thinking about her mother's question. She answered with resolve.

"I have watched this animal. When he was almost dying, I sensed fierceness as well as gentleness. I know you have told me that the wolf does not mate for life, but I sense he is different. We will do well together. If he chooses me to mate, I will accept."

"Then let it be done as you wish," Aloma said, nudging Jet with her muzzle affectionately. She nodded at her mother, who slipped noiselessly from her offspring's side and left to return to Kiya.

As Aloma had predicted, it took time for Kiya to change his mind. Initially, he remained solitary and illusive. Even though he witnessed them together, he avoided Jet and the wolf. He secretly watched as they hunted. He saw how the wolf was playful and affectionate with his offspring. He slept next to Aloma and remembered how he had fallen in love with her and how important choosing her had been. Finally, he approached the two as they sat in the afternoon sun, watching the butterflies buzz around them.

"What do they call you?" Kiya said to the wolf.

"My name is Cutter." the wolf said, wheeling around and standing upright in a manner of attention.

"How did you get that name?" Kiya asked in a guttural growl.

"Before I was injured, I was known for how fast I could come around and cut off our prey," the wolf replied.

"Where is your pack now?" gruffly responded.

"They left me. When I was trapped, they decided I was going to die. So, they left me." Kiya detected anger in the wolf's voice, as it should, he thought.

"Humph," grumped Kiya. "If you stay with us, you must follow the rules of our clan. I would expect you never to try to rejoin Wolves, and you must forever pledge allegiance to Jet. If you go against us in any way, I will be forced to kill you. Do you understand?

Cutter bowed his head in agreement. He spread his lips and peered over at Jet, who was crouching low, watching her father. Cutter bolted toward Jet, and the two animals ran together toward the desert boulders. Kiya watched as they went, sensing he had made the right decision to accept Jet's choice of a mate.

Jet and Cutter mated and became valuable members of their family. Cutter proved to be able to run with almost as much speed as Jet, despite being three-legged. He could still cut off an animal the pack would chase, and the group began to hunt bigger prey with his masterful instincts and skills. It was soon announced that Jet was going to have a litter. To Kiya's relief, Cinnamon and Cinder had also found mates, but they were coyotes. Two wolves in the family were enough, he often quipped to Aloma as they traveled together on their daily hunts. After a while, Cinder and Cinnamon announced they would split off with their mates to establish their own territory and build a den where they could have a litter of pups. Kiya, Aloma, Jet, and Cutter said goodbye as the four left the pack.

# The Desert Saga

## Chapter Thirteen

The night had been cold, and the coyote-wolf foursome knew their food supply was low. It had been a while since they had hunted. Jet exited the den as dawn rose, ready to look for prey. She had developed a ravenous appetite since the last moon rising. She then announced to Cutter that they would have a litter of pups. Even so, she remained one of the best hunters of the group and often was the first to sense nearby prey. This morning, she lifted her nose, smelling any nearby opportunities. The morning breeze blew in her direction, and her ears peaked in alertness. A sense of alarm filtered into her nostrils as she recognized an unfamiliar scent of an animal. She let out a high-frequency whine coupled with her howl of warning. Her howling continued when a colossal animal emerged from behind a craggy mound of boulders. She held her ground, daring not to show signs of panic.

"Who are you?" she growled. "You are a wolf. This is not your territory. You must leave or be prepared to fight my pack." Her eyes flashed defiance.

"You smell of coyote," Howler's voice spat out condescension. "And yet, I sense a wolf!"

The wolf's fur was covered with brambles, his stature overpowering, and his teeth exposing a malicious grin.

"Call your pack. I want to meet your mother," he paused, adding, "and your father."

He came closer than Jet wanted, and she howled louder this time, hoping one of her family heard her. Cutter first came roaring around the corner to slam into the wolf's right flank, knocking him off balance. The enormous wolf was stunned for only a second, unsure of what animal this was that attacked. Then, finally, he saw that Cutter was a wolf and looked at him intently.

"And who might you be?" he growled before lunging forth. He grabbed the smaller wolf by the throat. He picked him up and whirled him around like a paper doll. Jet poised to attack, but Cutter howled to command her to stay away. She was with pups, and he would fight to the death to protect his mate. Instead, Jet gave a high-pitched signal to the others of her family as blood spilled from her mate's gashes. The intruder was besting Cutter rapidly.

She trembled helplessly as Kiya and Aloma came around the bluff. Confusion momentarily slowed their approach as they looked at Jet and saw Cutter on the ground before a wolf attacker. Kiya lunged for the neck of the wolf while Aloma ran toward Jet to stand in front of her in protection.

"He came out of nowhere, " Jet screamed at her mother. "He's going to kill Cutter. Who is he?"

Aloma looked at the wolf intently. Her anger was clouding her recognition, yet she perceived to know him. She had sensed from the moment she ran away from the East that Big Grey would come for her. But this wolf was not him, and yet, was familiar.

"Howler," she screamed, "getaway." Aloma's call slowed the attacker to allow Kiya to embed his gnashing jaws into Howler's rump, which did little to stop the wolf from grabbing Cutter by the neck and pulling pieces of his flesh as he flung back his head.

"Hello, Aloma," growled a voice behind the dueling animals. Aloma swirled around to see a second wolf come into view. He was large and blackish gray in color, with huge yellow eyes glaring with rage.

"We've been looking for you for quite a while." He smelled of malice and revenge. Aloma looked over at him and froze with terror.

"Big Grey," she managed to whisper.

The wolf squinted with violent vehemence. Kiya spun away from Howler when he heard Aloma call out the wolf's name.

"Grey," Kiya growled. "I have been waiting for this." Kiya lunged for the wolf slamming his body into Big Grey's, bile erupting into his throat. He bit, thrashed, and clawed at the wolf, pulling off fur and tearing into his body with rage. Grey's size was massive, and although Kiya was the most powerful coyote Aloma had ever seen, she watched in horror as Grey sank his fangs into Kiya and, with his powerful jaw, ripped away the flesh from his neck, only to release his grip at the neck and land another blow into Kiya's left flank. Blood poured from the struggling body of the coyote, and Kiya fell to the ground.

Eyes filled with hatred and rage, Aloma sprang toward Big Grey with a force she never knew she had inside of her. All her loathing, hurt, and disgust for this wolf flung itself at his throat in a maddening fury. Big Grey's reaction was faster than Aloma's, and he grabbed her by the throat and oscillated her violently from side to side while blood was poured from her neck. He shook the helpless female wolf until she was limp and lifeless. She and Kiya lay side by side, unconscious and torn to pieces by a wolf so full of anger and dominance that nothing could have stopped his revenge.

"What have you done," Howler yelped at Big Grey. "We were to take her back, not kill her."

"She attacked me," Big Grey retorted. "She dared attack me. I had no choice." He examined the scene and surveyed the three animals helplessly on the battleground.

He looked at Jet, plastered against the bluff wall. She crouched, incapacitated as her mother and father, and mate lay on the ground before her. No movement was visible from their fallen bodies.

"We take the half-breed with us instead," barked Big Grey. "She will have to do in Aloma's place." He snuffed and growled as he turned to Jet, and the two wolves prodded her away from the attack site.

Cutter's eyes cleared enough to see the wolves shove Jet and lead her away. Gasping, he let out a weakened howl and shouted at his mate.

"Stay alive," Cutter cried to her, his voice barely heard over the wolf's yelps. "Whatever you do, stay alive. I will find you. Stay alive!" And then Jet heard no more.

## Chapter Fourteen

Cutter lay still on the ground. His shredded body oozed continuous blood, and his chest ached with grief.

"Jet, I'm coming," he whispered. His attempt to get upright failed.

"Aloma." he muttered. "Kiya!" He raised his head and tried to focus. He looked over and saw Kiya and Aloma motionless on the ground. Inch by inch, he pulled himself toward the two, his body vibrating with pain. He laid his head on Kiya's to feel any breath coming from his nostrils. A slight puff of air blew across Cutter's snout, and he saw Kiya slightly open his eyes when Cutter licked him across his face. Feeling hopeful of finding Kiya alive, he pulled himself toward Aloma. Again, he put his snout neck to hers and waited to feel the movement of air.

"Aloma," he said, shouting her name repeatedly, licking her face as he called to her. There was no breath, no movement, no sign that she had survived the attack. Then, with his last bit of energy, he mustered a yelp and howled until he fell unconscious.

The near-death bodies of Cutter and Kiya were unaware of the pack of coyotes that had found them. They protected their immobile bodies and the fallen Aloma from the giant vultures that loomed overhead. Cinder and Cinnamon had heard Cutter's howls, and they and their mates, along with two other coyotes in their pack, began the slow process of bringing the two back to life. They brought food and gulped water from a stream, getting mouthfuls to the two. They patiently licked away the dried ooze from their wounds and combed through their matted fur with their paws. They nuzzled beside them to keep their bodies warm, observing for signs of healing. They piled batches of dried branches over their bodies to protect them from the daytime sun. It took days before either became conscious of his surroundings. Cutter aroused sooner than Kiya. The six coyotes had pulled Aloma's body from the area to prevent Kiya from seeing her lifeless form when he awoke. The two female animals grieved in silence as they nursed Kiya and Cutter. Their mother had been an amazing role model. She was strong, intelligent, and compassionate. She showed humor when Kiya was being too stern. She had taught Cinnamon how to communicate when she was silent and Cinder how to survive against all odds. She showed the rest of the family how to be a clan. She had loved her mate with a fierceness that they wished to duplicate in their relationship with their mates. She was his alpha to the end. They had no idea how to tell their father that Aloma had been killed when, or if, he woke up.

But it happened. One day, after Cutter had been up and hobbling around for some time, Kiya raised his wounded head and spoke.

'Where is Aloma?" he called out, his voice confused. His eyes blinked as he tried to focus on his surroundings. He then saw Cinnamon and Cinders by his side.

"Where is your mother?" His eyes pleaded, panic filling his gaze.

"Father, you have awakened. You have been sleeping for days." Cinder said, and Cinnamon moved close to Kiya with gentle nuzzling and stroking. "How are you feeling?" asked Cinder.

"What has happened? Where is Aloma?" He tried to get up on his legs, but they collapsed immediately. "Your legs are weak, and your body has been torn with many rips and tears. You were attacked by wolves. You are still healing." Cinder's voice was in a whisper. Cinnamon was looking at her sister, questioning whether she should continue. Memory began to surface inside Kiya.

"Go on," Kiya said weakly, his heart beginning to pound. "And what else?"

"Cutter was badly injured too, and we have been helping him heal. He is better and is finally able to walk a little." Cutter sat immobile across from Kiya, his head down and tears moistening his eyes. He was silent as the females answered the alpha's questions.

"The wolves took Jet with them, herding her as if she was prey in a way she could not resist. She was not injured. Cutter has vowed to track them, swearing on his life that he will find her." Cinder hesitated to go on. Kiya gave a slight nod to Cutter's vow and deepened a big sigh.

"And Aloma?" It seemed that he didn't want the answer to this question. His heart was already breaking, realizing she would have been there if she were alive. Nothing in this world would have kept her from her mate, risking it all to be by his side.

"She did not survive the attack, father. She is dead."

The words coming out of Cinder's mouth rushed forth a cry from Kiya the world had never heard from a Coyote. The story has been told from coyote to wolf alike about how the world stood still at that moment. The howl was heard around the world, so the tale is told. The howl was long and furious, sounding like a million animals in unison, lamenting the sorrow piercing Kiya's soul.

His howling continued until the sunset in the West that day when his spirit could take no more pain, and he fell into a deep unconsciousness. There he stayed for days, breathing shallowly but steadily, his body motionless as if he never wanted to awaken again.

## Chapter Fifteen

Cutter didn't wait until he was fully recovered to travel. He bolted from the compound, ravaged with grief and anger. His three legs were wobbly, often falling in his awkward attempt to run. Initially, jumping over bushes and logs was too painful, making it harder to go as fast as his instincts demanded. His unhealed body required frequent rest, prompting him to eat plants and berries instead of hunting meat. Despite his injuries, he made good time. He immediately detected Jet's scent she had left to mark her path. Cutter knew she would be masterful at helping him find her. He recalled the "hide and seek" games they had played on days when they didn't hunt, trying to trick each other into finding the other, continually sharpening their skills. Cutter lost her scent when the group had crossed over streams but picked it up on the other side, Jet knowing he would follow. He hated the smells of the male wolves. His wrath grew as he pictured them pushing, prodding, and possibly injuring Jet. Cutter's maniacal urge to crush her captors pushed him faster and further than he would have otherwise. The time would soon be when Jet's pups should be born, and he knew how distraught she'd be not having a den for their arrival. These thoughts furthered his rage, also helping him move past his exhaustion.

The night was cold and dark. The moon was not in the sky, and Cutter could sense he was getting closer to Jet. He was a wolf and knew he could hunt like a wolf. Jet was half-wolf and half-coyote and had the intelligence and sharp wits of both. He stopped abruptly, picking up the scent of two wolves up ahead. Cutter surveyed the alcove surrounded by tall boulders where they were encamped. He smelled Jet with them and saw her silently huddled beside the rock wall.

"I'll take the first shift," uttered Howler.

"Make sure you stay awake," Big Grey shot back at his brother, his voice patronizing. Howler scowled back at him, ignoring his demeanor.

Cutter determined which wolf was the alpha, who moved to the other side of Jet, much too close to Cutter's liking. Cutter stifled a growl. He studied the foul-appearing wolf looking for his weakness. Vomiting erupted into Cutter's throat as hatred burned inside him. Jet remained in the shadows, blocking Cutter's attempt to tell if she was injured. He didn't want her to see him. Any reckless move on his part or hers could jeopardize her rescue. Eyes focused, ears alert, he watched. He did not sleep.

At dawn, the alpha wolf rose and shouted out to the other.

"Today, you hunt," the wolf commanded. "We need meat."

Howler growled and got up to all fours. He had just come back to the alcove after being on watch. His eyes drooped, and his tongue hung from his mouth. He stretched and lowered his head and slunk around the wall of the alcove. Jet was alone with the alpha wolf. Her head rested on her front paws, and her eyes were closed. She had no signs of injury, which pleased Cutter, yet when he witnessed the wolf marking the surrounding area with his scent, Cutter held back his surge of anger to attack, realizing the timing was not right. He settled his wrath and began to initiate his plan.

He silently inched away from his hiding place toward the open field. He spotted a mound of loose dirt and rolled in it to prevent the other wolf from smelling or seeing him. Then, he moved toward where a large animal was grazing in an open field the night before. The animal had large horns, and his body was twice the size of the wolf. His plan entailed herding the animal toward the alcove where Jet was captive, possibly luring the two wolves into a chase. Perhaps these two wolves were arrogant enough to be enticed to take the larger animal down. Nevertheless, it would be his chance to get Jet away.

Just as he had hoped, the horned animal was lazily grazing where he had last seen him. A burst of adrenaline flowed through his injured and exhausted body, and he ran yelping and howling toward the animal. His masterful skill herded the animal toward the alcove where the wolves were located. Cutter gave a muffled yelp as the two wolves chased the horned animal. Jet was left unattended. As Cutter had predicted, the large-horned animal turned in a different direction from the boulders and ran toward the open fields. Taking down such prey would take cleverness and cooperation on the part of the wolves, and It would give Cutter a chance he needed.

Cutter lowered his head, flattened his ears, and went to the alcove. Jet was still asleep, exhausted. Cutter quietly came to her side, softly calling her name, trying not to startle her. She lifted her head and opened her eyes, blinking in recognition at Cutter, giving a low bark and leaping to her feet. Cutter placed his snout to hers, momentarily forgetting the danger surrounding them.

"You came back for me," she said in a low voice. "Just like you said."

"You stayed alive," he answered. Time paused as they messed their heads together and reveled in the smell of their mate.

"We must go. The two will be back soon. Remember our game of hide and seek? That is what we will do now to escape." Jet nodded in agreement, joy, and terror rushing through her body. She stayed close behind Cutter as he raced away from the imprisoned surroundings and the fowl animals that had been her captors.

## Chapter Sixteen

Jet let out short howls and barks as she followed her mate. She was proud of how good he was at cutting and weaving through bushes and around rocks. His three legs never slowed him down, and she had trouble staying close. Her litter began swiftly kicking inside her belly as she ran and leaped, making it more exhausting to navigate the terrain as before she was with pups. Cutter sensed her difficulty and slightly slowed his pace. The two were marvelous runners, and the wind blowing in their faces and the smells of the prairie brought back memories of their first days together hunting as mates.

When nightfall came, Cutter found a deserted den that had previously belonged to another species of animals. He felt it was hidden enough to protect them for the time being. It had high walls to its back and a thick brush on both sides. Only a small opening allowed the two to enter. Jet fell onto the den floor, her body hungry and drained from the day of running. She snuggled next to Cutter, whose warm body radiated heat into hers. She let out multiple sighs and yelps, Cutter interpreting her relief. When her breathing slowed, and muscles relaxed, he began to ask her about her experience. They spoke quietly long into the night, Jet telling him everything she remembered about the journey. She related that they had not hurt her, only humiliated her. When she could no longer keep her head up, Cutter stopped asking questions, and the two lie side-by-side, exhausted.

In the following days, Jet spent long hours sleeping. Cutter would slink from the den to look for food, staying close so he could protect the den entrance. He brought back berries, insects, and pieces of meat from small prey he could capture. It gave the two enough sustenance to provide strength for a few days. Cutter knew they needed more. One evening, he settled next to Jet as the sun set and the day's warmth turned to a chill. Jet abruptly lifted her head and growled as pain spasmed in her belly.

"It is happening," she whispered to Cutter, another burst of pain taking away her breath.

"I am here," he said softly to Jet, licking away the sweat from her brow. The night remained cold, with brilliant stars blanketing the dark moonless sky. Cutter didn't move from Jet's side as she panted, puffed, and clawed the ground, frequently letting out faint moans. She clenched her jaws as the magnitude of the pain intensified. Cutter watched, not sure how to help her.

A smooth-skinned head popped out in front of Cutter, followed by the rest of a tiny body, and a second followed. Then, she gave a final, long grunt, and the pain was over. She slumped her head onto the den floor and sighed in relief. Cutter gave a loud and exhilarating howl. He looked down and nudged the pups, turning them over on their back and examining them closely.

"We have two male pups!" Cutter cried out. "They both look alive and moving." He touched his nose to hers and then went back to the pups. He inhaled the smell of their new bodies and licked away the mucous and blood. Jet looked up at him and then laid her head on the ground, closing her eyes.

Cutter continued licking the pups and watching them move in all directions, eventually finding their way to Jet's nipples. They latched on vigorously, drawing a yelp from Jet's exhausted body as they suckled their first taste of milk. Finally, jet and Cutter closed their bodies tightly around their new offspring, falling asleep wrapped in blissful fatigue.

Cutter hunted for food and watched for signs of danger. He kept Jet supplied with meat, trying to satisfy her unending hunger. The pups drank Jet's milk for ten sunsets, and when they became less interested in constantly suckling, Jet started giving them pieces of chewed meat. They loved the meat and always wanted more. During those ten sunsets, the pups' eyes remained closed, and Cutter could tell they couldn't hear. He spent time heading the pups back toward their mother when he wasn't hunting to keep them from wandering off. After two moon risings, they were no longer blind or deaf. They were impossible to keep inside the den. Jet was stronger, and the four would take short excursions outside their protected territory. The parents became restless to start their journey toward the West, away from the birthing den. They had to get out of range of wolf territory.

They feasted on a large wild turkey Cutter had captured before the designated day of their departure. Jet spoke quietly to Cutter, wanting his reassurance that the pups were ready for the journey.

"They are young, strong, and have good instincts," Cutter replied. "Of course, we must watch them carefully, but I have confidence in what we have taught them. They are part you and part me, Jet." Cutter

The Desert Saga

moved alongside Jet and laid his head on top of hers. She responded, leaning into him and sighing. The two were ready to go forward together.

## Chapter Seventeen

Cutter's hunting and tracking skillfully kept the little family moving along, his wolf instincts always on guard to look out for the possible pursuit of the two wolves they had left behind. He was confident that they could find Jet since they had found Aloma. He zig-zagged through streams and boulders to mask their scents, and he covered their markings and scat with other animal droppings attempting to confuse the wolves. The little pups needed frequent stops, were quickly tired, and were always hungry. They were too young to perceive danger, and Cutter looked forward to the day he could teach them the ways of the wolf and their mother the ways of the coyote. They would travel mostly at night and sleep during the day, hidden away from danger as they slept. On some days, Cutter would only travel half of the night, stop for cover to let the family sleep, and then begin their journey closer to dawn. On one such morning, they reached a large grassy field. Sounds of birds calling back and forth across the meadow welcomed the group to the beauties of the rising sun. Cutter's keen sense of smell alerted him to a scent that brought a warning to his nostrils.

"I sense animals ahead that we should avoid," he muttered to Jet. "They are animals called sheep, and a cloud of danger always surrounds them. We must go around this meadow."

Jet obediently followed her mate, directing her pups forward, cautioning them to make as little noise as possible. The path was narrow, with little space between the outskirts of the meadow and where the sheep grazed. Slowly edging by the herd, they heard loud howls from their rear. Howler and Big Grey had found them. Cutter barked in alarm to Jet, sending her and the pups ahead. "Stay down and out of sight," he yelled at her. "Don't let them see you."

"Cutter," she gasped as he turned back toward the howl. "We must stay together. You can't hold them off alone." She looked down at the pups, conflicted about protecting them and fighting with her mate.

"Go, Jet, now. Get to protection," Cutter growled in warning. Jet hesitated, then turned and herded the pups toward cover, anguish filling each step she took. She looked back at Cutter, who nodded, acknowledging she was obeying. He watched as Jet and the pups reached safety, then turned and ran in the opposite direction.

A loud, vibrating snap echoed out into the air. Cutter stopped abruptly, wary of going forward. A second similar popping noise rang out. This time, Cutter recognized the sound and turned and bolted back toward Jet and the pups. He ran as fast as he could, screaming at the top of his voice,

"Stay down, stay hidden!" he cried, approaching where his family lay concealed.

A third blast echoed across the meadow, again loud and crashing. Jet lay in the brush, motionless as she had been told. She expected Cutter to plow into their hiding place with the speed of his retreat, but he did not. The noise was no more. Nor did she hear Cutter call to her again.

She waited a long time, watching the sheep scattered in different directions. Finally, the quiet of the meadow returned, and she chose to creep forward to see what had happened. Her pups sensed her fear and stayed close beside her. Only yards away from where they were hiding lay Cutter in a pool of blood, a large hole visible in the side of his chest. He was not breathing. Jet gasped, laying her head on his chest, and could hear no heartbeat. Her throat was clogged, and she could not force air into her lungs. She raised her nostrils to the sky and struggled to breathe. Her eyes became blurry, and she fell to the ground. Her pups came up alongside her, their little bodies shivering in panic. She dug deep inside her being and relaxed enough to open her mouth and allow a breath to flow into her body. The pups both began a low rumbling sound that made Jet snap to attention. She needed to stay alive, she thought.

"Our pups, "she whispered to Cutter's lifeless body. "I'll live for our pups." She felt the blood once again starting to flow through her body. Her breathing became regular, and she leaned over and licked her mate, watching her two pups doing the same.

A little further, frightfully close to her loving mate, she saw the dead bodies of Howler and Big Grey, also with a hole in their chest wall, staring up at the endless sky. She went back to Cutter, lay by his side, pulled her pups close, and sobbed uncontrollably, realizing that she, too, had received one of the big holes in her chest.

# Part Three

## Chapter One

The sound of the chasers throbbed in Cache's ears, and his muscles seized, causing him almost to stumble. Sweat trickled down from his forehead into his eyes, momentarily blurring his vision and causing immense pain. His nose was clogged with dust, and his eyes watered from breathing the musty smell of prickly pear and jumping cholla plants. He sneezed, choked, and looked up to see a grouping of boulders ahead of him. Heart pounding and gasping for air, he dove between the small opening in the rocks and collapsed on the floor, licking his burning feet. He did not move. He adjusted his position in the cramped space in the rocks. He listened. The sound of the pursuers was gone. He slowly rested his head between his paws, carefully remaining silent until he was confident he was safe.

"Mother, Rafe," he mumbled in a low voice. "Where are you? I was being chased by coyotes, just like you told me they would do. I don't know what to do." The tears began to flow again. This time they felt cool and refreshed his vision. He closed his eyes and started remembering so many things.

Cache awoke suddenly, a small prairie dog sniffing at his nose.

"I'm sorry, I'm sorry. I didn't mean to wake you," the little critter jabbered." I was just seeing if you were alive. You know, many animals have gone missing lately, and some have ended up dead. So I was wondering if you were alive. And it seems like you are, and that is good." He took a quick breath and then continued. "And it is important you stay hidden because The Boss is out there close by, and he will probably want to eat you." Again, he took a breath.

" I have come to warn you, but please don't eat me. I know you like to eat critters such as I am, but I assure you that I am very nice and can help. You won't be sorry that you didn't eat me!" And just as abruptly as he started talking, he stopped, looking directly into Cache's yellow eyes and taking several more breaths.

Cache was enormously confused and almost speechless until he managed to ask boldly, "Who are you?"

"My name is Jabberrunner, and as I said, I am a prairie dog. But I have a lot of other friends who are not prairie dogs, such as snakes and rabbits and lizards and foxes, but not coyotes like you are. But I really would like to have a coyote as a friend, since, as I said, I don't have one. Do you think you could be my friend?" He spoke so fast that Cache had such difficulty following him.

"But that means you would not be able to eat me if we were friends since friends don't eat each other."

Finally, Cache was able to get his wits about him and yelled, "STOP! You are talking too much and too fast, and you are making me dizzy." Much to Cache's surprise, the prairie dog stopped. He slowly sat down beside the coyote and allowed himself to rest. Apparently, he had been running from The Boss, too, and was just as exhausted as Cache. The prairie dog slowed his breathing and ever so quietly asked the coyote a slow, drawn-out question.

"Will you please not eat me, and can we be friends?'

Cache chuckled. It felt good to laugh after all the tragic events that had happened to him. It might be nice to have a friend, even if it was a prairie dog. He didn't particularly like to eat prairie dogs anyway. He preferred larger prey meat like deer. But, in reality, most of his food consisted of berries, bugs, and pieces of animals that had somehow died in the desert. His mother had taught him how to be a scavenger.

My mother, he thought. What had ever happened to Mother? He must have said these words out loud because the little prairie dog again started asking him questions.

"Where is your mother? Do you have a mother? And what about a father? I had a mother and father and a brother and two sisters until The Boss and his pack wiped them all out, or it might have been his pack. I'm not sure. Now it is just me, and I am alone." He suddenly looked up at Cache, his eyes apologizing for talking so much and so fast again. He immediately put his head down, promising to be quiet.

"Ok," Cache replied, changing the subject. "I won't eat you, and we can be friends."

The little prairie dog jumped up and started licking the little coyote until Cache pushed him away with a gesture of YUK! After that, Jabber jumped around in circles until he fell back onto the ground, again exhausted from his efforts.

The two settled into a quieter interaction, dozing intermittently through the day's heat. When they were sufficiently rested, they began telling each other about their past. Cache talked about Rafe and his mother, Jet. He told Jabber how his mother had gone hunting not too long ago and never returned. She had never done that before. He had waited and waited. Finally, he became alarmed and impatient and decided to continue looking for her. She had spoken about going West, where they would find a home. So, all he knew was to keep going since she was nowhere to be found.

He told Jabber the stories his mother told him about his grandfather, who had died long ago, the alpha coyote of a pack. His grandmother was a wolf, and she and his grandfather were madly in love. They had three pups, one who had no voice, one who was a fantastic hunter, and his mother, whose name was Jet. Like him and his grandfather, his mother had a black streak of fur down her back. She told him tales about his father. His father had also been a wolf. His grandfather initially forbade his mother to mate with this wolf, prompting his grandmother to remind him that Jet was half wolf and half coyote, so he relented. His mother and father mated, and shortly after, she announced she was with litter. But then she was suddenly kidnapped by wolves and taken to the East, and his father had to rescue her. When he and his brother were born, his father and mother cared for them until they could travel back to the West. The story had poured uncontrollably from Cache's mouth. Suddenly, Cache stopped talking. Jabber looked up and saw moisture streaming down the little coyote's cheeks, his eyes staring blindly into space.

"Mother never told her any more stories about my father. She just stopped talking about him, just like she stopped talking about Rafe." Jabber remained quiet, waiting for Cache to continue.

"And now my mother is lost. I am alone, with only stories and nothing else."

The two sat in silence. Jabberrunner moved closer to the grief-stricken coyote and joined him, sobbing in a puddle of sorrow.

## Chapter Two

The little prairie dog sat up on high alert. Jabber heard noises outside the protected area where he and Cache were hiding. Cache was solidly asleep.

"A cougar, Cache," he said, poking Cache firmly, "You must wake up, but stay quiet."

Cache opened his eyes, confused but silent. Then, his ears lifted, and he heard the noise from outside their makeshift den. He looked at Jabber, who was barely breathing with eyes wide with panic.

"Couuu-ggerr," Jabber managed to whisper.

The cougar, as was the wolf, was one of the fiercest predators of a coyote. Cache had never seen a cougar but saw by its shadow that it could have easily overpowered the two huddled in the crevice. A paw batted forcefully into the rocky space swiping across Cache and sending painful gouges into the little coyote's flesh. He winced in pain and inadvertently yelped in surprise. Growls and hisses came from the animal outside. Encouraged by his first attempt at wounding the coyote, the cougar swiped his paw again, up and down, hungry for his prey. Jabber was frozen in his spot, unsure of what to do. There was no escape, and the more the cougar struck, the more he hit his target. Cache pulled back toward the back of the boulder crevice as much as possible, but the space was small. The next paw strike could hit the coyote's neck region, slashing into his arteries and proving fatal.

"We're supposed to be friends, Jabber. So what am I supposed to do.?" Cache whispered in panic.

Jabber, for the first time since they met, was speechless. He sat silently for a short time before an idea struck him, and he called to the little coyote at the top of his lungs!

"Howl, Cache. Howl like a coyote. Howl like a wolf. Just howl until you cannot howl anymore!"

And so, Cache began to howl. He sent "wow-oo-wow" across the territory. He sent woofs, growls, huffs, and barks like he had never done before. He had spent most of his life having to mute the vocalizations of a coyote-wolf because of the danger they had been in, and now, long periods of careful silence broke into howls he never knew were possible.

Shortly, over his howls, he heard other howls. He heard a cacophony of sounds bellowing above him that came together in a large symphony of howls. Jabber jumped up and down and tried to howl, too, little squeaks coming out of his mouth. Finally, the cougar stopped swiping his fangs or paws toward Cache. The hissing and growls ceased, yet other sounds of growling and howling could be heard outside the rock enclosure.

"Cache," came a voice calling to him." Is that you? You can come out. You are safe now."

The two trapped creatures remained frozen, uncertain, and cautious.

"Cache, it's me, your mother. I have been looking everywhere for you."

The young coyote put his nose into the crack of the hiding place, discerning the speaker's scent.

"My mother is gone. She left me." His voice mixed with anger and grief.

"I left to get us meat, but when I came back, you were gone. I've been tracking you for many sunrises. So come out little Cache. Everything is safe."

Jabber looked at Cache, who seemed unsure.

"She knows your name, Cache. Does her scent smell familiar?" Cache nodded, unable to take the next step outside the safe crevice.

"I'll go first if you want me to, "offered Jabber, trying to be brave.

"No," Cache said, puffing out his chest and laying his ears back. "I will go. Stay close, ok?" Cache nudged the little prairie dog and gave him a lick. He now understood what it was like to have a friend.

Cache and Jabber slowly emerged from hiding together and peered around the rock to see a tall, feral-looking coyote standing beside his mother. He had scars, cuts, and crooked legs on his massive body, but he also had a black streak running down his back.

Cache cowered down on the ground, Jabber trembling next to him. The large coyote stared down at them both. His eyes were fierce yet curious. Cache shivered in disbelief when he thought he saw the animal wink.

"When I was looking for you," Jet whispered as she ran to his side and placed her snout next to his, "I found a group of coyotes who took me to their alpha. This is your grandfather, little Cache. He is my father."

Cache blinked and surveyed the pack of coyotes surrounding him. Then, recognizing his mother's scent, he leaped toward her. His wounded body tried to slam into her like he used to do to his brother Rafe, but his strength failed, and he crumbled at her feet.

"You came back, Mother. You came back for me." Cache took deep, slow breaths.

"I am here, Cache. You are safe. This is the West. You have made it home!" Jet licked her cub with long strokes, clearing the blood and mud off his snout and trunk. Cache leaned in and shivered.

"I want to introduce you to your grandfather. His name is Kiya." Jet stood back as the large, aging coyote came forward. Cache saw his black streak on the old one's back, turned his head toward his mother, and lowered his head.

Donna Krutka

"Hello, grandfather. I am called Cache."

The long ordeal was over for all of them. He and his mother had made it home, and he was safe, gratefully reunited with his wolf-coyote family. Cache introduced Jabber to his mother and, carefully, to his grandfather, adding a little bow at the end of the introduction. Jabber remained silent, overwhelmed to be in the presence of The Boss, who Jabber had been told was the scariest animal in the world. Finally, Kiya greeted Jabber with a smile and regal nod as the sun set on the desert landscape, and the pack settled down to a feast of wild boar and deer meat.

Donna Krutka

# JABBERRUNNER

## Chapter One

Paco stood on the rounded mound of dirt that shielded the entrance of the extensive underground network of tunnels called the Prairie Dog Town. His family lived in a territory of the town named a coterie. In his coterie, he was the kingpin, with his mated female and four junior offspring, two males and two females.

Paco's nose rose into the air as his tan body and white belly stood on his hind feet, suddenly jumping vertically, and throwing his forefeet into the air. A bold "yip" bellowed from his voice as he warned nearby prairie dogs of the impending attack from a red-tailed hawk. He dove into his burrow just in time to thwart the sky predator from catching his meal. Mamasita ran to Paco inside the burrow and began kissing him, rubbing her nose into his.

"I was about to bring the little ones out of the burrow to feed. What would have happened if you had not been there? Oh, my goodness!" Mamasita's voice was high and harried. She moved her forepaws in multiple directions, indicating her anxious nature. Finally, she started spinning in slow circles, unable to contain her worry.

"It's okay, Mama," Paco gently responded. "I will always make sure the coast is clear before you leave the burrow. It is what I do, little Mama. I make sure you are safe."

He patted her on her head and then turned to the four wide-eyed pups, giving them a reassuring nod and kiss to alleviate their concern. He then slowly approached the ward's opening to see if the hawk had disappeared. He peered around and indicated that all was well, stepping out of the way as his little group filed past him to look for breakfast insects, grasses, and seeds.

"Mamasita," he called as she exited the burrow. "Stay alert. Use your keen sense of vision to watch for predators. Don't forget your grammar. Remember, you can be very specific about what the danger is all about. Your call can let me know if there is a coyote, a hawk, a snake, or whatever. Try not to get flustered if you come across such dangers. Remember, you have very sophisticated ways of telling me what's out there. You're not going to forget that, are you, Mama?"

"Now Paco," Mamasita slowly replied to her mate. "I won't forget. You have told me repeatedly that we are the best communicators in the animal kingdom, and I won't forget. That's what is in our nature. So now, don't you worry!"

Paco eyed Mama with concern. She was a worrier and sometimes easily flustered, yet always took the responsibility seriously to teach her pups about foraging. She was a master at finding food, even during a drought. Other prairie dogs would starve during winter because they could not find food. At the same time, Mamasita always returned from searching for food with a feast that defied the most accomplished forager.

"Papa Paco," a little squeaky voice called from under his father's prominent belly, looking up with wide entreating eyes. "Will you teach me how to watch for predators? I can run fast and get away quickly, but I need to learn to hear and see the way you do, so I won't have to run as fast. All my friends tell me you are the best chatterer in our territory. They say you have saved so many prairie dogs by warning them. So, I want to be just like you."

Paco looked down at his most diminutive offspring. He smiled with pride at the words he had just heard.

"I will teach you, little Jabberrunner," he told his pup. "In good time, little one."

Donna Krutka

## Chapter Two

"Now stand firmly on your two hind feet on top of the rim," Paco instructed Jabberrunner. "The ground beneath you is called a rim crater. We use it as an observation point. We can see a long way in every direction. Can you see that similar mound of dirt on the other side of the collection of cholla trees, the ones with the round prickly balls you got into your fur not long ago?" Jabber shivered with the memory of his Mama taking such a long time to pick out the painful stickers that had burrowed into his belly. He nodded to Paco.

"That is our neighboring group of prairie dogs. We are family since we share the same parents. So, we are friendly. Unfortunately, many prairie dog groups are not friendly."

He pointed far up the desert terrain to a large group of mounds clustered on a slope. Beautiful, blossomed bushes adorned the surrounding area.

"They have a male kingpin who will fight us. You will see them sitting upright on their mounds, staring, chattering their teeth, and making aggressive barks. It would be best if you always stayed away from them. There is nothing they want more than to fight and dominate. They will sometimes show challenging behavior 20 times a day."

Paco's mind immediately thought about Mamasita. That area had the tastiest berries in the territory. Mama continually defied the neighboring kingpin's threats by foraging the fruit. Paco had tried to forbid her from attempting to get blossoms from that area, but he was sure she ignored him. She had come home countless times with plump ripe buds, berries, and seeds that spoke of being foraged from the forbidden territory. Of course, she denied the charge. Paco felt fear when this happened, but he remained silent.

"Now smell the air," he said to Jabber. "Tell me what you smell."

"Well, I smell...," Jabber tried to come up with something to say. He didn't smell anything. Everything smelled like desert and dirt to him, but certainly not coyotes or bobcats. That is what he wanted to learn about.

"Follow me," Paco said. Jabber chased after his Papa. He came up alongside him, glancing over to see if Paco had acknowledged how fast he was running. He squinted his eyes and oversaw the ground, desperate not to trip and stumble like he did the last time he raced his brother, trying to match his Papa's speed. His chest felt tight, and his breathing was rapid as they climbed a steep hill and another. Finally, a large outcropping of boulders came into view, looking to Jabber like an insurmountable obstruction in their pathway. Paco then turned abruptly to the east and entered a dry, rutted depression in the landscape filled with sand and a collection of fallen cacti and limbs of mesquite trees, cluttered with mismatched rocks of all shapes, sizes, and colors.

"This is the Wash, Jabberrunner. The wash is where water pours into and down the hill after a big rain," Paco's voice sizzled with concern and warning. Jabber had never seen rain. Instead, it had been dry, hot, and sunny every day since his birth. His eyes widened as he looked around.

"Wow," he exclaimed to his Papa. "We're in the wash. Mama told us never to go into the wash and that Papa would kill us if we did!"

Paco laughed. "I would not kill you, Jabber, but some other predator probably would. This is where coyotes and javelinas, and bobcats live. Snakes are here too. Your Mama's warning is true. Never go into the wash unless it is an emergency. Do you understand?" He looked down at Jabber with a fatherly concern mixed with a warning.

Jabber nodded and asked, "But why are we here, Papa?"

"It is here you will learn the scent of all of our predators," Paco said patiently. "This step is critical in becoming a chatterer. You must first learn what the scent is you warn others about."

And so little Jabber spent the day learning each animal's scent. He was a quick learner, and Paco was delighted when Jabber confidently identified the different scents they encountered as they wandered through the wash. The two laughed and jabbered on their way home, Paco smiling that his pup was well suited for his name.

## Chapter Three

Jabberrunner stood on the rim of the family burrow, his hindlegs solidly anchored. His body stood as vertical as possible. From one of the four entrances to their burrow, his other siblings popped their heads out of the holes.

"What do you smell, Jabber?" his older brother yelled at him. "Do you smell a grasshopper or mosquito? Papa will be proud of you for saving us from a cricket!" He snorted mockingly.

"Stop teasing him. He is trying to learn what Papa is teaching him." His sister scolded their older brother. "Leave him alone."

Jabber ignored his brother. He stood still, detecting an unfamiliar scent. He cocked his head to one side, confused. He was sure the scent wasn't that of a coyote, hawk, bird, or snake. It smelled of danger, but he wasn't sure what kind.

"Get Papa," he yelled to his brother and sister, "Quick, get Papa!" His voice spoke of alarm.

"Stop being such a pest," replied his brother. "You don't know anything, Jabber!"

"Get Papa," he screamed again, this time with such force it prompted both the pups to submerge into the burrow and call Paco.

"What is it, Jabber?" asked Paco, who emerged from underground swiftly.

"I don't know, Papa. But it scares me."

Paco stood beside his youngest pup, smelling the air with concern. Without warning, he looked around and then let out a prolonged bark. The bark undulated a low and then high pitch, followed by a high-pitched call. Jabberrunner looked up at Paco and began making a similar call. He had no idea what he was warning about. Still, he bellowed in unison with Paco, mimicking the high and low sounds that Paco was chattering.

The rain suddenly appeared. It poured from the sky with a ferocity Jabberrunner had never seen. Lightning struck close to him, Jabber throwing his paws over his ears and tightly closing his eyes. Fear paralyzed his legs, and his father forced him into the burrow.

"Water is going to pour into our burrow. It will come fast and furious," Paco yelled at Jabber. "We must get to the furthest part of the tunnel. There is a chamber at the far end of the burrow that may save us from the water. We must hurry."

Mamasita was quietly grooming her youngest female pup. The two other siblings stood close by, uncertain of the alarm. Paco gently kissed his mate and calmly spoke to her so as not to get her panicky.

"Mamasita," Paco began. "The rains have come. Do you remember how we prepared the burrow for the rain? We built a broad chamber at the far end of our tunnel, allowing air in case our burrow is flooded with water. It is time we go there now." He spoke in a slow, gentle manner.

Mama's eyes enlarged. She shot a look at her mate, her eyes laced with terror. She started trembling and mumbling. Paco gently directed her to the lower level of the tunnel. They passed the chamber where she had nursed her pups. They passed the chamber where they slept at night. Mamasita hesitated, and Paco gave her a nonaggressive nudge, and she continued.

They reached the last chamber and climbed high into the air chamber just as water flooded the tunnel where they had been traveling. Mamasita huddled close to Paco, the four pups piled on top of her. The water rose into the air chamber, cutting off any escape. It came within inches of Jabberrunner as he looked down at the liquid predator.

"It was rain I smelled. Rain! " Jabber mumbled, the scent forever imprinted for the rest of his life.

## Chapter Four

It took longer for the water to recede than Paco had anticipated. He was continually reassuring his trembling mate that they would be okay. Their breathing became labored. The chamber began to get hot and stuffy. Deep inside their burrow, the sound was muffled. There was no way to know if it was still raining. Sometimes the downpour lasted only minutes, and at other times it rained for days, Paco told them.

"Papa," Jabber quietly asked after some time. His Papa did not answer. It seemed too quiet in the chamber to Jabber.

"Papa, wake up." Paco slowly tried to open his eyes but fell back into unresponsiveness. Jabber nudged his Mama, who had her eyes closed and was breathing in a jerking manner. His sisters and brother didn't answer when he called them.

"Everyone is so sleepy. What's going on? What's going to happen to us?" He looked down at the central tunnel filled with muddy water, allowing no escape from their chamber.

"We are not going to survive here much longer," Jabber whispered, hoping not to alarm his Mama. " I think I should start digging, Papa. What do you think?" He remembered helping his Papa burrow in the tunnel.

"I can dig out this side wall, down and then up, and maybe I can get to the top to see if it has stopped raining. Then, if I run into water, I will climb back up before it reaches our level." His father didn't answer. Paco's breathing was slow and shallow.

Jabber slowly began to claw at the dirt. He dug in a zigzag fashion, building small out chambers to pile the soil as he moved forward. He instinctively angled down and then turned upward toward what he felt was the surface. He worked swiftly but felt tightness in his chest as he struggled to breathe. Gasping, his tunneling met muddy dirt. He pushed his head against the mud and grunted with all his strength. His head popped out of the ground, and precious air flooded his dirt-clogged nostrils. Finally, he lay his head on the rim, sputtering and snorting. The rain had stopped. He looked around at the flooded desert terrain. He identified the domed opening to the family burrow, ringed in a pool of water. He climbed from his newly created entrance and stood on his hind legs to evaluate the danger. There was no smell of predators on the ground or in the sky. He dove back underground to rescue his trapped family.

"Papa, Mama," he exclaimed as he looked at the motionless group of prairie dogs.

"We must get out of this chamber. You must follow me." His Papa opened his eyes sluggishly, only to close them again.

"Papa, wake up!"

He turned to his brother and sisters, who were equally motionless.

"Wake up, wake up!" he yelled. His heart was pounding as he, too, began to feel groggy and overcome with inertia.

Jabber grabbed the leg of one of his sisters and bit down as hard as he could. She pulled back her leg and half-consciously muttered for him to stop. He bit down on his brother's flank, whose head slightly lifted off the chamber floor, releasing a subdued growl. He went back and forth, biting each one until all were awake and making annoying sounds for him to stop.

Jabber maneuvered close to Papa and shoved him with all his might. Paco's eye popped open, and he looked around, trying to focus on his surroundings. He took several deep breaths, and clarity oozed into his bloodshot eyes. Paco then started nudging his mate and biting her with his sharp teeth. Jabber and Paco pushed, shoved, and continued to bite the other three until they were all angled into the newly created tunnel that Jabber had dug. Slowly, they started feeling the fresh air flow down the tunnel and became more alert. They emerged onto the wet desert surface one by one, gasping and gulping air. Jabber and Paco were the last to climb out of the tunnel, falling exhausted on the ground alongside the others. They lay unmoving for an extended period, then slowly began sniffing and cuddling up to the others, chattering about what had just happened in the airless chamber.

Donna Krutka

## Chapter Five

"Usually, it takes many of us to dig a tunnel," Paco said to Jabber the following sunrise.

"You did it all by yourself. Well done." Jabber looked up and saw the smile on his Papa's face.

"I was scared," Jabber admitted. "I was terrified."

"You acted with a swift sense of urgency, Jabber. You saved our family."

Jabber's back extended a little higher, and he tossed his head up into the air. He felt a little older than he had the day before. His Papa nodded at him, and that was that. Nothing else was said about the rescue. The sun came out and baked the surrounding desert with heat that soon dried their burrow so that life returned to the regular routine. Paco observed the skies, and Jabber stood on their burrow dome, adding rain to his list of potential threats. He helped the family repair their tunnels, adding additional air chambers large enough to survive longer underground.

The rain had washed away the dust and dryness of the previous months. The air smelled of freshness and blossoms. Life in the desert erupted with insects multiplying by the thousands and other creatures feasting on the insects as they frolicked in the new-found moisture after the rain. Jabber noticed a strange, musty smell forming in their lower tunnels. A thick whitish substance started lining the walls.

"Papa," Jabber said to his father. "We have a problem down here in the tunnels. Something is growing on the walls, making my eyes water and smells bad. What can we do about it?"

"Leave it alone, Jabber," Paco replied. "My father told me the white material protects a prairie dog burrow. He was wise and insistent, and I have always been careful to leave the smelly stuff when I find it on our walls. So, it must be a good thing." The prairie dog pup scrunched his nose after smelling the thick white material. He then bounded to the top of the tunnel to play with the other family pups.

Jabberrunner continued to learn the skill of detecting predators. Paco let him practice the high-pitched call of the chatterer, alerting other prairie dogs of impending danger. He chattered back and forth between his cousins in the next burrow closest to theirs. He learned how to be a ventriloquist, confusing the predators as to the direction of the call. His Papa increasingly relied on him to be the family sentinel as he and the rest of the family reinforced their burrow and repaired the damaged sections from the flood. He had successfully warned the entire prairie dog township of impending attacks from a black-footed ferret, a fox, a golden eagle, and a red-tailed hawk.

The monsoon flood also destroyed the burrows on the rocky side of the neighboring territory where the kingpin lived.

"You must be careful, Mamasita, about foraging close to the rocky burrow next to ours," warned Papa. "I don't have good feelings about where his clan lives after the rains."

"We must eat, Papa, and an abundance of seeds and blossoms are growing on that hillside. I'm careful when I look for food. The last time I went there, I saw no sign of alarm."

She scampered off with her two female offspring. The sisters merrily giggled as they gobbled blossoms and seeds along the path, following close behind their Mama.

"I will rest for a while," Jabber said to his Papa, entering the burrow after standing watch for long hours on the outer dome. Paco kissed his youngest son on his nose and indicated he and his oldest offspring would take over the sentinel position.

Jabber laid his head on the burrow floor, quickly closing his eyes. His limbs relaxed, and the neck tension eased from the position he held while sniffing the air. He fell into a deep sleep, abruptly awakened by a loud screech and growl from the surface. Jabber jumped up in alarm. He ran toward the burrow's opening to see two large prairie dogs attacking his Papa and brother. They were biting and ramming his father and kicking his brother. The intruding prairie dogs were bulky and muscular, towering over Paco and his oldest pup. Jabber pulled himself onto the dome of their den, ready to smash into one of the hostile prairie dogs, hissing and spitting, prepared to join the fight. Instead, Paco pushed Jabber back into the burrow, screaming for his youngest to stay hidden. Jabber hesitantly obeyed, retreating, and peered over the burrow dome. His heart raced, and fear-laced tears streamed from his eyes. He blinked, trying to focus and calculate the strength of the attackers. His head jolted to one side as he picked up movement from the surrounding bushes. His throat went dry, and he unsuccessfully tried to swallow, unable to release a cry of warning. Four coyotes emerged from the brush, bodies lowered and ready to strike. Before his eyes, the coyotes snatched his father, brother, and the two attacking prairie dogs from the ground and carried them off as fast as the predators had appeared.

## Chapter Six

Jabber fell onto the burrow floor, unable to breathe. His body trembled, and his eyesight clouded. Neither his arms nor legs would move. He felt like one of the attackers had punched him in his belly, an indescribable pain burning inside him. He closed his eyes but quickly opened them, blinded by a vision of what had just happened to his family. Uncontrollable weeping came from deep inside of him. He took slow breaths, trying to calm down.

"Where are Mamasita and my sisters?" he heard himself say aloud as he continued to sob in paralyzing grief. The realization that he was all alone overwhelmed him. He would fall asleep and then awake with a start, plagued with nightmares of coyotes and prairie dogs. He looked around frantically to see if his Mama and sisters were back, but they were not there.

"Papa told you to be careful, Mama," he cried out. "He told you that leaving our family territory perimeter could allow a hostile, neighboring male prairie dog to steal you and my sisters. You could be forced into their clan. Did that happen to you, Mama? Where are you?" His head fell to the ground of the burrow, and his eyes closed. He remained motionless in the same spot for sunrise and sunset.

The colorful blue Lizard peering down at the shattered prairie dog was high at the top of the opening of Jabber's burrow. He studied him closely, extending his long tongue to catch insects as they attempted to enter the burrow. It appeared to Lizard that the prairie dog was dying as he watched him take shallow breaths and occasionally move his head. Finally, he decided he liked this little prairie dog and brought seeds and pieces of grass to lay before him. The little animal never ate the food before him, and the Lizard crept closer and closer to him to observe. The Lizard listened as Jabber talked to himself in rapid-firing sentences. He yelled out screeches and yelps, trying to drown out involuntary memories. The prairie dog repeatedly covered his face with his forepaws, then batted at the air to push something away. The Lizard began licking the prairie dog and then turned to nudge him. He still could not see any change in his alertness.

    As he sat watching Jabber, his eyes moved toward the burrow opening. A spindly black spider climbed into the tunnel, heading toward the immobile prairie dog. A bright red spot was plastered across its back. It was followed by another more enormous black spider, similar in appearance but with a red marking on the belly. The two spiders sensed the vibration of the Lizard and quickly turned around and ran out of the tunnel. The Lizard was familiar with these spiders, knowing they had a deadly toxin and would poison their prey. He had witnessed them spinning a robust and silky web around a stunned field mouse and saw them feast on the mammal for an extended period. He was confident they would try to harm the little prairie dog.

"Wake up, wake up!" he shouted at Jabber. "It is time to eat and wake up." He said this repeatedly, hoping to get a response from the prairie dog.

Jabber raised his head, growled at the Lizard, then dropped his head back on the ground. The Lizard continued to pester the little mammal until, finally, Jabber opened his eyes and scowled at the Lizard.

"What do you want?" he shouted at the Lizard.

"You must get up. Spiders are coming, and they will poison you and wrap you in silk, and you will die. So, it would be best if you got up!" exclaimed the Lizard, snapping at an insect that flew by him.

Jabber looked around as if seeing his surroundings for the first time.

"Where am I?" he asked.

"In your burrow. You have not moved or eaten for many sunrises and sunsets. It is time to start to move and to eat!" Again, the little Lizard used his most authoritarian manner of speaking.

Jabber tried to get up, but his legs felt like mush, and his head throbbed as if it would explode.

"Why am I here?" he again called out, then slumped back on the ground, remembering his family and hesitant to move again.

"I have had trouble sleeping. I feel irritable and angry. I am overwhelmed with guilt that I did nothing to help my Papa and brother. I have no idea what happened to Mamasita and my two sisters." Jabber took another breath and continued, his speech getting faster with each word. "I keep seeing the whole event repeat in my dreams. I don't want to get up. I don't want to eat. I don't want to live."

"Well," the Lizard mumbled, his voice cocky catching a tasty grasshopper with his tongue. "If you don't want to live, it won't be long before the giant black spiders sting and spin their web around you. There's also a tan-colored, coiled pit viper camped out at the entrance of your burrow. I think he's getting ready to swallow you head first. Are you ok with that?" Lizard looked up toward the opening above, trying to glimpse the snake.

"But more likely," Lizard continued, "the neighboring prairie dog kingpin who kidnapped your Mama and sister will come and take over your burrow since they haven't seen any activity coming from this tunnel."

Jabber's head lifted spontaneously, and his breathing quickened. He looked over at the little Lizard, and burning erupted in his throat. His eyes widened, and he tried moving his arms, then his legs. He spotted blossoms and grasses piled in front of him and looked up to see sunlight coming from the burrow opening. He slowly nibbled at the food before him and stretched his legs in all directions. He had once been proud of his muscular body. Now he felt like he was made of wilting branches. He struggled to lift his legs and reach a standing position, clawing toward the burrow exit. The little Lizard ran in circles around him, joyfully snapping up flies and gnats that buzzed around him. Eventually, the two creatures emerged from below into the open air above ground. Jabber sat on the dome rim of the burrow and smelled the desert wind, not seeing any signs of a pit viper anywhere around. He looked at the bright blue sky and felt the sun on his face. A heavy sadness lay across his chest, but the Lizard had helped him want to live, even if just a tiny bit.

"My family is all gone," he said quietly to the Lizard. "I am all alone."

"I don't have a family either." replied the little Lizard. "We can be friends if you would like." Jabber looked down at the Lizard. Then, he looked up at the dry, unfriendly desert land before his eyes. A shiver jolted his entire body, and he again turned his head toward the little creature below him.

"Yes," he said to the Lizard. "For sure, we can be friends."

## Chapter Seven

Jabber slowly began to eat better each day. He ventured cautiously into the open desert foraging for blossoms and berries. He tried eating roots and seeds he didn't think he would like. His little lizard friend was his primary social interaction now that his family was gone. The two lived together inside his spacious burrow. The Lizard feasted on the insects that drifted into the burrow, keeping the fleas and spiders safely away from Jabber. Jabber decided he would again begin to stand on the burrow mound and communicate with the neighboring prairie dogs. He exhibited the "jump-yip" display, stretching his body straight up and throwing his forefeet into the air as he called out. This sent a wave of "jump-yips" throughout the territory, encouraging watchfulness and vigilance for others to pay attention to approaching predators. He often asked if any other prairie dog coteries had seen his mother and sister. Still, no one admitted to knowing anything about them. Throughout his territory, his skill as a communicator was proclaimed.

"I am tired today, little Lizard. It has been a long day," said Jabber. So, he and the Lizard moved down into the lower part of the burrow to settle in for the night.

Lizard turned up his nose to smell the walls of the burrow.

"What is that thick white gooey stuff alongside the walls of your burrow?" he asked Jabber. "It smells awful."

"My Papa always insisted that it was necessary for our survival. He said we should leave it alone, never eat it, but never remove it." Jabber's head dropped a bit as he mentioned his Papa. He had to shake his head to keep from remembering too clearly.

"I always felt like it smelled awful too, but after a while, I stopped noticing it."

Lizard looked at it more closely and touched a small part to feel the spongy nature. "I hope I stop being able to smell it too," he said and again scrunched his nose in disgust.

"We should rest, my little friend," Jabber later said. "I need to look for berries and roots tomorrow. I want to start early."

Lizard lowered his head onto his forelegs and nodded in agreement, both fast asleep within the shortest time.

The two friends exited the burrow the next sunrise to find a clear blue sky and a warm breeze out of the north. Jabber stood on his dome surrounding the burrow and made his morning calls. He called and called but was perplexed at not receiving any responses. He repeated his routine, and again, he heard no familiar answering chatter from the neighboring burrow. Lizard sat alongside the prairie dog, equally surprised.

"Where is everybody, Lizard?" Jabber's voice sounded frightened.

"We are up early in the morning. Do you sense any danger?" Lizard asked, also concerned.

Jabber lifted his head up into the air, smelling the wind while standing on his tiptoes. He then looked far and wide and saw no raptors, coyotes, or ferrets that would have wiped out a town of prairie dogs.

"I don't smell or sense any impending danger, Lizard, but I do smell something. It smells like...." his voice trailed off.

"What does it smell like?" Lizard yelled back at him, impatient with terror.

"It smells like...DEATH!"

Jabber looked at the Lizard, who stared back at the prairie dog.

## Chapter Eight

Jabber started running, instinctively plowing across the desert terrain. Lizard worked to keep up with the prairie dog, trying to determine what Jabber was chasing. Jabber abruptly slowed as he approached the neighboring burrow. He mounted the rim crater, confused that there was no greeting from another prairie dog. The quiet coming from the burrow spoke of abandonment. Suddenly, a foul smell filled Jabber's nostrils, and he choked. Lizard started rubbing his nose into the ground.

"It's here. It's coming from here," whispered Jabber. Slowly he started to descend into the burrow. Lizard grabbed Jabber's tail with his sharp teeth and stopped him from going below.

"I will go first, Jabber." Lizard declared. "You stay here." The prairie dog instinctively obeyed, moving his head in agreement.

Lizard disappeared into the burrow. Jabber began trembling as he waited for the longest time before the lizard jumped from the burrow opening. His eyes were wide with horror.

"They are all dead, Jabber. Every one of them."

"Dead? What was it? Spiders or snakes?" Jabber could hardly breathe.

"Their faces were puffed up, and large lumps were under their necks. Yet, they all looked the same. Their eyes were wide open and oozed blood. Their bellies were bloated." Lizard looked closely at Jabber as he reported his findings.

"And there is something else." He gulped and shuddered. "They were all covered with fleas!"

Jabber's jaw dropped, and his eyes stared with disbelief.

"Fleas?" he said, his voice quiet and confused. " I've never heard of this happening."

Jabber made a move to go into the burrow when Lizard stopped him.

"For some reason, I don't think you should go there."

Jabber hesitated and then obeyed. His head fell onto his paws.

"What are you thinking? "Lizard asked expectantly.

"We never had fleas in our burrows. Papa talked about keeping the fleas away, but I don't remember why that was so important. None of this makes sense. So, I don't know." Jabber's voice trailed off. He looked out over the terrain.

"Let's go examine another burrow, Lizard. I don't hear chatter from the other neighboring burrows. We should check."

Jabber slowly moved toward a different ward, hesitant to get there too fast. Lizard followed, trying to get ahead of the prairie dog to prevent him from entering the burrow first.

When they arrived, Jabber stood back and allowed Lizard to descend. Again, the prairie dog had to fight his instincts to plow under the surface.

Lizard ascended from below, shaking his head.

"It's the same. They all are dead, and they look the same. They are all puffy, and their eyes are bleeding." he rubbed his nose on the surface of the dirt, appearing to try to mask the smell. "And they are covered by fleas!"

After going through the entire Prairie Dog town, which included over 20 family groups, they could not find survivors.

"They are all dead!" mumbled Jabber, each footfall feeling stuck in the mud and nearly impossible to pick up. His head hung near the ground, and each breath was slow and forced. Lizard followed close behind, his eyes staring straight ahead. Finally, they reached the burrow, and both moved deep into the lower tunnels. They laid their head onto their paws and fell asleep.

When Jabber awoke, he looked around at the tunnel. The white spongy lining of the wall was visible where they were sleeping. His head popped up, and he woke up Lizard.

"Did you see any of this white stuff in any of the other burrows? " Jabber sniffed the musty scent of the walls. "I wish I could remember all Papa told me about the white outgrowth."

Lizard opened one eye slowly, then the other. "I'm still tired, Jabber, and I don't want to wake up!" He sounded annoyed and unfriendly.

"Lizard," Jabber again exclaimed." Did you see any of this white stuff in the other burrows? Or could you smell it in any of the tunnels?" His voice was higher pitched and more excitable than usual.

Lizard lifted his head and used his tongue to wipe the sleep from his eyes.

"Jabber, the smell of death was awful in the burrows." Lizard raised his eyes. "I couldn't pick out that type of smell."

"You said that there were many fleas in the burrows. I have never seen a flea in this burrow." Jabber's eyes widened. "I noticed many prairie dogs spend much time rolling in the dirt and pouring dirt on their fellow mates and pups. They do that to get the fleas off them. Papa told me when I asked him." Jabber jumped up and headed toward the top of the tunnels. As he went, he touched the white substance lining the walls.

"It's the white stuff, Lizard," Jabber said excitedly. "Papa said it would protect us. It must keep the fleas away."

Lizard suddenly got to his feet and followed, noting the white lining throughout the burrow.

"So, what does keeping the fleas away do with anything?" Lizard said in confusion.

"Don't you see, there are no fleas here, and we have never had to pour dirt on each other to kill the fleas. The white stuff is doing that for us. It's killing the fleas. And the fleas must have something to do with killing the other prairie dogs."

"Papa did it again. He kept me alive." Tears rolled down Jabber's cheeks.

"But, if I am the only prairie dog left in this territory, how will my kind ever return?" Jabber turned his head from one side of the horizon to the other. He stood up and onto his hind legs. He sniffed the air and gasped in alarm. The scent of rain hit his nostrils. He "jump-yipped," throwing his forefeet into the air while making the call. There was no answer from the surrounding burrows.

"No one can hear you," Lizard whispered, standing motionless by the lone prairie dog.

"I know," Jabber answered, looking out into the valley. His arms dropped to his side. "Nobody's out there."

"What are you going to do now?" Lizard asked as a bolt of lightning flashed across the sky.

Jabber looked up suddenly as the rain started splashing into his face.

"You can come with me, Lizard." Jabber took a long breath in and exhaled slowly. "I'm going to look for another place to live, away from death and fleas."

Jabber peered out over his devastated territory and then turned and bolted away, looking back to see that Lizard was following.

Donna Krutka

The Desert Saga

# LENNY

## Chapter One

Dark clouds formed across the sky, obscuring the bright desert sun. Cool air mixed with droplets of moisture filtered over the warm rock where Lenny, a Western Diamond-backed Rattlesnake, was perched, taking his mid-afternoon nap. He suddenly awoke, startled by a flash of light followed by a booming clap of thunder. He looked up just as sheets of rain pelted him from the sky. A wall of water rushed over him, knocking him high into the air and cascading him down the front face of the boulder. His senses tumbled along with his body, making it difficult to get a bearing on his direction. His head bashed against a stationary object and then another. Tossing around in a grove of mesquite trees at the bottom of the gorge, he quickly gulped air while rapidly moving water carried him through sharp cactus spikes. He smashed against boulders, choking, and twisting his body in every direction, finding it impossible to get out of the flow of the muddy water. Exhausted, he became limp and hoped for snatches of air as he rushed down the wash inside the torrent of the newly formed river. Time was difficult to calculate, and he had no idea how long he tossed and turned.

He opened his dirt-caked eyes and perceived his momentum slow until he came to a stop. A gentle flow of water continued to flow over him, shallow enough so he could raise his head out of the water, then lay it back down onto the soft sandy surface. He remained motionless, drifting to sleep, losing any sense of threats from predators. The sun popped out of the clouds and formed a hovering layer of steam, dissipating the rain. When he awoke, Lenny was unable to raise his head. Thick, brown sludge encased him in a sticky goo hardening around his body. The squawk of a red-tailed hawk screeches across the sky, and Lenny again tries to wiggle away to cover.

A loud whooshing sound occurred, and Lenny could pivot his head in time to see a rusty-colored badger suck him from the mud. The badger's teeth were firmly implanted into the snake's long trunk. With a burst of instinct, Lenny lunged his vicious teeth into the badger's neck, startling the attacker, who promptly dropped the snake back into the muddy wash.

With no time to waste, Lenny slithered toward a nearby outcrop of boulders and dove between two rocks. The badger rolled into the muddy wash and rubbed his neck into the sand. The badger was immune to the poison of snake venom, but the bite hurt enough to anger him, and he quickly bolted upright to try to catch his prey.

Lenny burrowed deep into the crevice, remaining coiled and still. The badger pushed his snout into the gap, unable to reach the snake. Finally, after repeated attempts, the larger mammal became bored and ran away.

Donna Krutka

The Desert Saga

## Chapter Two

The day's light dimmed, and the snake remained wrapped in his rocky crevice until his need for food overwhelmed his senses. He emerged cautiously into the open wash, looking for the usual source of insects. But none were found. He spotted a tiny field mouse lying on its back along the muddy bank, legs quivering and twitching haphazardly. Lenny watched for some time, determining that the flooding water had injured the mouse. The movement of its limbs stopped, and Lenny slithered closer, opened his jaws, and grabbed the mouse into his mouth. The animal gave no fight. A rush of relief rushed through his hungry body. It had been several days since he had last eaten, he remembered.

Bruised, exhausted, and now no longer hungry, he moved toward the grassy brush away from the wash area and coiled to rest. The moonless night brought bright stars to adorn the cloudless night, and the smell of mustiness and freshly washed sand allured Lenny to fall fast asleep.

His exhaustion brought him dreams of sunning on his favorite rock under the 200-year-old giant saguaro. Dread, the red-tailed hawk, soared above and made wide circles in the sky, looking for prey. He felt a shiver through his body as he saw Burley, the colossal king snake known to be able to swallow a rattler. Burley was immune to the viper's poison.

Lenny boasted to all who knew him around his desert terrain that someday he would explore his world, see new places and have new adventures. The others around him had only laughed, saying he was all talk and no action. They were right; he had never shown any effort to move from his 5-mile circumscribed territory. But he told them over and over he would someday explore a new country.

A sudden vibration jolted him awake from his dreamy state into alertness. From somewhere close by, a foul smell hit his nostrils. It was the scent of a king snake, like Burley back home. He steadied himself for an attack, slowly moving forward in the sand. But, to his surprise, the large predator moved away from Lenny.

Another scent filtered through the air. In the direction the repulsive, fat king snake crawled, a female rattler was coiled, unsuspecting of a possible ambush. Infused with an instinct of purpose, Lenny let out a slow, hissing sound and began jerking his body back and forth. He kept his head down, angling slowly toward the larger snake. The commotion alerted the female snake, who looked up to see the danger and, with lightning speed, shifted positions and pushed off nearby rocks in time to abort the king snake's assault.

Lenny's body bridged back and forth, sending an invitation to combat. The king snake abruptly turned toward Lenny just as the rattler slammed his body into the hulky predator and knocked him off balance. Lenny kept his head low and his body high to prevent the king snake from his killing technique of swallowing the rattler by his head. Pounding and hissing occurred, and the two snakes engaged in an ancient form of a snake dance to prove who is dominant, wrapping their body around each other, and keeping their head high. The smaller snake was repeatedly pummeled but kept his resolve until the king snake tired of the game and slithered off.

Lenny lay plastered in the sand, bruised and exhausted. Pieces of his precious rattle lay in the rocky area next to him. He slowly lifted his head to look around to see if the female snake was anywhere close. He could still discern her scent from where she had been resting, yet he needed clarification about her escape route. Wounded, body spent, and confused, he slowly started moving on a random path, hoping to find the little female.

## Chapter Three

The frightened female snake didn't stop, her muscular body grabbing the rocks and propelling her forward, undulating back and forth swiftly, smoothly, and seamlessly. She traveled through the sandy desert and over rock outcroppings until her trembling body sensed no further threat of danger. Shortly, she spotted a thick pile of leaves and brush and buried her body until she was well camouflaged.

The feeling of danger was new to her. She was a young snake with little experience in defending herself from predators. She coiled her body into a tight knot and tried to relax so that she could rest.

Vibration from her surroundings warned her of something approaching. She lifted her head and sensed another snake close to her, moving in her direction. Panic filled her coiled body, and she was poised to flee when she heard the intruding snake speak.

"Are you all right?" he said. His voice had no threat in its hiss.

"He's gone. The big snake is gone. I saw him go the other way."

He hesitated and then asked again, "Are you ok?"

The female snake slowly emerged from under the brush into the sunlight and looked at the advancing snake, cautious but calm. The snake appeared injured, with purple marks visible on his muscular body and a portion of his rattle hanging loose.

"You're the snake there when that big black snake threatened me. You're injured. What happened? I, I...I left as fast as I could. I didn't know what else to do!" Her voice was apologetic.

"It was good that you moved so fast. That malicious snake would try to eat you." Lenny's manner surprised the female. She thought he should be angry at her for leaving.

"Eat me?" she gasped. "A snake would eat another snake?"

"Yes, and he would have eaten me, too. We're what that snake eats, rattlesnakes. We have no defense against them. Our poison doesn't work on them. So, they overpower us and eat us, headfirst.

" He paused and watched the female's stunned reaction. "And then they swallow our body whole."

"It was good that you ran," he added.

The female snake shivered, stunned into stillness. Lenny worried that she would turn and leave, but instead, she spoke softly.

"You're not from around here, are you? I haven't seen you before."

"I'm from a long, long way away." He paused and reflected for a short time. "I'm uncertain where it is. I'm not sure where I am now," he said, anxiety filling his response.

"What are you doing here if you don't live here?" the female snake said, puzzled.

"I was sunning on my favorite rock by my beloved green monster, the old grandmaster saguaro when a huge torrent of water washed over me and sent me a long way down in a whoosh. I landed in a pile of mud, was almost eaten by a badger, and then I saw you." His voice got a little quiet on the last part. He looked away from her when he said that.

"My name is Greta." the little snake said.

Lenny looked curiously at the female snake, then answered, "I'm called Lenny."

The two snakes remained silent for a while, each not knowing what to say. The afternoon was hot, and Lenny wanted to get out of the sun and into some shade.

"What are you going to do now?" Greta said shyly, breaking the silence.

"I feel lost. At my home, I told everyone I wanted to seek adventure. But now, I'm unsure if that's what I want."

"I could show you where I live. I have never seen a big black snake, badger, or a whoosh of water where I live." Greta paused, a little uncertain of how he would answer.

Lenny lowered his eyes. What was left of his injured tail slowly and rhythmically began to rattle. He slightly tensed his muscles and moved from side to side.

"I'd like that," he said and followed Greta as she took off toward her territory.

## Chapter Four

The terrain they traveled together was different from what Lenny had known. There were large boulders with steep, rocky faces and jutting, ragged peaks. His familiar landscape of ribbed green saguaros was missing. This smell of the terrain had a different fragrance than the desert where he lived. It gave off a sweet scent, and trees were peppered with woody, scaly ornaments growing from the branches. The trees stood tall and straight, with no fleshy leaves but bunches of spiny green projections jutting off the tree's arms.

The snakes talked as they went along, telling the others about their experiences. Lenny learned many things he had experienced that Greta hadn't known, and she was eager to learn from him. She, too, told him about her world, and he listened attentively.

Suddenly, Greta stopped and looked high toward a towering cluster of rocks.

"This is home," she said, turning to see if she had Lenny's approval.

Lenny raised his eyes toward the layered, piled rock before him.

"You live up there?" he said with a puzzled voice. "How do you get up there?"

"Come on," she beamed, "I'll show you."

Her agile body quickly climbed the steep face of the rock. Lenny had to work hard to stay with her as she maneuvered through loose rocks, around trees growing from the side of the cliff, and even straight up a sheer drop-off. Then, after a long climb, she abruptly stopped and slithered through an aperture that would have been invisible to Lenny if he hadn't seen her enter.

"Ingenious," he said half to himself as to her and followed her in.

Once inside, a large atrium opened with high ceilings surrounded by cool, moist walls. A tingling rush overcame his body as he slowly moved around the spacious cavity.

"This is where you live?" His voice was in disbelief as he continued to survey the site before him.

"This is perfect. No badger or hawk or bobcat could find you here. How did you find this place?"

"It's the only place I've ever known," Greta answered. "I lived here with my mother from the start," a twinge arose in her voice. Then, she became silent and looked away from Lenny.

"It seems like a long time ago," Greta began, "when my mother told me she was going out to find us food, and then she never returned. I waited and waited, not sure what to do. I had only left the cavern on a few occasions before that with her, but not often. Finally, I decided one day that I had waited long enough. I was hungry and frightened and went out to find her. I never did. To this day, I am not sure what happened. I had to learn to eat and forage on my own. I did ok, I guess, until today. I decided to go further, and that's when the big black snake found me." Her voice trailed off, and Lenny could sense her shudder recalling the event.

"I'm glad I came along," he said, moving closer to her.

They remained silent for a while. Lenny cautiously moved closer, longing to coil next to her, and Greta didn't move away. Together, they shut their eyes, falling into a deep sleep.

## Chapter Five

Lenny awoke with a start, sensing something was amiss. Greta was not next to him. A sense of urgency pulsed through his body, warning of danger. He found the cavern's exit and emerged, forgetting how high Greta lived in the mountains. It was as if the whole world lay in front of him. He perceived Greta's scent on the rocks and followed it to the right.

He had been reckless about watching Greta's route when she entered her cavern, uncertain he could find his way back. A loud screech bellowed from above. A red-tailed hawk circled close to the rocks, spotting prey. Lenny looked over and saw Greta coiled up close to the rock wall, trying to camouflage herself. He shot toward her with sudden urgency, knowing the hawk's keen eyes could see her. The hawk began his dive, and Lenny reached Greta in time to sling his body over hers. Greta's breath was shallow, and her eyes were plastered shut. The hawk struck Lenny, grabbing the snake's sleek body with his sharp talons. A solid grip failed, and he picked up Lenny, then dropped him again on top of Greta. The female snake attempted to break toward her cave, and Lenny hissed at her to stay where she was. He knew the hawk was faster than she was and would grab her before she reached safety. The hawk again plunged for the two snakes. Lenny remained tightly coiled to Greta's body, hoping the two snakes' bodies together would thwart the bird's attempts. This time, the hawk struck, and his talons pierced into Lenny's scaled, muscular body. The male snake was lifted high into the air, swinging his body from side to side to escape the raptor's talons. The hawk's grip was solid, and try as he could, Lenny could not break his hold. Looking down, Lenny saw Greta peering up at him in horror and disbelief. He was too high in the sky for her to hear him yell to return to her cave. Fear and uncertainty encased his body. Where did a bird, the likes of Dread, take their prey? What would become of him?

Never seeing Greta again encouraged him to twist violently in his captor's claws. The sudden flailing of his prey caused the hawk to lose hold of Lenny, and the snake felt his body falling through the sky, tumbling in the air end-over-end. A jolt thundered through his body as he felt claws dig into his sides again, aborting his freefall. Looking toward the sky, he saw the hawk flying far above him, circling back in his direction. He looked up and saw his captor clearly, a brown-faced owl who had caught him as he fell toward the ground.

The red-tailed hawk made a pass toward the owl, hitting him head-on with a force that tore into Lenny's body. The impact was so quick and fierce that the owl dropped Lenny, and he was again plummeting toward Earth. He was closer to the ground now, landing on a looming mesquite tree laced with thick leafy branches and sharp spines. Lenny winced as the spines pierced his thick, scaly skin. He lay motionless, mangled in the tree. The two birds continued to ram their fierce bodies into each other, angry at the other for losing its prey. The battle went on while Lenny watched from the tree below.

Battered and breathless but alive, Lenny maneuvered through the spines of the tree and made it to the ground. He slithered his injured body toward shelter and coiled, closing his eyes. Sleep did not come, only thoughts of Greta. Finally, he turned his torn, bruised body in a direction his instinct felt was towards finding Greta.

# The Desert Saga

## Chapter Six

"Get over here quickly," a high-pitched voice shouted at Lenny.

"Hurry up, hurry up. Are you crazy for being out there moving so slowly? Hurry up, hurry up!"

Lenny wasn't sure which direction he was going to hurry up. He looked around, trying to discern the source of the voice.

"I can't understand why your kind can sometimes move so quickly, particularly when you are trying to eat me, and then at other times, you move so slowly. You must promise not to eat me, but hurry up, will you."

A tiny, tan face peeped out of the bushes to his left. It appeared to be a prairie dog, hastily calling him.

"What's my big hurry," Lenny scoffed back at the little creature, slumbering along as fast as he could with his injured body.

"It's The Boss. He's coming, and he's coming fast. So, you have to hurry before he gets here. He is mean and vicious and wants you for a meal!"

The voice spoke so rapidly that Lenny had trouble understanding all the words. The prairie dog's urgency prompted Lenny to move faster and reach the bushes where the creature hid.

"Who is The Boss?" Lenny managed to say as he breathlessly slipped under the camouflage of the desert weeds. Moving that fast made him realize he was exhausted, and quite frankly, the brush covering was a welcome place to rest.

"Who's the Boss?" the creature spouted. "He just happens to be the meanest coyote, kingpin of the largest coyote ring in the entire desert." His voice dropped a few notches as he added, "Or so his gang told me, but I never stuck around long enough to verify if that was so. So, I get out of his way and continue going as fast as possible. See that burrow over there?" He pointed to a hole a few feet away from Lenny.

"The Boss and his gang wiped out the entire prairie dog town. The only reason I know is that I met one of the inhabitants who were away when they struck and missed being eaten just by chance. It was awful, I was told. So you don't want to meet The Boss and, of course, not meet his gang."

The little prairie dog kept jabbering and jabbering, talking as fast as Lenny could follow, telling him all kinds of stories about the coyotes. Before long, the animal abruptly stopped talking and listened.

"He's there. Be quiet," he whispered as if Lenny had been talking.

Lenny was not going to take any chances. He slowed his breathing and stayed as still as he knew how to. To his surprise, the little prairie dog stopped talking and stood like a statue, his front paws perched in front of him as he balanced on his back legs. Lenny heard sniffing on the other side of the bushes. He could feel the vibration of many animal feet. The animals, presumably The Boss and his gang, weren't making any noise. They were good hunters, knowing the right tricks to sneak up on prey. They would soon find the two helpless creatures if they were as ferocious as the little prairie dog had indicated. Lenny wasn't sure he had it in him to give a fight at this time.

The sound of a red-tailed hawk screamed overhead. He must have won the fight, Lenny thought to himself. He was still looking for Lenny, having chased away the Owl. The vibration from the coyotes' footfalls seemed to go away from Lenny and the little prairie dog. The hawk was scaring away the coyotes, and for once, Lenny was grateful for the Red Tail's timing.

It wasn't long before the little creature started talking again.

"That was close. We were fortunate. I told you to hurry up, and it was a good thing you did," the prairie dog said, continuing the conversation unbroken by any drama.

"My name is Jabberrunner. What's your name?"

"Lenny," the snake replied, grateful the coyote and the hawk had not found him. He chuckled that a prairie dog, usually a possible meal for a snake, kept him safe.

"Now you have to promise me you won't eat me. I don't think I would be very tasty, by the way. I was always told that I was kinda stinky, and if I am stinky, I'm thinking I wouldn't taste very good."

The prairie dog kept on talking and talking. Lenny closed his eyes, not able to listen anymore. He was tired and hurt and wanted to rest to find Greta. He started dozing off to sleep, his last thoughts of finding Greta and fell fast asleep.

## Chapter Seven

Lenny awoke, and Jabberrunner was still talking. Lenny raised his head just as the creature was telling him again not to eat him. Lenny started slowly moving, checking his muscles, his sense of direction, and in particular, his sense of smell. He would need that sense, in particular, to find Greta.

"You are so right," Lenny said to Jabberrunner. "You do smell awful. Why?" He wished for a little of the mud and sludge that had clogged his nostrils in the river.

"I smell like that on purpose. I figured that eating Javelina's poop every day would keep the coyotes from finding me. They would expect to find a Javelina, which they love to eat so that they wouldn't be looking for a lowly prairie dog. So far, I haven't eaten, so I figure it has been working. What are your thoughts about Javelinas? Do you like eating them? Does my smell keep you from wanting to eat me?" Jabberrunner looked warily at Lenny, watching closely for his answer, ready to run if Lenny said the wrong thing.

"No, I don't like to eat javelinas, and I don't want to eat you, so you can stop asking me. And stop talking for a while. I need to think." Lenny sounded annoyed for the first time. He needed to figure out how to get to Greta.

To his surprise, the little creature remained quiet. Lenny looked out from under the brush to see if all was safe. He needed to get moving.

"I must find my new friend, Greta. She's also a rattlesnake; the last I saw her, she was in danger. I'm not sure if she is ok." The snake turned and looked at the prairie dog. "Would you help me find my way to her?"

Lenny slithered out from the brush toward the mountains without waiting for Jabber's answer. Jabberrunner rushed after him, unsure if he wanted to help, but then he realized he had nowhere to go. He didn't have any family or friends. Maybe this snake and the other snake could be his friend. He started to ask Lenny not to eat him but stopped abruptly before the words came out of his mouth. He suddenly realized that if Lenny had wanted to, he probably would already have been eaten. So, he let it go.

"Well, sure, I guess. I mean...I can come along," he stuttered, " and... try to help you...I have never helped a snake before. I'm not sure why I started helping you in the first place. But, ok...I'll come along."

He scampered alongside Lenny, now with a new sense of purpose. He was going to help two snakes. He knew snakes love to eat prairie dogs. But no matter.

The desert was dense with plant life making it difficult to maneuver. Each plant seemed to have treacherous thorns that reached high into the sky and then plummeted to the desert floor, making it hard to find a clear path. Jabberrunner proved to help find a route that both Lenny and he could safely negotiate. Lenny angled closer and closer to the high rocks, the only landmark he remembered. The terrain became rockier, requiring climbing over boulders. Lenny's body still ached, but Jabberrunner scampered over even the highest obstacle. They came upon a small pool of collected water, and both stopped to drink to their fill.

# The Desert Saga

The sun was starting to lower in the sky, and the day's heat settled as night was imminent. Lenny would have no problem traveling at night, but Jabberrunner would be more vulnerable in the dark. Sensitive to the prairie dog's needs, he spotted an opening in a group of rocks, nestled beside bushes resplendent with seeds and flowers.

"We'll stop here, Jabber," his eyes followed the insects that buzzed around them. Jabber jumped up and down, gobbling up the abundant, luscious purple and orange flowers while Lenny lopped up insects with his long tongue. Finally, night descended on their hide-out, and both headed in between the rocks, eager to rest.

## Chapter Eight

A low, guttural screech sounded into the night, awakening Lenny and Jabber. Then they heard a demonic growl Lenny had never heard before.

"What is that?" whispered the snake, paralyzed by the terrifying sound.

He looked over at the prairie dog and saw him sitting straight up and shaking.

"It's a bobcat," answered Jabber, his voice quivering. "I hate bobcats," he continued. "They are enemy number one. It is tough to get away from coyotes, but I have almost been caught twice by a bobcat." He continued to tremble, holding his paws over his ears. The terrifying sounds continued.

"Do you think he knows we're here?" asked Lenny.

"Not sure, not sure, not sure, not sure!" Jabberrunner continued to repeat.

Lenny discretely stuck his head out from under the brush and surveyed the area, activating his infrared senses to look for the bobcat. Thermal images from his pit organ showed him the cat's location. Yellow eyes with round, black pupils stared straight at him. Its face was sleek with long whiskers, and its ears were pointed with streaks of black on the tips. It remained perfectly still, ready to strike. It was tracking Jabberrunner, who was no match for the cat. It was up to the snake for the little prairie dog to survive. He would have to fight.

It had been a long time since he had fought an animal of this size. He calculated his strike angle and the amount of venom needed to immobilize the animal. The bobcat was bigger, but Lenny knew he was fast and clever. He had to try. He could not let the cat get Jabber.

He moved forward in a stealth-smooth manner. His crucial element of the attack was surprising. He tracked right and left, hoping the cat concentrated on Jabberrunner straight ahead. He needed to strike as close to the neck as possible, enabling his potent venom to immobilize the cat quickly. It would probably take three strikes, he surmised. The first was not the most potent but would weaken the animal so he could go in for the 2nd and 3rd bite. He must be quick, smooth, and accurate. He had done this before, he told himself.

The cat remained stationary, focusing on the prairie dog. Lenny approached the cat from the left. Lenny plunged and missed. The cat turned and saw the snake strike from his left, pulling back. He hissed and came around behind Lenny, attempting to grab and sling him in the air, maneuvering to stun the snake. Lenny was too quick and undulated away from the cat and twisted in time to strike at the cat's neck. The bobcat was dazed momentarily, then leaped again toward the snake. This time, Lenny struck fast and hard, releasing all his venom into the undersurface of the cat's neck. The cat pulled back, stupefied, and veered off to the side. He stumbled away weak and wobbly. Lenny considered striking again, but most of his venom was depleted from the previous strike so that he could be vulnerable to a direct blow from the cat. He looked up to see the attacker disappear into the night. Lenny turned back slowly to find the little prairie dog.

Jabberrunner had not moved. He was in the same place Lenny had left him, still holding his paws over his ears and now with his eyes closed. He shook uncontrollably, not sensing Lenny was back by his side.

"It's ok, Jabberrunner. It's ok. He's gone."

Jabber opened his eyes. He slowly lowered his paws, and Lenny saw a tear roll down his cheek as his body slowly stopped shaking, and he fell to the desert floor in a puddle of fur.

"Thank you, Lenny!" he whispered, his voice almost inaudible for Lenny to hear. "Thank you, Lenny!"

## Chapter Nine

Even if he wanted to start his journey to look for Greta, he couldn't make himself move. His body was devoid of energy. Using his venom for the attack had sent his body into a downward spiral, and there was nothing he could do but allow his body to heal and resupply the poison. Jabber went out to find food and brought fresh supplies of insects into Lenny, laying it carefully before his immobile head. He had even captured a live field mouse and tried to get Lenny to eat it. Lenny didn't look toward the mouse, and Jabber let it run off, almost glad he didn't have to watch a snake eat a fellow mammal. Jabber wasn't sure what was happening and didn't know how to help Lenny. All he knew to do was stay by his side, looking closely for possible danger, which didn't happen. In his usual fashion, he talked and talked, telling Lenny the many stories he knew repeatedly until he ran out of anything to say. The sun dropped in the sky and then rose on two more occasions. Jabber sat next to Lenny, quiet for one of the first times in days, when Lenny suddenly lifted his head, gobbled down the insects set before him, and asked Jabber if he was ready to go. Jabber jumped at the sound of his voice, thinking some creature had burst into their place of hiding. Then, blinking in amazement, he gathered his composure and told Lenny he was ready.

Lenny slithered out from under the extensive brush that Jabber had piled on him to protect him and started on their way.

"You are better," sputtered Jabber, unsure if he should be happy or frustrated that Lenny was up and going so abruptly.

"Yep,' Lenny replied. "I'm better."

And just like that, they were on their way.

Lenny got stronger and stronger as they went along. With improved stamina, he could keep up with Jabber, and the two traveled faster. Jabber loved seeing new territory. Having been a loner in the past, it felt new and fresh to have a companion. However, Lenny remained so focused on Greta that he rarely talked. Jabberrunner didn't mind, feeling like the two were silently becoming friends.

On the second day of their journey, Lenny abruptly stopped and surveyed his surroundings.

"This spot seems right," he said out loud to Jabber. He looked up and recognized the massive rocks where Greta had taken him the first day they met.

"She's there, high above us. It's her scent." Lenny started climbing, Jabber close behind. He concentrated hard to find the opening in the cliff wall that Greta had entered. The higher he ascended, the stronger and sweeter Greta's scent became, pulling him forward urgently.

The traveling companions slithered along the cliff's edge. Jabber knocked off loose rocks as he lost his balance, catching himself before falling over the side. Lenny abruptly slowed, looking back to be certain Jabber was safe. Jabber nodded, and Lenny doubled his pace and identified the crevice in the rocks that Greta had shown him. A second scent, different from Greta's, filtered into Lenny's nostrils as he approached the opening. It was foul and ominous. Lenny hurled his body into the cavern. He saw Greta curled in a tight ball huddling in the middle of the atrium. A large, male

Mojave rattler danced around her, nudging her head, rubbing, and touching her sleek body, coaxing her to move. Greta kept her head buried tightly inside her coil. The male snake swayed in a bizarre ritualistic fashion. Greta raised her head momentarily and flicked at his extended tongue in an irritated manner, rebuking his advances.

Lenny burst forward with fury.

"Greta, are you all right?" he hissed.

Greta slung her head upright, exhilarated in her movement.

"Lenny," she said in surprise.

His eyes met hers and flowed over her coiled body, sensing she was alive and unharmed.

He turned to the other snake.

"What are you doing here?" Lenny accosted sharply.

"Who are you?" the Mojave rattler spit out. "I am here to mate with this female." His voice was slimy and condescending.

Lenny glanced at Greta, who exhibited a look of horror and disgust.

"And I refuse your approach," Greta snapped at the snake. "I have told you for days, and you have not left me alone."

"She has refused your approach," Lenny repeated. "Did you not hear her? Now you must leave." Lenny moved closer to the other male.

"I will mate with her. I have found her first, and you are the one that must leave." The Mojave retorted, malice in his voice.

Lenny darted toward the other snake. He wrapped the anterior portion of his body around the Mojave, his head and neck held vertically. The other snake acknowledged the combat pose, raising his head high and vertical. Greta moved back against the cavern wall as the two males fought with ferocity. They bumped and hit each other with loud, forceful blows. Greta gasped as the large Mojave pushed Lenny toward the cave floor in a dominant move. It seemed like an eternity to the female snake as Lenny hovered in the lower position. But with resolve from his fiery spirit, Lenny pushed against the more muscular snake until he was upright again. The combat continued until both showed exhaustion, and finally, the other snake pulled away, not a match for Lenny. He moved out of the cavern, sluggish and defeated.

"If you come back here or ever approach her again," Lenny hissed slowly at the snake," You will not leave alive."

Over in the corner, away from the snakes, Jabberrunner huddled against the moist cave wall during all the verbal exchanges and the combat. His eyes were wide as Lenny fought for dominance. He knew his friend's strengths, yet he trembled as they fought. The petite female snake remained motionless, and Jabberrunner found himself drawn to her, understanding why Lenny had so desperately wanted to return. He shivered, thinking about what would have happened to Greta if their arrival had been delayed.

Lenny moved closer to Greta, who extended her body lengthwise, and Lenny wrapped his body lengthwise around hers. They remained still, entwined, disregarding all that had happened. Jabber gazed at the two snakes, paused, then quietly slipped

The Desert Saga

out of the cavern, Greta and Lenny never noticing he was there.

## Chapter Ten

The following morning, the emerging sun basked the side of the rocky boulder with warmth. Lenny and Greta slithered out of the cavern to find Jabberrunner snuggled alongside the cliff.

"Greta, this is my little prairie dog friend, Jabberrunner. And Jabber, of course, this is Greta," Lenny beamed.

Jabber jumped onto his hind legs and rubbed his forepaws together nervously. He bowed in a formal greeting, surprisingly speechless.

"I have much to thank you for, Jabber." Greta gushed to Jabber. "Lenny has told me about your journeys, the coyotes, the bobcats, and you nursing him back to health. How can I ever thank you?"

Jabber's face flushed, and he continued finding it difficult to say anything. Finally, he nodded and bowed again, Lenny amused at his lack of speech.

"We have decided to return to my home territory, Jabber," Lenny said as he looked over at the little female snake. "Greta is worried that the large Mojave rattler might return."

"I am not willing to have Lenny engage in such combat again." Greta blurted out. "That all was so frightening." She twisted her body playfully around Lenny. The two snakes coiled and uncoiled as they moved along the edge of the mountain face.

"At one time, I had longed for adventure," wheezed Lenny in a quiet voice." But now, I have had my adventure. I am ready to return to the land that I will be glad to call mine. I am eager to show Greta where I came from."

The two snakes noticed the prairie dog hung his head in disappointment. He cast his eyes to the ground.

"But we want you to come with us, Jabber," Lenny quickly added. "Will you come back with us? There are prairie dogs that live there. So, you could have a family."

Jabber looked up, and a thrill rushed through his body. He started jumping back and forth, words flowing out of his mouth in a torrent of jabbering. He told them he was confident he could find the best and safest path to travel. He would avoid red-tailed hawks and coyotes. He talked about meeting new friends. The two snakes eventually tired of his ramblings and slithered back into the cavern, allowing Greta to spend more time in her beloved home.

"Are you sure?" Lenny asked, gentleness and understanding in his voice. "You would leave all this behind?"

"I'm sure!" she said softly. "I want to come with you. I want to be your mate." She looked at Lenny, her eyes filled with anticipation.

Lenny slithered toward Greta and coiled his body around hers, the two interlocking, while the world around them went silent.

The sun rose the following day, and the snakes uncoiled, ready to begin their journey ahead. With Jabber beside them, the three set off together to travel to a place to call home. Whatever adventure was up ahead, they would be ready.

Donna Krutka

# DREAD

# THE RED-TAILED HAWK

## Chapter One

The female hawk dove toward the desert floor with lightning speed, the tiny field mouse screeching in terror, trying to escape the capture. It ran around the brittlebush and prickly-pear cactus, but the hawk was too fast. She scooped the mouse in her claws and carried it high into the cloudless sky. The mouse squealed and wiggled, arms flailing, trying to escape, but within minutes, the hawk landed on a tree branch and tore the mouse apart. Her arrogant countenance looked over the desert as she licked her beak with pleasure. She was satisfied, at least for now.

She lifted her sleek, muscular body from the darkly colored branch of the Mesquite tree and soared above her desert territory. She scanned the ground below, seeing everything that moved under her flight path. Then, she angled her body flat against the updraft and floated effortlessly up and down. Dry air drifted past her nostrils, and the hot sun warmed her mighty wings. She made wide circles in the sky, the prey below rushing for cover to stay hidden from her. Her name was Dread, and she was the terror of the sky.

Her eye caught a group of coyotes feeding on a fallen mammal. She circled above the predators, listening to their yelps and watching closely. She clicked her tongue to join the feed and dove toward the grouping ferociously, letting out a screech heard for miles. The coyotes caught sight of the bird and scampered away from their prey. Dread grabbed a large hunk of the carcass with her talons and lifted it toward the sky, allowing the coyotes to surround their prey again. She screeched with haughty delight when the more prominent animals gave way to her presence.

The day's bright sun rays began to dim, replaced by orange, red, and blue shadows. Dread lowered her head, noticing cooler air temperature and calmer wind. She landed high in the branches of a mesquite tree and gobbled down the meal. She had eaten well today. Tonight, she was content to rest and watch. She observed the jackrabbit occasionally stopping to glance from side to side, then continuing to nibble on the blossoms of desert plants. Her keen eyes spotted the pig-like family of Javelina. Parents led four pups through the wash; their snouts raised upward to smell for danger. Dread scoffed. Their poor eyesight could prove their doom, making them easy targets for those with vision like hers. The desert spoke tales of prey and predator; she was at the top of the food chain and, thus, a top predator. Yet, it was hard for her to shake off a sense of sadness at times surrounding her. She stood more erect and shook her head from side to side, masking a secret hurt she held inside. Finally, she screeched a loud cry into the desert, warning of terrifying anger layered with a vengeance and a hidden hint of loneliness.

A sudden sound came from the nearby giant Saguaro, and she peered into the intimidating, yellow-eyed stare of a great-horned owl. It was Conn, a rival dominant predator in the territory. He was a night hunter, and the two birds had consciously agreed to hunt at different times of the day to avoid constant battles over prey. She acknowledged his gaze and then looked around, curious to see if there were a nearby meal the owl would hunt. Conn wouldn't need to see his catch. He located his next meal by sound alone and approached it in silence, the sound of his wing beats muffled by the soft edges of his specialized feathers.

Dread looked out to the desert to see what he would hunt. He winked, nodded, and lifted from the saguaro in hushed flight, heading toward an inattentive, small king snake slithering on the desert floor. Dread saw him grab the snake and fly to his perch within seconds.

"We are much alike!" she mused under her breath. "But in the sky, we are not. I will forever be dominant." Dread turned away, ignoring the Owl, and rested for the night.

The first light slowly rose above the mountains. Dread stood on one leg, then the other, wings stretching in a habitual morning routine. The musty desert air smelled of dirt, dried brittlebush, and cactus. Lifting from her perch, she relished the air pressing against her chest, outstretched her wings, and angled toward the sky. The field below, peppered with giant saguaros, shrank in size as she lifted upward to make the rounds of her beloved territory. The higher she soared; the more exhilaration swept through her body. From below her, the creatures on the ground could see her hooded, brown head and could make out the hooked bill that characterized this raptor. She screeched, aware that she was overhead and could see everywhere in her territory.

Her eyes settled on a prairie dog scurrying along the desert floor. She angled her sleek body toward her prey and began her dive. Out of her left field of vision came a dark, flying blur. She was startled and momentarily lost her concentration as the Great-horned Owl flew past her, diving for the prairie dog. She let out a harsh shrill cry realizing Conn had encroached on her hunt, deliberately trying to outsmart her. Her wings pulsed in anger, and she circled to visualize where Conn had traveled. He landed on a tall Saguaro and swiveled his head to see Dread flying overhead. Confident she was observing, the owl lifted the little prairie dog into the sky again and flew back to the desert floor, placing him carefully back on the ground.

She recognized the prairie dog. It was Jabberrunner, the creature she had been trying to capture for weeks. She screeched, realizing Conn must have been watching her. She felt her head pulse and lifted her wings.

# The Desert Saga

## Chapter Two

Conn bellowed a long, triumphant screech as he set down the frightened prairie dog close to his burrow opening. Then, a cacophony of gurgles sounded like laughter from the owl.

"I love doing that to Dread." he boomed, Jabberrunner quivering as he stood frozen beside Conn.

"She has self-proclaimed her presence in the skies as most powerful, most dominant," Conn continued, "But I can out-fly her, out-smart her and out-hunt her any time."

"You've been perching near my burrow, owl. Have you been trying to eat me?" Jabber spoke with a quivery voice.

"No, Jabber. If I wanted to eat you," the owl scoffed," I would have done so sunsets or moons ago." Again, Conn hooted comically.

"I just love taunting Dread. She is furious she hasn't been able to catch you, and I have." He peered down at Jabber, remembering he had grabbed the little prairie dog, flown him high up in the air to his nest, and plunged him back to the ground. Jabber was probably terrified.

"I was trying to protect you, Jabber. I meant no harm," Conn said, sounding almost remorseful. "But you better watch yourself." The owl leaned his face close to the prairie dog and spoke slowly and deliberately. "You are definitely on Dread's list of future meals. First, however, you must remember our agreement. You will flush out as many field mice and snakes into my hunting territory as possible, and I will spare you from Dread and myself."

Jabber nodded nervously in the Owl's direction as he looked down to the sandy ground. Then, as quickly as he appeared, Conn flew away, not saying goodbye or acknowledging what he had just done for Jabber. The little prairie dog blinked in confusion, scurrying back into his ground hole, grateful he was not a victim of the food chain.

Conn flew back to the perch on the tall saguaro he liked to call home base. He hunted through the night, finding several snakes that filled his belly, satisfying his hunger. He watched the skies for other predatory owls, only recently having to ward off attacks by several hostile species of owls attempting to take over his territory.

His senses shifted to his witty interaction with Dread. She now would be on the watch for his thwarting activities in the future. He would stay alert to find other stunts that would annoy her, if not just to make her have to notice him. He liked it when she conceded his presence in their shared territory. He outstretched his massive wings and felt a shiver filter down his body. The night darkness was fading into shades of pale blue. Dawn, and he needed to rest. He closed his eyes, perched comfortably on the tall saguaro, and settled into the approaching warmth of the sun to wait for his next hunt at nightfall.

## Chapter Three

The crow flopped around on the ground, unable to get up. His wing had broken as he dropped from the sky, plunging into the boulder at an uncontrollable speed fleeing from the hawk. His mate landed beside him, squawking and pleading for him to get up. She peered at the sky, seeing the hawks circling over their heads.

"I can't fly," he told her. "You must go and leave me. Otherwise, she will get you too." His voice was desperate and weakened.

"I won't leave you. We've hunted in this territory for some time. It's as much our territory as it is the hawk's." Uncertainty rang in the female crow's response.

Within seconds, the dominant red-tail hawk landed next to the wounded crow. His mate spread her wings and puffed her feathers.

"Stay away," squealed the female crow. "He is injured." The crow's voice was desperate. Dread callously took a step closer.

The defending crow lunged toward the hawk, shrieking and thrashing. Dread pulled back and swatted the crow with her wing. Then, the red-tail swiftly grabbed the male crow into her claws and lifted it off the ground, tearing into the sky. The female crow screeched in agony and took flight, losing sight of the hawk and her mate within seconds. She landed on a mesquite tree branch, her beak open with a panting breath. She looked upward, where her mate had disappeared into nothingness. Then, she pierced the heavens with a harrowing cry of retaliation.

## Chapter Four

The dawn brought eerie shadows over the landscape, giving a layered appearance to the mountain topography. Dread stared lazily over the desert, warm air bathing her rested feathers. She stretched her wings, as was her morning routine, readying for her dawn hunt. The Grandmaster Saguaro, where she perched, seemed to creak in the wind. She suddenly heard a thud as Conn landed close to her on an adjacent arm of the saguaro. Dread scowled, taken aback by his boldness.

"Are you here to try to see what I will hunt this morning so you can get a jump on my choice of a meal?" her voice was sarcastic and unfriendly.

"Not this morning," he replied, turning his head slowly to look into Dread's angry eyes.

"I want to sit on the Grandmaster as you do to look out at our resplendent territory.!"

Dread turned her head away, choosing not to give up her perch.

"I noticed your flight speed has been suffering as of late." Conn quipped. He was larger than the female hawk. His upper body and wings were a muddy brown with dark horizontal markings throughout his camouflaged body. His head sported a reddish-brown facial disc made up of a concave collection of feathers that channeled sound into his ears. His eyes were piercing, and his overall appearance was foreboding.

"So, you are referring to your catch of the prairie dog? I give you no credit for that victory. You had been preparing to thwart me." Dread stared straight ahead, not wanting to acknowledge Conn's comments. "I have always been able to outfly you, Owl."

"Would you like to test your abilities?" Conn spoke as if Dread were eager to continue in conversation. "If so, I have a suggestion. I am proposing that we race." The Owl again turned toward the hawk and watched for her response.

"A race?" Dread said incredulously. The idea sounded so unbelievable that she turned and stared at Conn.

"Yes. A race! I propose we start from this spot and fly to the far point of the Black Canyon. We then make an aerial turn and return here to see who is the fastest." His voice sounded excited and already triumphant.

Dread looked out toward the Black Canyon. She knew of the narrow canyon and the tales of the intense updrafts and head-blocking winds that made them dangerous. Choosing the wrong flight path through the canyon could knock you against the walls' sides and prove perilous. She turned her head back to Conn, locking her gaze into his.

"And if we do this race and I win?" she said with a question.

"I will leave you alone and stop harassing you. I will give up daytime hunting." Conn had trouble not showing his delight that she might be considering his proposal.

Dread took some time to ponder the offer. She wanted to flippantly dismiss Conn's presence over her desert skies. The two birds were rivals in their territory, both wanting to be owners of the skies. However, she was not one to back down from a challenge. Conn's proposal sounded like an easy feat to win, and she was confident that she was undoubtedly the faster raptor of the two.

"Are we to do this now, at this time, Conn?" Dread was feeling well-rested and calm, and since it was now dawn, the Owl might be tired from hunting most of the night. But, on the other hand, she had not yet had a morning meal. Beating Conn at his own game was quite tempting.

"Yes, now," Conn answered. "Your call when we start!"

Dread momentarily paused, then nodded in agreement, and Conn acknowledged her nod. Both birds took deep breaths, stretched out their wings, and took off from their perch with reckless abandon.

Dread soared through the air with majestic ease. The wind rushed by, feeling cold. Her wings weaved right and left, accelerating her body to produce a bolt of electricity. She dared not look to see Conn's position in case it would slow her down. Instead, she looked ahead, the Black Canyon looming far away. She knew she had to pace herself since the distance of the round trip was lengthy. Her wings functioned with precision. Her usual wing beat was slow and deliberate, but now she used a faster cadence to gain speed. Her breathing rate increased, blood rushed to her head, and her vision sharpened. The canyon walls enlarged before her.

"Steady," she whispered. "Focus! Embrace for updrafts."

She accelerated, ensuring she would enter the canyon before Conn. With a near-fatal mistake, she ducked her head back toward her chest to scan for the Owl. Her body swerved to the right, missing the canyon wall only by inches. She steadied her flight, controlled the updrafts, and cleared the walls safely. She hissed, sensing Conn was right behind her. She reached the canyon's end, sighting where they were to make the 180-degree aerial turn. Her body torqued with maximum speed, and her turn before Conn put her in first place.

At the turnaround, a massive headwind took her breath away. Her eyes moved to the canyon sidewalls. She flapped her wings to near exhaustion, making little progress. Finally, she ducked her head and straightened her body, fighting the updrafts that blasted her from below. She emerged from the canyon wall, breathing rapidly and her heart pounding.

The headwind continued to pound at her. Her wings flapped and fluttered uncontrollably, and her body bashed against the hot air currents. Resolve weakened when she looked over to see Conn pass her, quickly taking the lead.

Unexplainably, her exhausted body tucked behind Conn, and the effort it took to fly eased in his draft. She slowed her breathing and momentarily was able to rest. She looked ahead and saw the Grandmaster's silhouette in the foreground. She bobbed to the right, but when she got out of Conn's draft, she faced a solid wall of air again. She knew the timing was everything.

She had to choose with care when she would make her move. She waited. She waited. With only a short distance, she hurled her body forward with all her might and went around Conn, landing on the Giant Saguaro exactly when Conn landed.

The two raptors collapsed in absolute exhaustion. Their heaving chests pushed blood to their head, so they had to fight against passing out. They lay motionless for a long time before Conn lifted his head and managed a hiss toward Dread.

Conn's superiority appeared to be matched by Dread's audacity. The two predators would have to allow the other to live in their claimed land.

"That was quite a race," Conn said with mumbled words. "The drafting was pretty smart. I almost had you, and I'm impressed with your speed. I take it back. You are not slowing down in flight!"

Dread raised her head and looked at Conn, and he almost thought he saw a smile in her peering hawk eyes.

# Donna Krutka

## Chapter Five

The snow swirled frantically. The biting cold tore into the male hawk's underside as he flew into a stiff south wind, unusual for this time of year. Rogue planned the departure to leave before the wind shifted to the south, anticipating a tailwind for most of his journey. Optimal travel from north to south would be easy if the wind were at his back. But it had changed direction early. He scanned the land below for food but spotted none. He urged himself forward, despite hunger, searching for the territory where he could survive. He was tired of the cold and dark, cloudy skies. Instead of tall, densely packed trees and high snow-covered rocky mountains, he wanted sun, warmth, and open plains. He pressed his chest into the wind and tucked his head, making slow progress, happy to see the land below him change in appearance: less snow and dense pine tree forests replaced by open pockets of green grass. He scanned the ground for field mice. Finally, he spotted a lone white-tailed rabbit nibbling on tree nuts. He plummeted to the ground with incredible speed, scooping up the startled rabbit in his claws and lifting him off the ground. He landed on a nearby tree and fed, exhilarated after being so long without food in the snow-covered land in the north.

His rest was quick, and he felt the nourishment pulse through his wings. He swiftly took flight, resplendently happy to fly south. He was a migratory bird and passed high in the sky above other hawks, flying over their territory, giving them no provocation to challenge their dominance. He dropped to the ground when he needed to feed, spotting the abundance of small mammals emerging as he traveled into warmer areas. His strength improved after finding prey.

He slept fitfully in the warmer air perched atop a tall, multi-branched tree. His eyes opened to spot a pair of eagles flying closer and closer. Suddenly, they dove in unison to attack. He lifted off the branch at the last possible moment in a cunning move prompting the eagles to slam into the tree where the hawk had been roosting. He rose high in the sky, circled 360 degrees, and with speed as fast as lightning, outmaneuvered the two eagles, disappearing before they spotted his direction. He was stealth in the sky, using similar skills often on his migratory journeys. He wasn't afraid to do battle. He would confront the dominant predator when he found a place he wanted to settle. But not until that time. He looked back and studied the birds that had attacked. He would remember them!

After days of flying, the sun was a brilliant yellow, and the sky was a deep, welcoming blue, almost cloudless. The terrain turned sandy, with jagged mountains and fat boulders dotting the terrain. The plant life was more sparse than up north. He marveled at the tall, green, tree-like columns populating the landscape. Some trees had dark, blackish barks and others green bark. All appeared to have spikes that made him cautious about landing. He noted abundant wildlife as he flew over.

He landed on a prickly tree branch growing from an outcropping of boulders. He peered through the gnarled limbs over the desert valley, camouflaged by his reddish-brown coloring. The hot sun warmed his muscular body. Insects buzzed around, and he snapped at several, gulping them down like misty droplets of water. Multiple holes peppered the desert floor, burrowed by small rodents. He puffed his feathers as his eyes followed a field mouse ripe for capturing.

He spotted a female hawk perched casually on the arm of a giant green columnar cactus, appearing to be the grandmaster of all the plants in the territory. He watched her from afar, not wanting to be conspicuous or threatening. She seemed to be alone and content. He watched her hunt, taking note of her ruthless style. He also saw a large Golden Horned Owl flying over the territory. The two birds appeared to live in the same region without hostility.

He decided he would stay in this territory for at least a while. The female hawk intrigued him, and he loved the open sky with the abundant sun. He glanced around for a more permanent place to roost, choosing a secluded giant saguaro. Its uppermost arm showed a large opening. Yes, he thought, this seems like an excellent place to stop. He needed to feed soon, and if he did, he wondered how the female hawk would respond. He lifted off, climbing high into the air, and plunging precipitously, only to reverse directions and rise again. He did this several times, conspicuously, then vanished from the sky, confident that the female hawk had seen him announcing his presence in her territory.

## Chapter Six

Conn sat on his favorite tree outpost as the day turned from dawn to a hot midday temperature. He had done his hunting during the night but didn't want to rest yet. The morning bustled with a different array of animal activities than did the night. He looked to the sky to see if Dread was in the air, disappointed when he couldn't spot her antics.

The exciting race of the previous morning still lingered in his thoughts. He fluttered his wings, working out the stiffness present. The female hawk had surprised him. Dread was smaller in size but mighty in flight. He mused they were much alike: the top of the food chain with any prey choice. Somehow, they managed to hunt in the same territory and have plenty of meals. Dread was a fierce bird. She had no mate and was self-sufficient. He had noted anger in her spirit, wondering if that was from her past.

The winter months were coming. If he were to mate, haste was necessary before the colder temperatures overtook the desert. His eyes scanned high trees for abandoned nests. It was in his Owl nature not to build his own nest but to use nests of other large birds of prey before their mating season.

He looked down and sighted Jabberrunner eating blossoms on the ground below. He smiled at how simple it seemed to collect berries, grasses, and plants rather than hunt for meat. But his thoughts were interrupted when a soft whoosh came from above, and he witnessed sharp talons grab Jabberrunner and hoist him into the sky. Conn's feathers flared, and he twisted his neck, expecting to see Dread having made her catch. But instead, he saw a formidable golden eagle dangling the prairie dog in its claws. Jabber wiggled in desperation to try to get loose.

Conn didn't recognize the eagle. It was from a neighboring territory. He instinctively followed and took flight, not giving away his presence. The eagle flew higher and higher until he reached a cliff and dropped Jabber into an expansive nest snuggled into the side of the hill. Conn plowed into the belly of the eagle at top speed and snatched Jabber out of the nest before the eagle could react. A second eagle flew toward the owl, and Conn realized this was the mate of the first eagle. Conn tucked the shivering Jabber in one of his claws and reached out the other claw to land a slash across the oncoming attacker. A heinous shriek came from his other side, and Conn felt a shearing sensation in his right wing-prompting him almost to drop the prairie dog. He steadied his flight, keeping Jabber in a tight hold, and with a wince in pain, forced his magnificent wingspan to lift off into the sky. The two eagles followed closely behind. The Owl swirled and dodged the attackers, breathing heavily and blinking his eyes to clear his vision. He needed an escape route, but the extreme pain in his wing was clouding his instincts.

A high-pitched screech came from above the owl, and Conn looked up in time to see Dread and another hawk swoop down toward the eagles. The two hawks struck the eagles in unison with the downward force of their bodies and locked talons with the eagles spinning them over onto their backs. Dread loosened one of her talons and sliced it across the belly of one of the eagles while the second hawk grabbed the other eagle's neck in his beak and pulled back with deadly power. Squeals and cries rang out in every direction in the sky as the birds fought, and then abruptly, the eagles pulled away from the fight and flew away. Conn kept the terrified Jabber tucked close to his body, each wing flap more difficult than the last.

Dread and the second hawk flew up alongside the owl, assessing the injuries of Conn and the prairie dog.

"Can you fly home?" Dread squealed at Conn, noticing his unsteady wing. "Did the prairie dog make it?"

Conn nodded, dangling Jabber gently from his claw. The red-tailed hawks followed behind until Conn flew to the desert floor, landing near Jabberrunner's opening to his burrow. He carefully opened his claw and gently set the prairie dog on the ground.

"You ok?" Conn managed to say, his voice weak and shaky.

Jabber looked up and nodded. His body trembled uncontrollably.

"Thank you, great owl," Jabber said, hesitating as if he wanted to say more. He then plunged into his burrow.

Conn hooted, then slowly pivoted his head toward the sky, trying to catch sight of the two hawks. But unfortunately, they were nowhere to be found.

## Chapter Seven

The two hawks flew upward into the sky, side by side, after ensuring Conn reached his perch safely. The adrenalin of the fight still hung in the air between them.

"My name is Rogue," the male hawk finally said. He took glances at the female hawk as they flew.

"You were following me," Dread said indifferently.

"I saw you take off, and I was curious." Rogue remained cautious.

"I have seen you circling in the sky. You're not from around here. What are you doing here?" Dread's voice was stern and unfriendly.

"I am from the North. Up there, there's too much snow and no prey. So I decided to come south. I have passed over many lands. I like what I see in your territory. The sun is warm, and the sky is blue. Prey is abundant." he answered. He hoped she noted he referred to it as her territory.

"What's your name?" Rogue asked as they continued flying. There was a long pause.

"They call me Dread." The female hawk appeared to snort. "The creatures of this territory named me that name."

"I understand. I've seen you hunt." Rogue gave her a nod. "Where were you when the eagle attacked? You appeared from nowhere."

"I was scouting for prey when I witnessed the eagle grab the prairie dog. His name is Jabberrunner," Dread elaborated. "The Owl and the prairie creature are friends. I followed when the Owl took flight, sensing his concern." Dread's banter was curt.

Dread was certain the eagles they had fought were the two birds that had attacked her nest. Her rage had consumed her for so long after that attack. Countless flights around the surrounding territory had proved unsuccessful in sighting the attacking eagle or her chicks. Now that she had seen these eagles, she would find their nest and watch for her chicks.

Dread had become quiet again, content to remain on course flying with Rogue.

"I know those eagles. I have dealt with them before." Dread's voice was angry.

"When I saw them attack the Owl, a surge of vengeance ran through me." She stopped momentarily, then looked his way. "I was glad you joined me. Thanks for your help."

Rogue turned his head in surprise at Dread's acknowledgment of his help. He was sure this was a rare remark from the dominant female hawk.

"I haven't been in a good fight for a while. But, in truth, I found myself enjoying the experience." They flew further into the desert before he spoke again.

"How do you know those eagles?" His question was tentative, wondering if she would answer.

"Thanks again for your help," she said, ignoring Rogue's last remark. She nodded and then abruptly pivoted in her direction and flew off toward the east. Rogue stayed his course and returned to his home perch.

Dread spent days flying toward the eagles' nest, remaining hidden, camouflaged, and silent as she watched them hunt and prey. Her eyes scanned the skies for two recognizable hawks.

She flew back to her territory, trying to find updrafts to lift her spirit. Above her, the male hawk made wide circles over the land. Instinctively, she followed, the rush of air clearing her senses. She gently beat her wings, allowing a smooth and gliding ascent to the height of the other bird, watching as he shot toward the ground with lightning speed. Exhilaration filled her body as she matched his movement and plunged toward the earth. Rogue saw her following and changed his flight angle, again shooting back toward the sky. Dread followed, and the two circled in synchrony. Then, Dread took the lead, and the male hawk followed. She went wide and made a sweeping oval pathway in the sky, mapping out the territory she had claimed. Rogue, in synchrony, locked onto her line of flight.

Rogue broke away from Dread's flight plan and circled slower. He partially closed his wings and dropped his legs with his talons spread. He moved his body, tilting from side to side. Dread flew above Rogue, creating slower circles in the sky. She watched as he climbed higher in the sky with deep, exaggerated beats of his wings, then closed them and dived precipitously at an incredible speed. He shot back toward the sky and repeated his plunge toward the earth, this time not as steep. Dread observed his behavior and continued a slow glide. She recognized the invitation to engage in a sky dance, a quest for courtship. Her wings pulled her toward this strong, bold Red-tail Hawk. She was eager to participate in his invitation but struggled with restraint.

She slowly angled her flight away from Rogue. She was not yet ready to mate. Before joining a mating courtship, she had to complete what she had set out to do. She put her head down into the wind and headed toward her perch, not looking back at Rogue, who continued circling in the sky.

## Chapter Eight

Conn perched on a high outcropping of a massive collection of boulders. His eyes frowned, and his breathing quickened as he watched the two hawks in their flight antics. The arrival of this male hawk had made him feel unsettled. The hawk had played a part in fighting off the eagle attack, but he felt sure that Dread had been the bird to intervene to help him. He wrestled with his anger and hostility. His usual tolerant nature turned intolerant, and he had to suppress an urge to drive this intruder out of the territory. He sat brooding while the two hawks made annoying circles in the sky. He quietly closed his eyes, blocking his mental images, and awaited nighttime. He would feel better when he could hunt.

The two red-tailed hawks returned to their perch. It was late in the night when Conn flew quietly to land next to where Rogue rested. Rogue, not surprised at his arrival, sensed that the Owl had a territorial claim on the territory and a unique attraction to Dread.

"Hello, Owl," Rogue said. He waited for the Owl to make a threatening hiss.

"My name is Conn. You were with Dread when the eagles attacked me." Conn hesitated before he added, "Thank you for your help." Conn's voice resounded with indifference.

"It was Dread who saw your plight. I merely followed," answered Rogue.

"I am aware of that." Conn continued," But I acknowledge your help!" The owl fell silent, but Rogue knew there was more he wanted to say.

"What is your intention here in this territory?" Conn said curtly.

"I think I am going to stay for a while. I am attracted to the sun and warmth. I am pleased with the plentiful prey." Rogue glared purposefully at the owl. "I don't intend to be a threat to you, Conn."

"And what are your intentions with Dread?" Conn was perceptive. He knew there was more to Rogue's intentions.

"I'm not sure yet. We are learning about each other. Why do you ask, Owl?" Rogue was beginning to become annoyed.

"She is a strong, dominant bird of Prey, Rogue. I would hate for anything to happen to her." Conn had a warning in his answer.

"My feeling, exactly, Conn. I'm glad we agree." Rogue peered menacingly at the Owl and made a motion of his wing for the Owl to leave. Conn hesitated but decided to go without further confrontation. He still could not shake the uncertainty and hostility toward this hawk.

"I will be watching you, hawk!" he managed to say as he flew off.

"I am sure you will be," Rogue screeched in reply.

## Chapter Nine

Dread's initial antagonism toward Rogue's presence in her territory began fading. The two hawks began to work together to catch prey. They spotted small groups of mammals and would attack from different directions, trapping the prey from a line of escape. They followed each other flying above the land much of the day and settled together in a shaded part of the hot desert sun to rest.

"How do you know the two eagles you are tracking?" Rogue one day asked as they took off for a morning flight.

Dread was silent for a while.

"You've been watching me?" she said as they flew together over the desert. Rogue gave her a nod.

"I'm interested in your past. There is more to you than just being a fierce predator, Dread." Rogue waited for a response and added, "I sense you are hiding a secret."

After thinking about his question, something inside broke loose and encouraged her to reach out to this hawk. Dread decided to answer. She looked straight ahead and began telling Rogue her story.

. . . .

Before she had been named Dread, she lived in this territory, roaming the skies and enjoying its beauty. Her parents had moved away, giving her the land, they had once dominated. Her dark-brown wing coloring and white chest feathers quickly attracted another red-tailed hawk, and after a ritualistic courtship, the two mated. Together they reigned over the territory, hunting and soaring in the sky without competition from other birds.

The mated Red-tailed hawks began the process of building a nest. They wanted the highest vantage point in this desert land.

"The Grandmaster," exclaimed the female hawk. "It is the tallest and oldest saguaro in our territory. So, it would be perfect!"

The majestic saguaro had six arms extending off from the center of the cactus. It was on a sloped hill filled with boulders and smaller saguaros. It overlooked the territory they had claimed as their home. They collected mesquite tree branches and fallen ocotillo skeletal spines for the outer walls. They carefully selected dead or dried prickly pear plants to reinforce the walls. It took one and a half-moon cycles to build the nest.

The birds settled inside the spacious nest. The bowl was so deep that their heads remained hidden from predators. They felt it was perfect.

"We have another full moon before it is my time to lay our eggs, " said the female hawk. Then, exhausted, she nestled down to get comfortable in the nest. "It will easily fit the 3 or 4 eggs I will lay."

The male red-tail moved close to the female, eager to keep her warm. "What's it like to have a clutch of eggs?"

"I lay one egg, then wait for the sunset, and if we are fortunate, I will lay another egg. I continue until there are no more".

Time passed quickly, and the female laid three eggs, each white with a few speckles. The female hawk surrounded the little eggs, keeping them warm with her body. It would be a full-moon cycle before she could leave the eggs while her mate hunted and brought her food. On occasion, he took her place and gently sat on the eggs enabling her to stretch her legs and fly around the saguaro keeping her wings active and fresh.

"Do you hear that? Scratching and poking are going on beneath me." The female nudged her mate in excitement. "It's the time!"

The male hawk rushed to her side, looking below her breastbone to visualize the tiny creature emerging from the cracked egg, beginning to try to make faint peeping noises.

"It is making noise already just as it is hatching," exclaimed the male hawk with a chuckle.

She nudged the little chick with her beak, helping it break through the shell. The parent hawks hovered close as two more emerged over the next two sunsets.

The three chicks had strong necks, opening and closing their beaks, peeping, bouncing and waving their wings. One was smaller than the other two but no less active. The male parent flew off to hunt and dropped pieces of meat into the nest while the female tore the catch into smaller pieces to drop into the open mouths of the hungry chicks.

The chicks grew fast. It was hard to keep them contained in the nest with all of their bobbing and flapping.

"What a commotion they are making!" the male hawk said, fluttering around, snapping up insects before they landed on the chicks. "How long does this go on before they fly?"

"It will be a full moon's revolution before that happens," she replied.

"I think I can tell the difference in their sex," the male said excitedly. "The little one is a male, and the two larger ones are male and female." He puffed out his chest at his discovery.

"Let's name them." the female said. She looked at them intently, thinking of names.

"How about "Mighty" for the little one." the male suggested. "Maybe that will help him outmatch his size," shoving his beak gently into the smaller one's delicate frame.

"I like Dante and Wren for the other two. Family names," said the female.

The personality of the chicks began to be apparent. Mighty lived up to his name, continually pecking at his larger brother and sister. Dante started showing slight aggression toward the others, striking out with his talons and claws. Wren was eager to fly, stretching her wings and needing more exercise than the others. She watched her parents with wide eyes when they took to the sky, anxious to join them.

"It's time to teach them to fly," the female hawk one day said to her mate.

The male hawk looked at the three chicks.

"Which do you think will take off first?" he asked.

"Wren," the female answered. "I was worried she would fall from the nest before she was ready. She ignores my warnings about injury or predators."

The male hawk studied his chicks. He was the protector; they would be alone when they learned to fly. He shuddered, thinking of the danger they might encounter.

"Tomorrow it is!" he said, resigned to what lay ahead.

The night was quiet after the parents settled the fledglings to sleep. The parent hawks wedged their lean bodies close to each other, looking out over the beautiful night sky, where a new moon was rising over the surrounding mountain-scape. A surge of satisfaction filled the air as the hawks looked upon their offspring and the home they had built. The chicks were strong and about to learn to fly, soon to leave the nest and join the parents in soaring and hunting.

"A family of hawks is invincible," the male hawk whispered to his mate. "We will dominate the skies, just as you dominated the skies before we had mated. We will be a force to reckon with as a family of red-tailed hawks."

A piercing screech sounded out from above. Two large shadows flew at the nest from overhead, hurling an attack with magnificent speed. A pair of Golden Eagles slammed into the male parent- hawk. In an instant, razor-sharp talons tore at his throat while another swipe ripped apart his wing, slicing his feathers from their insertion. The female hawk draped her body over the chicks as clawed talons dug into her back and beaks dug into her sides. Heinous squeals enveloped the nest as the female hawk looked over to watch the eagles fatally gouge the tiny Mighty chick and lift the larger Dante and Wren in their claws to fly into the sky.

The female slowly inched her injured body toward her mate, who lay immobile close to their most diminutive offspring. Then, finally, she let out a weakened cry and fell in desperation on top of the lifeless remains of her shattered family.

........

Dread flew silently for a long distance after telling her story to Rogue. It was a long time before either spoke.

"I am certain those were the eagles that had killed my mate, the tiny fledgling, and stole my chicks." she finally said aloud. Rogue looked puzzled. Dread continued.

"Eagles whose eggs are destroyed by other predators, or whose chicks are taken as prey, will steal hawk chicks and raise them as their own." Her eyes spit out a fire as she looked over at Rogue.

"I'm sorry," Rogue managed to say to her. But then, the anger he had sensed in Dread since he first met the female hawk became clear.

"I can help you look for them," he said as the pair glided aimlessly in the sky.

Dread's attention suddenly landed on Rogue.

"What did you say?" She responded, surprised at his words.

"I can help you look for your chicks," Rogue repeated.

"You'd help me? Why?" Dread's voice was high-pitched.

"I told you I haven't had many satisfying fights lately, and this seems like a battle worth taking on. " He waited for her response.

"We know where they have nested. So we can watch for your fledglings in stealth and intervene when we see them. I am good at stealth," Rogue smiled.

The desert air was warm and reassuring. Dread looked over at Rogue feeling an ounce of hope for the first time in many moons. Rage and revenge had consumed her for so long.

"I haven't thought of anything except looking for my chicks since that attack.

I have been unable to trust another creature." Dread looked over at the hawk flying next to her. Rogue was silent. Dread finally whispered: "I feel like I can trust you, Rogue. Maybe with your help, we can make it happen. I accept your offer."

## Chapter Ten

The two hawks flew every night back to the site where they had encountered the eagles. They sat on a neighboring saguaro, tucked behind one of the giant arms extending off the thick trunk. They spoke in hushed tones, telling the other stories about their encounters. Dread enjoyed Rogue's description of the lands he had flown over. She had never known a migratory hawk and was amazed at his description of the worlds he had seen. Little by little, she related more and more to him about who she was and what she wanted. But there were times when Rogue would be gone for hours. Dread looked out toward the desert, realizing she missed him when he was gone. She wasn't sure she wanted to be attracted to this strong, independent hawk. Any day he could resume his journey to places unknown.

"I must feed," one morning Rogue told Dread. "If you want to continue the watch, I will find us both food."

With a quickening in her breath, she looked at Rogue. When a male hawk offered a female food, he was giving her an invitation. It was a very specific invitation, Dread knew.

"You hunt first," she said in response. "Then I will hunt."

Rogue nodded, a tinge of disappointment in the rebuff. Then, he flew off in a similar direction to what he had been flying the last few days.

## Chapter Eleven

The sun hid behind the mountains, casting a pink glow on the clouds. Rogue flew high into the sky to visualize what he was tracking. Rather than looking for prey to hunt, he scanned the northern sky for other birds. Two red-tailed hawks were slowly circling below him. He lowered his altitude to approach, not implying an attack. Cautiously, the two hawks stayed close to each other. Rogue turned toward the south and left their territory so as not to suggest his hostility.

The next day, he flew the same course, again high in the sky, not arousing concern. The two hawks took off from their perch, circling below Rogue in defense. Again, Rogue descended to their altitude, not in a pattern of attack. He determined one of the hawks was female and the other male. He flapped one wing signaling a greeting, then left the territory.

On the third day, he took to the sky with a lower approach, flying directly into the two hawks' claimed territory. The female and male red-tails lifted from their perch and flew toward Rogue. The male was more compact than Rogue, eyes fierce, and his beak and claws ready to attack. Rogue spotted a multibranched tree below and dropped toward the tree, avoiding combat in the skies. The two smaller hawks followed, landing on a neighboring branch.

"What are you doing here?" the male hawk screeched. The female's eyes were bold and angry.

"I am from the south. I am looking for two red-tailed hawks: brother and sister." Rogue remained calm and non-confrontational. "I know their mother.

She has been searching for them for some time. Could you be orphaned hawks raised by eagles?"

The female choked and gawked, looking over at her brother.

"Who are you, then?" the young male hawk asked.

"My name is Rogue. I have migrated from the north to this warmer territory. The female hawk I am speaking of is from the territory south of here. I told her I would help find her chicks. I think you are her stolen chicks."

"Stolen?" the female said with disbelief. "Eagles raised us. Our parents abandoned us, and the eagles saved us. We are not the chicks you want. Our parents are dead."

"Are you sure about that?" Rogue questioned. "My friend tells a convincing story of two eagles attacking her nest, killing one of her chicks, and stealing the two others: a male and a female. The female hawk who told me her story said the eagles killed her mate and left her for dead. Thankfully, she survived."

The mention of another chick prompted the male hawk to turn to his sister.

"Remember I told you of another chick somewhere in my memory," he said. "Could it be our mother, alive?"

"Fly south with me," Rogue said in a convincing plea. "See if this could be true. See if she is the mother you thought was dead."

A surge of wings and accompanying squeals rose as the three hawks took flight, the two younger hawks following closely behind Rogue. Then, they picked up speed, gliding effortlessly, with a speed that defied resistance, heading toward the possibility of a reunion.

It had been some time since Rogue had left, and Dread took off from her usual perch. She soared and glided into the west wind, expanding her wings to their full width, creating sweeping tumbles in the sky. An unfamiliar sense of exhilaration clouded her awareness when a cacophony of screeches suddenly came out of nowhere. She looked up to see hundreds of crows mob, ram, and bombard her with ruthless force. She twisted and turned, zigging and zagging, up and down, using her claws to strike and tear. More and more birds flew at her, ramming and confusing her sense of direction.

The flock of crows parted, and a single bird flew toward the hawk. Vengeful eyes locked onto Dread. It was the mate of the injured crow she once attacked, seeking revenge. She flew straight for Dread, aiming to gauge the hawks' eyes. Dread tucked her head and continued clawing and scratching. There were so many birds, and she was losing ground.

Somewhere from outside this mass of crows, she heard other screeches. Sounds of multiple birds reached Dread's perception. She snapped a glance and saw three hawks battling off the crows. No, there were three hawks and one owl. Their screeches and loud squawks became louder than the cawing of the crows, and slowly, the crows began to fly away. Dread spotted a nearby saguaro and flew down onto an outstretched arm. Four raptors landed close to her. Rogue and Conn were there, but she didn't recognize the other hawks. Her vision fogged with the blood dripping from her gouged head. Then she heard their voices call out, and she passed out.

Donna Krutka

## Chapter Twelve

Dante and Wren stood guard over Dread as she slowly recovered from the crow attack. Rogue and Conn would individually fly overhead, keeping the skies clear of other threats. Dread finally opened her eyes and peered into the probing eyes of her female offspring.

"She's awake," Wren called out, and Dante quickly came closer. Dread shifted her body with difficulty, moving her wings to allow blood to flow.

"Wren, Dante, is that you? I've searched for you for a long time. So how is it that you are here? ", Dread's voice was muted.

"A swarm of crows attacked you," Dante explained. "They mobbed you, flying from every direction, gouging you with their claws and pecking at you with their beaks. You couldn't have survived much more of their ferocious attack."

"But how did you get here? How did you know it was happening? Where did you come from?" Dread had so many questions. She couldn't ask them quickly enough.

"Some time ago, a male red-tailed hawk flew in and out of our territory. We braced for an attack of dominance, but it didn't happen. Eventually, the hawk landed near us and asked who we were and our background. He spoke of how two golden eagles had taken your chicks, and you have been searching far and wide for signs of the chicks."

"Rogue," Dread whispered, looking around to acknowledge he had been helping her search for her chicks when he had left the territory.

"Go on," Dread said slowly.

"We told him that we were fledglings raised by eagles. The eagles told us our parents were dead and they had saved us from other predators. The story they told us was that we were from the north, not the desert." Wren spoke rapidly and with emotion. There was a long pause before Dante continued.

"Wren had always believed that our parents were alive." he said. "We flew north, often searching for hawks who might have been our parents. We never found any such birds. As long as we can remember, the eagles would watch us closely, stealing our catch and leaving only small pieces of meat for us to eat. We hated being in the nest."

"Until Dante stood up to the eagles one day," Wren said in excitement, "showing them that he was not afraid." Wren looked over at her brother, who abruptly puffed his feathers.

"We decided to leave their nest. We were careful not to be seen for many moons by the eagles. Even if they raised us, we would be treated as enemies if they found us" Dante's eyes peered out to the desert in anger.

"We found an abandoned, red-shouldered hawk's nest and stayed there for some time." Wren continued. "We had a routine we performed daily. First, we would soar in all directions looking for signs of a parent and then hunt for food."

"It was during one of those times that we spotted the male red-tailed hawk," Dante said. "We were cautious at first; then he approached us cleverly. We hoped we had found our missing parent when we listened to what he told us."

"We were flying back to find you when we saw the crows mobbing you," Wren interrupted, high-pitched and excited. "Rogue realized it was you. We panicked."

"Then we saw a Golden Horned Owl coming to help." Dante blurted out. "You couldn't have held out much longer." He gazed intently at his mother.

Dread slowly lifted her head. She looked at her two young hawks, warmth infusing into her injured body. Anger lessened inside her. She gently edged toward the two birds and laid her head on each one's tall body. The two younger hawks buried their heads into their mother's chest. The three stayed in that position for a long, tender moment.

## Chapter Thirteen

Conn watched three birds flying in a streamlined formation toward him. When they were closer, he recognized one as Rogue and the other as unfamiliar smaller hawks. Rogue signaled to Conn to follow urgently. The Owl sensing something was happening, feared Dread was in trouble.
He fell into a paceline with the three birds, rocketing across the sky. Conn looked below, his eyes spotting a massive flock of crows attacking a single bird. The bird was Dread, he realized. Terror and rage possessed his flight as he and the three raptors dove into the middle of the horde of crows, tearing flesh and ripping wings. The crows' reaction was swift and defensive as they lifted en mass, flying away from the attacked hawk. Dread slowly descended to a branch of a saguaro, weakened and injured. Rogue, Conn, and the two smaller hawks landed nearby. Conn perched motionless as the three hawks surrounded Dread, wings fluttering in protection. His piercing eyes observed the group.

He stood alone, not acknowledged by the other birds. He was not a hawk. He was an Owl. He was an outsider.

His eyes shifted to Dread, focusing on her features. She was injured, but she will heal. She is a robust and fierce bird. For a brief instant, Dread's eyes caught Conn's. He bowed his head. She briefly returned the gesture and turned back to the other hawks.

He would forever feel an attraction for this extraordinary female red-tailed Hawk named Dread, and they could be friends, but nothing more, he sensed.

He stayed on a nearby tree branch for a long time, watching as he felt something inside of him relinquish its hold on him. He would allow the male red-tail hawk, named Rogue, to stay in the territory. Dread and Rogue would mate and have chicks. They would be a family.

"I, too, need to find a mate," he said with conviction. "And I will build a family. A family of Great Horned Owls!" A sense of relief coursed through his sleek body. He lifted from his perch and flew high into the sky, leaving behind the three hawks to ensure his friend Dread would recover.

## Chapter Fourteen

The little prairie dog sat perched on the high boulder. It had been over two moon rises since his plight with the eagles. He looked over the beautiful lower lands of the desert. He sniffed the air, which smelled of dirt and wind mixed with potential rain. He looked up at the cloudy sky, surveilling the shadows that had passed over him. The temperature began dropping, and the wind picked up, blowing forcefully at his back. He looked in all directions, alarm pulsing through his senses. Rain began to fall. He stood paralyzed as a deep, rumbling sound filled his ears. He turned to run back to his burrow when he was broadsided by a blast of water, knocking him off his feet. He tumbled over and over, unable to get a breath of air. He surfaced, then sank, sputtering and choking, rocks and sticks hitting him from all sides. He tried grabbing ahold of anything in his path but soon was exhausted, uncertain how long he could keep from drowning.

Then, suddenly, he felt his body lift out of the rushing water and into the sky. He snorted and coughed, spitting mud and murk, clearing his nostrils, and took a deep breath. He continued to choke and gasp, half unconscious about what was happening. Sheets of water poured from the sky, making visibility difficult. Finally, he landed on solid ground and shoved under a protective rock ledge out of the downpour of rain. His thinking and vision cleared as he looked above him and stared into the stern gaze of a red-tailed hawk. It was Dread. His body trembled, and he was unable to move. Fear paralyzed his body.

"Are you all right?" he heard the bird say.

Jabber was unable to form words.

"Are you all right?" the hawk repeated.

"Yes," he squeaked. He was surprised at how frail his voice sounded. He was never without words, but now, he couldn't think of anything else to say.

"You're cold." The hawk raised her wing and draped it over the shivering prairie dog. Jabber's trembling body calmed, and his breathing slowed. He stared up at his rescuer. Then, gradually, his mind cleared, and he could speak.

"I'm ok. I was drowning. You saved me. Are you going to eat me?" Jabber was tentative in his question.

Dread looked down at the frightened prairie dog. Her stern countenance softened.

"I'm told they call you Jabberrunner. Is that right?" Dread asked.

Jabber nodded, continuing to have difficulty talking.

"There once was a time when I obsessed over catching you, little prairie dog. You are amazingly fast, and I knew catching you would take cunning and skill. But, of course, you were protected by a very skilled owl who saved you on several occasions!" Jabber thought he perceived a chuckle coming from the fearsome hawk.

"I've realized that you are much too important to eat. I want to be your friend," Dread added, "and I humbly apologize for terrorizing you as I did in the past. Will you accept my apology?"

Jabber blinked his eyes, stunned by what he was hearing. The great, dominant ruler of his skies had asked him to accept her apology.

"I accept," he answered and gulped again, hoping this was not a dream. The rain stopped. As quickly as they had occurred, the flood waters cleared. Jabber looked out over the wet desert land and then at the hawk.

"Thank you for saving me," he managed to say.

Dread nodded and fell silent. Jabber looked up at the sky and saw another red-tail hawk circling, and when it landed on the boulder where they were perched, Jabber moved closer to Dread, unsure if this bird would be as friendly as Dread had declared to be.

"This is Rogue," Dread said to the prairie dog. "He, too, will be a good friend to you."

Rogue squealed a hello to Jabber and nodded. Then, he squawked with jest, "This is a rather odd sighting, don't you think? A large red-tailed hawk's wing protectively draped over a potential prairie dog prey."

Dread attempted a smile and then asked Jabber if he was ready for her to take him home. Jabber wobbled his head in agreement, and Dread carefully picked the prairie dog up in her talons and flew toward Jabber's burrow, Rogue following. Then, safely placing the prairie dog down on the ground, she and Rogue flew away, leaving Jabber to wonder again if this was all a dream. But, even if it were, he decided it was a very delightful ending, which was the best way to end a nightmare!

## Chapter Fifteen

The air was crisp and smelled of openness and freedom. Dread and Rogue circled above the land below them, peering down at the creatures that made up their territory. They spotted the javelina parents leading their six babies across the wash. They saw the coyote roaming with their pack over the cactus-studded hillside. A bobcat was sunning on a large outcrop of boulders. They watched the prairie dog gobbling down blossoms from a thorny plant. There were lizards, rattlesnakes, roadrunners, and gamble quail, all representing the place they wanted to call home. Dread had accepted Rogue's invitation to mate, and together they began building a nest to prepare for their future family. They had started the nest building early and had invited Conn, the owl, to use their nest before they were ready to lay their eggs. Conn had found a mate and was grateful for the offer. The great horned owl's nesting period came several months before the red-tailed hawks' time, and the three birds agreed to use the same nest. Dread spent days flying over this same territory with her two offspring, Dante and Wren. Her heart was grateful for their return and that her anger and vengeance had melted from her spirit. The desert continued to burst with activity and promise, the cycle of life as always moving forward.

Donna Krutka

# THE DESERT BOBCATS

## AMARA THE STRONG AND MAGNUS THE GREAT

## Chapter One

A N eerie scream belted over the desert canyon, reverberating off the granite boulders and sinking into the rugged sandy wash. The female bobcat stares at the trespasser and releases a shrill hiss sending a warning not to come any closer. She lowers her body into a striking pose, the sun outlining shadows and ripples of her muscular body. The intruder, also female, pulls her upper lip backward and bares her sharp teeth, growling in defiance. She scoffs at the threats of the first bobcat and urinates on the ground where she is standing. She turns to run off when a tan and black blur of fur lands upon her, rolling them both into the barbs and spikes of desert plants. Blood gushes onto the ground, and snarls of ripping and tearing flesh can be seen and heard from the battling females. The larger bobcat, Amara, pushes forcefully down on the other.

"Who are you? This is my territory. Leave now." The threat was real and final. Amara held her tight grip and asked again. "Who are you?"

"My name is Stripe. Milo's mate." The trapped female twisted to get out of the hold.

"Milo's mate? He has mated?" Amara's surprise prompted the other cat to bite the paw holding her down, only to be painfully again pinned hard to the rocky ground.

Amara hissed. "Once more, this is my territory. I allow Milo to cross my land, but not you. You won't be allowed, despite being his mate. If you ever return here again," Amara growled at the intruder, "you will not leave alive." Blood continued to ooze from Stripe's ear, seeping into her eyes. Amara lightened her hold on Stripe, who rotated and snapped back to all fours.

"I will someday challenge you for your territory, shrew," Stripe said in a low growl. "Your time here is limited."

Amara scowled in amusement, her eyes following Stripe's retreat as the intruder turned and bounded onto a nearby boulder, out of sight. There were countless times when a female bobcat threatened to take Amara's space. Milo and Magnus were permitted to roam in her territory, but not other females.

Orangish-blue light settled over the desert. Warm temperatures were replaced by cold when a chilling wind blew from the north. The brightly sun-lit landscape became filtered with shadows of blue and gray. Amara's thick, tan fur kept her comfortable during the change. She quickly forgot the encounter with the intruder and continued her march around the perimeter of her domain. She scratched her claws into the black bark of the mesquite tree and squatted to reinforce her scent, marking the border of her land.

She usually traveled from dusk until dawn, covering nearly seven miles.

She negotiated through desert plants with sharp barbs and climbed rocky outcroppings. She sniffed the musty smell of desert bushes and bypassed the cottontail rabbit she spotted nibbling on freshly bloomed flowers.

She climbed onto her favorite lookout perch, feeling the last of the day's warmth radiating from the rock where she settled. She rested her head on her paws and looked over her beloved desert. The wind swirled dust and debris in front of her. The full moon illuminated the terrain making it easy to see prey.

She jumped to her feet when she saw movement on the boulder outcropping above her. The familiar scent of Magnus filtered down to her.

"Hello, Amara," he said casually.

"Hello, Magnus. It's been a while since I've seen you here."

"As usual, my rounds take me days. You? How are you?" Magnus replied.

The female bobcat slumped back onto the rocky ledge. She slowly licks her paws, tasting the salty grime deposited from her day's journey.

"I don't like the dryness and heat. So I look forward to the monsoons. Cooler and better feeding. You?"

"The same. We need rain. It's been a while." Magnus strolled closer and sat opposite Amara, glad to sit for a while.

Amara remained quiet, then one of her ears perked.

"So, Milo has a mate?" she asked with annoyance.

Magnus looked up, appearing slightly amused.

"You met Stripe?" he snorted to cover up a laugh.

"She attempted to defy my boundaries," Amara answered. She was not pleased with Magnus' attitude.

"I'm not surprised," Magnus replied. "She has been testing Milo's patience, too. She wants more than he has to give."

"What does that mean?" Amara's brows lifted in interest.

"She has been telling Milo to claim more territory. She wants him to expand his range beyond this one and into neighboring lands. She's not happy with him sharing this space with me. I think she is encouraging him to challenge me." Magnus' response was neutral, with no acknowledgment of a proposed threat.

"And this doesn't concern you?" Amara hissed as she thought of Stripe.

"Milo has been my closest companion since he was born. I have considered him a brother, even though he's not. He has been forever a peacemaker and negotiator. So I'm not worried about him defying me."

"So, how'd he choose Stripe as a mate?" Amara retorted, furrowing her forehead.

"Personalities are not often discussed during mating season," Magnus said, again with a sly smile.

Amara hissed. The thought of not choosing the right mate made her shudder.

"I will have no mercy on her if she again challenges me." rang Amara.

Magnus smiled and looked at Amara with interest.

"I would expect nothing less," he exclaimed and stood up.

He nodded with his usual brevity and leaped off the rocks where they were lounging. He had many miles to cover and Amara was used to his short visits. She nodded goodbye as he moved out of sight. She lay her head back onto her forepaws, considering their conversation, then rose, resuming her markings around her perimeter.

## Chapter Two

Magnus spotted the lone rabbit at first light. The crunch of dried brush made the bobcat hungrier. He crouched, licked his lips, and remained still and soundless. His eyes followed every move of the rabbit. His pounce was both magical and terrifying. Magnus grabbed the rabbit in one flawless snap and then sauntered off, ready to lay down and digest. He turned toward a pile of boulders and climbed high, then nestled in between a small crack in the face of the rock, partially hidden from the sun and other animals. He sensed it was going to be hot. He dozed off, suddenly awakened by a pack of coyotes scavenging below him on the sandy desert floor. One of the animals looked up, yelped out to the others, and in unison, ran off. Coyotes in a pack rarely confronted him, and he, too, was content to avoid the Coyote.

A foul, raucous smell drifted into his nostrils. He rubbed his nose back and forth in the dirt in front of him. A small herd of hoofed animals with stiff, blackish-gray bristled hair slowly emerged from behind a prickly-pear cactus. The larger of the group raised his pig-nose high into the air to smell the status of the coyote pack. Magnus counted six of them in total: two parents and four offspring. The little ones nudged their parents, staying close, as the parents moved out into the open sunlight to graze on the blossoms of the surrounding plants. The bobcat wasn't interested in

Javelina meat, primarily because of its aversive smell. Impatient for sleep, he laid his head back down on his front paws, closing his eyes again, avoiding seeing tempting prey before him.

He smelled the two bobcats before he heard their hissing. His agile body sprang to alertness, and he skillfully rolled out of the path of the attackers who flew high toward Magnus. Missing his target, one of the bobcats slammed into the rock shelf and gave a weak moan. The other landed on fours close to Magnus' perch. The smell of hostile pheromones flooded into the air. The fur coats of the transient bobcats were darker than that of Magnus, but their yellow eyes with black pupils matched his.

"You are from the upper land. You must be having hard times in the north,"

hissed Magnus. "Was this your feeble attempt to seek another territory? This one is called for. You need to move on."

"We like what we see here. We like the sun." The standing cat hissed.

"You're on my land!" Magnus said, issuing a guttural growl.

"We think we'll stay. There are two of us. Maybe it's time for you to leave." The first bobcat snarled with his threat. The second one moved alongside the first. Magnus snorted and swiped his sharp claws across the face of the larger cat, knocking him off the ledge with lightning precision. The second one backed up in hesitation, then lunged toward Magnus, both front paws swinging and clawing. Magnus sent a powerful blow toward the attacker, batting him off the ledge with forceful precision.

The two bobcats lay stunned, then moved to rescale the rocky outpost. Magnus emitted piercing screams across the valley, reaching over his 30-mile territory. The two invading bobcats halted their ascent, terror in their gaze. Magnus' silhouette towered above, magnified by the sunlight. His stare warned of his dominant power. The cats hesitated, turned, and bolted down the side of the boulders, disappearing in different directions. Magnus followed their retreat, only moving when they were gone from his territory.

He turned back toward the ledge of the outcropping, eager for rest. A gust of wind blasted thick sand into his eyes, and he blinked in annoyance. The weather was changing. The wind would become fierce. Instinctively he headed toward protective cover and maneuvered down the rocky terrain into a desert collection of bushes and plants. Laying his head onto his tired paws, he fell asleep immediately, ignoring the blustering winds outside his secluded hideout.

Donna Krutka

## Chapter Three

Magnus awoke with a start at the smell of coyote. He peered out from the brush, shaking off the sand thickly layered on his fur coat. The winds had calmed, and he was surprised it was already sunrise. He stretched his rested forepaws and let out a satisfied yawn.

There were six of them—a pack. Magnus took a deep breath, clearing his thinking. He surveyed his surroundings, spotting the piled rocks to his left and the open wash to his right. The bushes were thick where he slept, making an escape difficult. Magnus knew how the pack operated. Two coyotes would be positioned in the rear while the other four would attack from the front. He was confident he could outmaneuver the first four but was still determining the direction the back two would attack.

He glanced at the sun. It was angled at his disadvantage, blinding his vision if he were to exit his hideout. The first two coyotes began to creep forward. It was now or never, thought Magnus, and with speed befitting his species, he bolted out of his hideout directly toward the front coyotes. He moved toward the rocks but was cut off before he could leap onto the boulders. He cut back toward the wash and then, in a surprise move, did an about-face toward the rocks. The coyotes hesitated, and Magnus bolted toward the base of the cliff. He readied for a leap high onto the outcropping when two coyotes appeared at the top of the abutment, blocking his possible escape from on top. He sensed the coyotes behind him closing fast and tried to visualize another path to safety. Movement above him caught his eye as the two coyotes flew off the top of the cliff in an uncontrolled freefall. They landed, stunned on their backs, whimpering and moaning. Another bobcat stood at the top of the abutment, peering down on the scene below. Magnus reacted in response and sprang ten feet into the air onto the bluffs, landing successfully on all fours. He stood alongside Amara, the two cats staring down on the thwarted retreating coyotes.

"Was that a body slam?" Magnus said, still breathing hard from his jump to safety. Amara looked carefully at Magnus, a glint in her dark eyes.

"Is that a thank you, Magnus?"

"It is, indeed, Amara. A humble thank you!" He bowed playfully and then resumed his stance. Amara lifted her head, trying to match Magnus' towering height.

"It was windy and sandy last night. How did you end up being so close after such a storm?" Magnus shook his coat again, freeing another layer of sand.

"I have been watching that pack. They are reckless in their attacks, so I have stayed alert. This morning their yelps and howls made me suspicious, so I followed them. They appeared to be hunting a large animal. I had no idea it would be you." Amara looked over at Magnus. He was staring at her as if for the first time. His gaze surveyed her tan coat, black streaks down her trunk, and dark bars circling her forelegs and tail. Amara's pinkish-red nose was blotted with sweat, and pointed ears laced with black tuffs. Her yellow eyes encased round black circles that were open wide, staring up at Magnus. He could smell her scent that spoke of mustiness and cactus blossoms all in one. Amara blushed at his stare, her lips moving slightly upward as if in a smile.

"You were brave, confronting those two coyotes." Magnus continued looking ahead, rehashing the scene as they strolled alongside each other.

"I wasn't afraid. I've had practice." Magnus turned his head to study Amara as she continued.

"My father spent hours when I was a kitten showing me ways to escape predators. He always said the bobcat doesn't have many predators, but we must prepare to stay alive in case it happens. Mainly, my father warned of the threat from the coyote and the wolf." Her pace quickened when she mentioned the two larger animals.

"Hmmm, your father?" Magnus said. "My mother was the one to show us how to hunt. Sometimes it would be days before we could find a meal, so we had to learn to eat anything around, roaming long distances over our large territory". Magnus was quiet for several steps, then added more.

"She made us run fast repeatedly as if chasing a rabbit. But often, there was no rabbit. As a result, we often were starving." Magnus paused and then continued. "She knew what she was doing. We, however, sometimes didn't."

The two continued walking side by side, legs moving diagonally, with one of the front legs and the opposite hind leg moving in unison. They instinctively picked up their pace to a trot, their sleek bodies moving in a symmetrical flow.

"I felt cornered today, Amara. Almost frightened." Magnus said, "That hasn't happened to me very often. I am in your debt."

Amara gave a slight hiss, nodded, acknowledging Magnus, and then jumped up on a six-foot rocky alcove and was out of sight.

# Donna Krutka

## Chapter Four

The desert morning was alive with mice, rabbits, and moles scurrying past Magnus. He crouched and waited for prey to wander close, pouncing in a silent quickness that provided his morning meal.

Another larger male bobcat settled next to Magnus, clutching his newly acquired prey tightly in his jaws.

"Hello, Milo. Haven't seen you for a while." Magnus said.

"Hello, Magnus. 'Been making my rounds." Milo gulped a hunk of meat into his mouth and chewed quickly. "Word is out you had a run-in with a pack of coyotes." A sheepish smile plastered across his face. "Wish I'd been there to help."

Magnus growled. "Since you know what happened, other animals will likely confront me." He growled again, and both continued eating, tugging at the meat between their paws and swallowing noisily.

"Heard Stripe challenged Amara," Magnus said, watching Milo's smile become a scowl. "How'd that go?"

"Not sure what to say about that, Magnus," Milo answered, frowning as he spoke. "Stripe is insistent that she wants her own territory. She talks about it all the time." Milo pulled off another piece of meat.

"Your thoughts?" Magnus listened intently.

"She told me all this after we mated. She insists on claiming a territory before having a litter. She wants me to help her stake out a range of territory. She wants

Amara's." Milo took several rapid breaths and then snorted.

The two males were quiet for a while.

"Are you going to help her?" Magnus finally asked, not sure he wanted to hear his answer. He and Milo were like brothers. Magnus had allowed Milo's range to overlap his own, repelling any other male bobcat intruder.

"She's going to have my litter, Magnus. What else can I do?"

"You could both leave and find another territory. There is plenty of land around this desert."

Milo looked hard at Magnus, uncertain how to respond to his good friend. Magnus was telling him to leave. Milo swallowed hard, trying to get his composure.

"Magnus, you would have us leave? I can't believe you would say that to me." standing up and looking directly at Magnus.

"I can't have you taking Amara's territory," Magnus continued. "I don't even think it could be done. She is strong and would not allow it. I won't be a party to expelling her off her land. Not for Stripe. Not for any female."

"You would defend Amara over me?" Milo hissed in anger. "She is not your mate. Stripe is my mate. Your loyalty should be to me over Amara." Milo's body trembled. He cocked one ear and slightly lowered his gaze. "We go back a long way, Magnus. How is this happening?"

Magnus focused on his friend as Milo paced back and forth. His head began swinging from side to side, emitting a low growl as he paced.

"What about all the time we spent roaming the land together? How often have I had your back, Magnus? We've spent hours together. We played and hunted together. Are you forgetting all of that?"

Milo stopped and leaned against a nearby Mesquite tree, rapidly breathing, accelerating to panting. Magnus followed Milo's movements. His body seemed frozen in response to all Milo was saying and then quickly thawed as his thoughts shifted to Amara.

Magnus cautiously stood up and peered into Milo's blood-red eyes, surprised at his own words when he slowly answered Milo. "You are right, Milo. Amara is not my mate.... now! But she will be!"

Milo stood still for a long time next to his lifelong friend. Then, finally, Magnus heard a deep sigh when both turned from the other and bolted away. The sun beat down, and the wind picked up as the desert territory where they both had ranged somehow became smaller and more hostile.

## Chapter Five

Amara crouched under a bush, eyes closely following their activity from a distance to not frighten the little creatures. The kittens looked scruffy, and their fur was matted with desert burrs. It appeared that one was female and one male. The male was feisty, jumping at grasshoppers and trying unsuccessfully to catch a tiny field mouse. The female kitten lay motionless, her head draped over her paws. Amara judged their age to be about two moon rises. She remained hidden and silent, waiting until after dusk to see the mother, but the mother never joined the kittens.

The screech of a great horned owl sounds from above the kittens, circling overhead, spotting the easy prey. Looking to the sky, Amara instinctively moved out of the bush to confront the cubs.

The male kitten stopped his playful activity and hissed in a high-pitched squeal when he saw the large bobcat move out of the bushes. He lifted his head high in the air readying himself to pounce. He lunged forward and landed in a splat, all four paws going out from under his tiny body. The female barely lifted her head despite her brother's commotion.

"Where is your mother?" Amara said, attempting not to sound scolding.

"ARRRHH!" said the little male bobcat. "Go away!"

"I will, little cat, when you tell me where your mother is so you can meet up with her." Amara looked up to the sky to see if the owl had left. He was still circling overhead.

"She doesn't talk to us anymore," the female said, her little voice laced with sadness.

"Where is she?" Amara said, coming closer to them both despite the continued hissing of the brave male kitten.

"Over there, out in the field. She told us to stay hidden and not come out until she came to get us. I listened to what she said, but my brother didn't. He's been chasing all around, not staying hidden." The little female gave her brother a frown.

"What are your names?" Amara said, nudging toward the female who didn't complain as she laid down next to her.

"My name is Spot because I have more spots than my brother. Mom named him Kicker because he is always kicking everything. I am surprised he didn't try to come up and kick you."

Amara looked up and saw the male kitten kicking at rocks. He then kicked the base of a cactus and immediately pulled back and started licking his paw.

"Ah, so!" Amara said with a chuckle, watching Kicker dig and dig at his paw.

"Do you think you could show me where your mother is?" Amara masked her concern to the little female. She sensed something was wrong.

The owl screeched, and the female kitten turned toward the sky. Her eyes filled with panic.

"That is a Great Horned Owl," Amara said. "He is a predator to you while you are a small cat. So you should always try to stay hidden when you hear its call." The kitten inched closer to Amara on all fours, crouching low.

"He won't attack you as long as I am here," Amara reassured her. "He is afraid of me. I will protect you until your mother returns. Can you show me where your mother is?" Amara asked again. The female kitten slowly got to her feet, heading toward an opening in the desert prairie land.

"I'll take you there," she said.

The male bobcat followed along, still hissing, kicking, and chasing anything that moved. Spot was cautious as she approached the open field, Amara smiling at the kitten's early instincts.

"Over there, "she yelled as she ran, this time throwing caution to the wind. "She still hasn't moved. She said she would come and get us. 'Mom, Mom, here we are. You didn't come to get us!' "

Amara momentarily stopped breathing. The mother bobcat lay motionless, eyes wide open. A purple-colored leg was mangled in a large metal-toothed contraption, and a dark pool of dried blood pooled under her body. Amara circled the captured bobcat, hoping to see a sign of life. Nothing. She was not coming for her kittens.

"She's still not talking," Kicker said, inching closer to try to kick at the metal teeth. Amara grabbed him just before his foreleg made contact with another similar contraption. The male kitten let out a high-pitched growl.

"Kicker, that is dangerous. It has hurt your mother, and it will hurt you, too. Stay back." Amara screamed.

Kicker instinctively felt Amara's alarm and ran behind his sister, trying to keep from crying. However, Spot, startled and alarmed, did burst out in sobs.

"The two of you must come with me. Your mother won't be able to come with us, and we must leave here quickly." She looked at the sky and spotted more birds of prey joining the owl. They were circling over the mother bobcat, as well as her kittens. She shoved the kittens back toward the brush just before two large red-tailed hawks descended swiftly toward the lifeless bobcat.

## Chapter Six

Frightful sounds of howling wailed in the background, startling the kittens as they followed Amara through the desert brush. They rushed up alongside the large bobcat, bumping into her as they walked.

"Those are the calls of the coyotes. They are far from us. You are all right at this distance." Amara smelled the desert air to pick out signs of impending alarm. She looked at the sky and watched the high branches for signs of hawks or owls. She hissed in frustration, confused about what she would do with the kittens. Their pace slowed, and they became quiet.

"You're tired. We'll stop here for the night," Amara said, directing them into a rocky outcropping with a large overhang.

"I'm hungry," Kicker said, his juvenile voice sounding tired and whiny.

"When was the last time you were fed?" Amara asked, realizing the kittens may not have eaten for days. "Have you learned how to catch prey?"

"I'm hungry too," said Spot. "Our mother feeds us her milk." Amara stared down at the cubs. Her eyes widened.

"You still were drinking your mother's milk? So you haven't yet been catching prey?"

The two cubs looked back at her with little recognition of her frustration and disbelief.

"Have you ever eaten meat?" Amara asked.

"Mother gives us pieces of her meat sometimes. We like it." Spot's voice was low and sleepy.

"You need to sleep now. In the morning, I will feed you meat. I have no milk to feed you."

Kicker began softly crying, and Spot lay her head on his trembling body. The two shortly fell asleep, empty bellies groaning.

Amara rested her chin on her paws and looked at the two cubs. She took a slow breath, filling her lungs with air to clear her head. Her instincts were not yet prepared for kittens. She had no milk to feed them and was not inclined to teach them to hunt. Moreover, she didn't want to be responsible for kittens.

"They won't survive on their own," she mumbled, wishing the thought would disappear.

She stood up from the protected outcropping and strolled out into the night. The moon was bright, blunting the usual spectacle of the night stars. She looked at the familiar land around her and let out a prolonged sigh, then caught sight of a scampering field mouse wandering past.

"Breakfast for the two kittens," she reluctantly concluded, catching the mouse and heading back toward the sleeping kittens.

## Chapter Seven

"Follow me closely," Amara said for the second time to Kicker. "Watch Spot. She is doing it right." She skillfully jumped onto the short ledge, uncertain if the boulder was too high for the kittens to mount. Spot hesitated for a moment, then lunged forward and cleared the ledge. Kicker stood, looking up, and shouted up to Spot.

"How'd you do that? That's too high!" Kicker made little jumps around the base of the outcropping.

"No, Kicker," Amara yelled to the little male kitten. "Big jumps. Squat down and use all fours to lift you high into the sky."

Kicker turned as if to go backward, then pivoted to face the rock and ran as fast as he could. His leap was miscalculated, and he slammed into the rock face halfway up the side. Amara hissed but then cheered as he moved back to retry another lunge. This time, his knees coordinated with his effort, and his body flew through the air, reaching the top of the ledge. Spot gave out a kitten's roar and ran to Kicker, pouncing atop him. Amara grabbed him with her teeth before he was knocked off the ledge again. She sighed and nudged both the kittens affectionately.

The two wanted to practice the leap over and over again. Amara eventually lost patience and redirected them to something else. It was time to teach how to sense prey. She worked on sight, hearing, and smell. They learned quickly, pleasing Amara. She chuckled at their antics, despite giving the outward appearance of being annoyed. She continued making her way along her path around the outside of her perimeter, looking back to make sure the two small bobcats followed close behind. Each time she marked her territory with her scent, the kittens giggled and squealed, squatting close by to imitate the large female. The pace was much slower than she was used to. Her keen eyes watched continually for signs of predators. She forced herself to stay alert to danger, even though her attention was distracted by the kittens.

The day turned to evening, and the temperature dropped. Amara herded the cubs toward a thick collection of the brush. She tucked them inside the multilayer of bushes as they fell asleep, and she retreated to hunt for food. Her usual routine would be to move for long distances hunting from dusk to midnight. She then would rest, again roaming from dawn until sometime after sunrise. Tonight, she will stay close to the kittens. She crouched down in silence, smelled the air, watching for prey to wander close.

## Donna Krutka

## Chapter Eight

"She's there," Stripe slowly hissed to the two male bobcats crouched beside her. "In that brush are the two kittens. If you rush the enclave and grab the small cats, I will handle Amara. You can do what you want with the kittens if you distract her enough by taking them away. I have been watching her. She is showing more and more that she has an attachment to them. She will fight for them, even though they are not hers. Be aware of her strength. She is strong and will be determined."

"And what is it in return that you will do for us if we do this?" The scruffier of the two bobcats asked.

Snipe growled. "I already told you that my mate and I will help you claim Magnus' territory. Milo has agreed to allow you to share his territorial range. But first, you must help me take Amara's land. There is no deal if that part doesn't happen. If you fail, Milo will ensure you never come close to this area again." Stripe glared at the two transients with a vengeance in her eyes.

The transients nodded and turned to watch Amara. Her black-tipped ears pointed in regal attention. The cat's tan body was significant for a female. She stood head erect, scanning the area as a guarding sentinel.

"We should be able to take her easily," the one bobcat hissed to the other. "She's no match for the two of us." The other bobcat frowned, observing her ferocious countenance.

"Do you think Stripe will be good to her word?" one whispered to the other.

"Only if she can distract the other female. That one over there is larger than Stripe," looking toward Amara. "But not as ruthless. Powerful, but not as mean. If Stripe does what she says, she can take the other one down, and we can easily get the kittens. We've snatched other kittens before. This is no different."

They both stared out at the scene before them. Unfortunately, the bright moonlight would not be in their favor. They would need to calculate their timing carefully.

"I see hate in Stripe's eyes," one of the males growled at the other. "That should get her through the attack. I'm in if you are." The second male nodded, and the two began to inch forward. The night was too quiet, releasing no warning to Amara, who was unsuspecting of the attack.

A fierce hiss and guttural screech resounded into the air as Stripe pounced on Amara. Her claws slashed at Amara's neck, causing massive hemorrhaging. Her perfect timing allowed Stripe to continue biting and gauging until Amara was overpowered, bleeding, and breathless.

The two transient bobcats snatched the kittens from the brush enclave and headed toward the open desert fields. The stunned Amara wrestled with her attacker, looking up in time to glimpse the kittens being rustled away. She let out an eerie scream, but her distraction allowed Stripe to bite and claw another tearing blow into Amara's hind leg and trunk. Blood sprayed up into the air as a release of fury and rage

The Desert Saga

countered Snipe's hold on Amara, and she twisted violently to get from under her attacker to wield a clawed, vicious blow across Stipe's face. Then, she bolted toward the abducted small bobcats, vowing she would deal with Stripe later.

## Chapter Nine

The little male kitten kicked, scratched, and hissed as the two bobcats carried him and his sister toward a large rock outcropping. His eyes focused as he recognized the rocks where Amara had taken them to practice their jumps. He called out to Spot to see if she was all right, and she answered with a feeble noise, trying to duplicate one of Amara's eerie screams.

"Let us go, you mean monsters!" Spot finally hissed at the two kidnappers, giving up trying to scream. They held the kittens in their teeth as they ran, making it impossible to silence the taunts the kittens barraged upon them. The cat holding Kicker almost dropped him several times as the little cub swung around and tried to bite his captor. The bobcat would growl and hiss, but Kicker persisted.

The path they took was rugged, traveling a great distance. The kittens eventually, tired of struggling, became exhausted and fell asleep. When they awoke, a sizeable female bobcat with bloodied and gaping face stood over them.

"They are awake," she yelled out to the other bobcats. "You better be glad you didn't kill them." She huffed and turned away abruptly. Spot and Kicker looked up as a larger male bobcat came into view. He bent down, sniffed the two kittens, and let out a low pitch hiss. His deep yellow eyes peered into the frightened faces of the two little bobcats.

"So, this is your plan, Stripe? To use these kittens?" Milo's voice was laced with agitation. His eyes burrowed in on the little bobcats.

Stripe stared at Milo intently. She sensed hesitation. Stripe slinked next to Milo, rubbing her soft furry body against his. She licked his face and purred gently.

"You haven't changed your mind, have you?" she said, again licking his neck and ears, purring louder. "We talked about how all this land should be yours, Milo. I am just following our plan." Stripe moved her head up and down against her mate.

"Remember why we are doing all this, Milo," she said cunningly. "You are much stronger and wiser than Magnus; it is your time to dominate this territory. Together you and I can mark the perimeter, and all of this can be ours." She continued, watching her mate's reaction. "We are only using the small cats to lure Amara and Magnus to come to find them. That's all. What happens to them afterward is of no concern, is it? I told the others they could do as they want." She rubbed her body along the length of Milo's shimmering coat.

Milo strode away from the cubs and Stripe, growling under his breath. His head hung low as he exited the bramble den. It would soon be dawn. He stared up at the dimming stars, watching as they silently were slowly being extinguished by the morning light.

"No, I haven't changed my mind." His reply was to no one in particular.

Donna Krutka

## Chapter Ten

Amara followed the trail of the kittens, pain slowing her pace to almost a crawl. Oozing blood from her wounds left a trail behind her.

She looked back often to watch for followers, seeing nothing but shadows from the moonlit night. Her breathing became erratic and labored as she reached the large outcropping of rocks, her mind visualizing the small bobcats jumping up and down on the ledge the previous days. The pain in her side and back leg grabbed her, and she fell to the ground, uncertain if she could go further. She pulled her struggling body toward the lower part of the climbing wall and collapsed in agony, unable to care if she was not adequately camouflaged. The wind picked up, and a soft rain began to fall. Amara's injured body began to tremble. Being injured was new to her. She lay her head on her paws, trying to stay alert and awake.

Her head lifted in alarm as she smelled the approaching coyote. Her eyes were clouded, and her vision would not focus on the predator. She lifted her hind legs but fell back to the ground, unable to get upright. She growled, attempting to give off a sound of warning. She turned her head to the left, smelling another animal, this one an ally. Magnus leaped from the rocky ledge, landing before her, staring out toward the coyote. A fiery scream sprayed toward the coyote, and Magnus stood protectively in front of Amara until the scent of the threat was gone. He turned toward the injured female and sat beside her, eyes filled with concern.

"What happened? Was it Stripe?" he asked, certain he knew the answer. Amara nodded, feeling difficulty in moving her head up and down. Magnus surveyed her wounds, scowling.

"They are deep. The ones on your neck are still bleeding. Your hind leg is gaping. It will be a while before you can run."

Magnus' presence calmed Amara. She laid her head back onto her paws. Her breathing relaxed, and her heartbeat lowered. She could rest for a while with Magnus next to her. She slipped into a fitful sleep, images of Spot and Kicker filling her with unrest.

Amara awoke to Magnus licking her oozing neck wound. She pulled back instinctively, not clear what her response should be.

"The wounds must be tended to, Amara. I see no other way." Magnus waited tentatively for Amar's response.

She blinked in recognition and lowered her head to allow him to continue. He slowly cleaned the neck wound and then turned to her hind leg. Redness and swelling had set into her leg. His tongue felt heat as he moved the matted hair from the wound. Amara winced when he touched the bleeding hip. He stopped momentarily, allowing Amara to consent for him to resume. He continued through the night, unable to judge if she would improve.

By dawn, Amara's entire body felt warm. She had short, shallow breaths. She needed water, Magnus sensed. A water hole was far away. She would be unable to travel there. His gaze took him to a cluster of dried brush partially hiding a plant with long blue-green leaves. Jagged red spikes rested on the ends of the leaves. He jumped up to move toward the plant. His mother had used that plant to heal his injured paw when he was a kitten. He grabbed a branch between his sharp teeth and tore it from the ground. He gently aroused Amara and laid the plant before her. With closed eyes, she instinctively licked the sweet fluid from the plant and gulped a small portion of the pulp into her dry mouth. Her swallow was difficult but easier after the second gulp. She looked up at Magnus, nodding, then lowered her head back onto her paws, exhausted.

Magnus moved tirelessly back and forth between the healing plant and Amara, feeding her its sweet fluid. He rubbed the plant's pulp onto her wounds, recalling the warm rush of sensations he had felt when his mother had done that for him. The hot sun beat down on the two animals as night turned to day. Dusk settled over the desert, bringing cooler temperatures that bounced off the surrounding rocks. Amara could raise her head from her paws as the night darkened and lift her neck to catch the wind. She looked around and saw Magnus lying next to her.

"Magnus, how long have we been here?" Magnus jumped to alertness, surprised she was awake.

"This is the second sunset. How are you feeling?" He leaned over her on all fours.

She took a prolonged, slow inhalation. The earthy smell of dirt mixed with the musty scent of creosote met her nostrils. She looked around, recognizing the rock outcropping where she had collapsed. She rubbed her head on the nearby granite and moved her paws back and forth in the sand before her. The sweet taste of Aloe lingered in her mouth. She looked over at Magnus and nodded.

"What...exactly has happened to me?"

"I found you injured. Actually, badly injured. It was Stripe. Do you remember anything?"

Amara swallowed and hesitated, rotating her head in different directions to attempt to recall the previous events.

"Stripe attacked me." Amara slowly recounted. "I should have been more aware of my surroundings. I was preoccupied with the kittens." She looked at Magnus, noticing his confusion.

"The kittens?" Magnus asked, one eye raised with interest. "You have kittens?"

Amara gulped, slightly embarrassed.

"Well, they're not mine," she answered shyly. "I came upon them in the desert. They were alone. Their mother was nowhere around. I wasn't sure what to make of it. I decided to watch them for a while. The mother never showed up, so I approached them."

Amara began telling Magnus how she had found the small bobcats. She admitted to initially wanting to walk away, letting their mother look out for them.

"So why didn't you?" Magnus asked, quite surprised about what Amara was telling him.

"I don't know. Something made me hang around for a while and watch. First, they were in my territory, and I didn't want another intruder or challenger like Stripe. Second, I spotted a golden-horned owl flying overhead. An owl can descend upon a small bobcat, like the two of them, and snatch them in a flash. I guess I didn't want that to happen." Amara softened her gaze, her voice equally soft.

"I told them to take me to where they had last seen their mother." Amara continued. "When we found her, she gave no response. Her hind leg was caught in some metal claws." She shuddered, redrawing the scene in her thoughts.

Magnus's eyes widened. "I have seen those metal teeth in the past. I was almost trapped by them once." Magnus hissed. "Go on," he said, encouraging her to tell him more.

"I found out they had been still drinking their mother's milk. They had not been shown how to hunt or jump. I didn't know what else to do, so I started teaching them how to do both" Amara stopped talking and looked at Magnus. His face showed wide ruffs of extended hair tangled beneath his ears. Yellow eyes and round, black pupils stared at her. Reddish-brown fur surrounded his nose and continued toward the sides of his head and back. He was appealing, she thought. Her eyes traced the black streaks across his trunk, forelegs, and tail. She looked for a smile or a look of scorn from her friend. She saw neither.

Guttural noises and growls came from the area before them, and both cats became alert. Again, the coyote had returned, and this time with others. A pack of four stood before the bobcats. Magnus rose to all fours and met their gaze. Amara tried pulling her hind legs upward from her crouched position, falling back to the ground when she attempted to bear weight. She hissed in pain, and Magnus knew she could not fight or run. He looked in all directions, trying to envision how to protect Amara and ward off the coyotes. The four coyotes slowly moved forward as Magnus braced for combat.

A piercing howl shot into the night from atop the rock outcropping above them. The four coyotes stopped advancing abruptly. Magnus twisted his head to look up. He squinted his eyes, seeing a silhouette of a large figure towering over them all.

"The pack leader," Magnus exclaimed with a low hiss. "The alpha!" The howling continued over and over. The attacking coyotes backed away one by one, slinking into the night. Magnus never took his gaze off of the figure who lingered high above.

"Kiya," he said out loud. The coyote nodded to the bobcat, and Magnus nodded back. When Amara looked up, the coyote was gone.

"What just happened?" Amara whispered, sure she would not have survived a coyote attack.

"It was Kiya. He called off the attackers."

"Who is Kiya?" Amara asked, still looking up at where the coyote had stood.

"'The Boss' to the other coyotes, the alpha. Fierce and deadly, others have said. Yet I have met him. He is fair-minded and scoffs at unjust animal threats." Magnus stood looking out to the night, and Amara thought she saw his body tremble.

"We are safe now," he said to Amara as he lay beside her. Amara detected a shiver from Magnus' body and warmth countering the chill of the night air. Cautiously, she placed her head next to Magnus, leaning closer to him. A slow, soft purr came from Magnus as he shifted his weight toward Amara, both content to remain motionless for the rest of the night.

## Chapter Eleven

The two kittens were hungry but unsure of how to ask for food. In the past, Amara had carefully placed pieces of meat in front of them, partially chewed. Kicker cried for his mother's milk, and Spot nudged him, whispering that there was no more milk to drink. Their tongues felt dry, making it difficult to lick their sore paws and matted fur coats.

Kicker began making a high-pitched whining sound that provoked a hiss from one of the two male bobcats. The other large bobcat growled and slapped a large paw at Kicker when he did not stop his noises.

"I'm hungry," Kicker said, continuing to cry softly.

Another blow from a cat paw swiped across Kicker's face, who then jumped onto the larger bobcat, biting his ear with tiny cub teeth. The larger bobcat leaped to all fours and grabbed Kicker by the neck, slinging him into the air. The tiny male cub landed forcefully on his startled sister, who grabbed her brother's tail to prevent him from lunging toward the rough captor once again. Kicker backed down as he saw both bobcats with their paws ready to strike.

"How long are we going to have to deal with these two scruffs?" hissed the larger of the two captors. "We should grab them now and run away from this whole mess. There are other territories we can explore and claim without being beholden to that pompous Stripe female."

"Where're we going to find a territory with everything this one has?" The second bobcat growled as he answered. "The sun and the warmth and the endless prey. We can't go back to the north after being driven out by all the other bobcats." He looked over at the trembling cubs and continued. "Besides, that female, Stripe, is cunning and clever. I'm afraid of what she'll do if we cross her. So I say we do as she says, follow her plan, and hope she will come good with her promise." He looked at the cubs, a smile curving on his lips, hunger in his voice. "I'm willing to wait a little longer."

## Chapter Twelve

Amara awoke the following day with a sense of urgency. She weighed her injured limbs and pulled herself to a standing position. The pain in her trunk and hindleg felt tolerable. Magnus had stayed beside her the entire night. She was grateful.

"I think I can walk and possibly run. I want to find the kittens."

Magnus yawned, stretched his forelegs, and lifted off the ground. His eyes followed her movement around the rocky ledge, nodding in approval.

"I think you are better." He looked up at the sky and frowned. Dark clouds moved overhead, blocking the sun. He sniffed the air, nostrils flaring, taking in musty moisture. "Rain is coming. We should hurry so we can still pick up their tracks."

Magnus followed Amara as she cautiously tested her limbs. Her pace quickened, passing amongst the musty-rain smell of the creosote bushes.

She climbed over a rocky mound. The warmth of the rock soothed her injured paws. She tucked her head under her chest to look for Magnus and leaped ahead faster than she had been moving. Magnus matched her speed, and then the two simultaneously bumped into the other, a tangle of sweet and musty scents mixing together.

Tiny droplets of water glistened in the air as the sun peeked around the clouds above. Amara suddenly stopped, looking up into the sky.

"There, in the sky! Look!" Amara exclaimed.

Magnus cocked his head upward to see an arc of color, red on the outside, changing through orange, yellow, green, blue, indigo, and violet on the inside. He moved closer to Amara, settling his stance close to her without knocking her from her feet. The two stood looking up, each feeling their exhaling breath move across ruffs of hair extending below their ears.

"I knew your father, Amara," Magnus said, breaking the silence that had lingered between them. "I was there at the attack." He spoke in a low voice, almost a whisper. Amara turned quickly to look at Magnus. Her round, black pupils widened to study his facial image. She stood perfectly still as he continued.

"He was the fiercest bobcat I have ever known. He taught me how to hunt and saved my life more times than I can count." Magnus watched Amara's response carefully.

"There were so many other cats that tried to take his territory. He became such a legend that they would come from miles around to fight and attempt to take away his legacy."

Amara kept her eyes fixed on Magnus as he continued.

"He mated with your mother and no other. There were other males who attempted to mate with your mother and other females around that, who tried to attract your father, but both remained loyal to the other. "

Magnus was close enough to Amara to hear her pull breath from her lungs.

The scent of oil from the desert creosote bush lingered on her furry coat.

"It was when you were a tiny cub that they attacked. There were several cats. Two attacked your mother. She died protecting you to her death. The larger one stayed hidden and pounced on your father while he was defending your mother. Your father was severely injured, the big cat grabbing his neck and ripping at his throat. "

Amara gasped, and moisture filled her eyes.

"I came too late. I was unable to save either your mother or father." Magnus lowered his head and stared at the ground.

"I was still barely older than a cub. Rage overwhelmed me and gave me strength that I never knew I had. I gouged one of the attacker's eyes, blinding him, hoping he would never see to hunt again. I ripped at his ears so he could not hear. He released a terrifying scream and ran off, and I never saw him again."

"When I went back to your father before he died, I promised him I would defend his territory as long as I lived." He stopped talking and then looked at Amara. "And protect you."

Amara shook her head, letting out a low growl and deep hiss. She turned her head from Magnus walking a short distance away. She paced back and forth, her eyes darting from one rock to another. The growling and hissing continued until she swung toward Magnus and spat on the ground.

"I have known you for a long time, cat, and you have never revealed this to me." Her voice was filled with fury." I have learned how to hunt and survive on my own, no parent still alive to teach me. I fought for my territory alone, defeating countless other females trying to claim it from me. And now you tell me you have been here all along: "to keep me safe!"

"Your skills are your own." Magnus retorted. "I never interfered. I was there to make sure, as a cub, that you were safe. A male bobcat knows little about raising cubs. The female usually raises the young alone. My job was to keep you safe."

Magnus moved closer to Amara. The female cat rebuffed his approach and backed away. She stood looking out over the desert. Her desert. She hunted here. She had claimed the territory by her markings. She had held off challengers. Now, she wondered if it was hers to claim. Had it been claimed for her without her knowledge?

She turned toward Magnus, eyes dark with purpose. "I will find the kittens. I will repel Stripe's attacks, and I will reclaim this territory! Don't follow me." She leaped away from Magnus, a loud hiss and scream echoing in the wash as she departed.

## Chapter Thirteen

The rain burst through the dark clouds, pounding the dry desert ground with a vengeance. Amara could not tell if the water flowing off her face was tears or rain. Heaviness pounded in her chest. The blowing wind angled the sheets of rain directly into her eyes, causing her to lower her head to see where she was going. She should take shelter, but she could not stop her assault on all that had happened to her. By all rights, Stripe had bested her and could claim her territory. She had lost the two kittens fate had given her to protect and raise. She had found herself wanting Magnus to be by her side and now realized that would never happen. She could not mate with a cat that had deceived her about who she was and where she had come from. She let out a hiss, trying to expel the emotions battering her in the face.

Over the noises of the storm, she heard muffled, whining sounds somewhere in front of her. She crouched down, slowly inching forward. Ahead of her, she squinted to make out a tall rock abutment surrounding an open area. A shadow of two small figures huddled in the center of the unprotected area. The rain and wind plummeted the figures, and Amara could hear soft hisses and cries as they pressed together. The cubs were positioned so that rescuing them would allow for an ambush. Her heartbeat quickened as she sensed the tiny creatures shivering in the cold of the night, the downpour of the rain battering them.

She turned slowly to her right, sensing Magnus coming alongside her. Her fur bristled, and she pulled away.

"Amara, you will not survive an attack by yourself. There are four cats, all determined to beat us both."

"What do you mean, both of us?" Amara whispered, anger lacing her reply.

"You left before I could tell you the rest. Stripe wants us both deposed. The cat I blinded was her father. He died shortly after his attack. She has hated me for ultimately killing her father and you for surviving. She has set Milo against us both. She will stop at nothing to claim our territories and get revenge. "

His voice cut knives into Amara, overpowering the pelting of the harsh rain on her body.

"It was Stripe's father who had killed my mother and father?" Amara focused on the kittens as she processed Magnus' story.

There were four bobcats to fight. She knew she could not win alone. Her heart raced, and the sense of Magnus beside her ignited an explosion of emotions. A surge of repulsion and attraction filled her body toward Magnus. Inner turmoil weakened her independent certainty. She felt an attraction to this powerful, dominant male that she had previously never felt. This was Magnus, she reminded herself. This was a bobcat she had lived around all her life. She also felt an overpowering pull to protect the two kittens held captive sitting in front of her in the drenching rain.

As if an explosion went off all around her, she released the fear, hesitancy, and confusion trapped inside her. She turned and acknowledged the penetrating gaze from Magnus' eyes and nodded toward the kittens.

## Chapter Fourteen

Magnus whispered his plan into Amara's ear. He leaned his head gently into hers and then shot off in a different direction. There were so many things that could go wrong with his ploy, Amara thought. She paused, then confidently strolled toward the two kittens from the far side of the opening. The rain was still falling but had lifted in its intensity. She could not discern Stripe or Milo's scent. She scanned the area for any clues as to the whereabouts of the kidnappers. Trusting Magnus, she strolled into the opening and stood in front of the cubs.

"Stripe and Milo," I am here to take the kittens. Her voice was strong and loud.

"Amara," Spot screamed as Kicker tried to stand and shake off the rain. The little bobcats' voices were weak from the rain and hunger. Amara strolled up to the kittens and rubbed her head against theirs. She whispered a command into their ears, and they sat back on the ground obediently.

She spotted Stripe first, high up on the rock abutment behind the opening. Milo came from the opposite side of the opening on the desert floor, and the two intruding bobcats followed.

Stripe hissed. She outstretched her claws and made deep cuts into the rock where she stood. She screamed in triumph mercilessly. "Do you give up your territory, Amara, or do we take it from you." Stripe hissed. Milo moved closer, growling.

"That's not going to happen, Stripe. Not today, and not ever." Amara's eyes scanned the shadows, ears poised straight up to listen to her surroundings. Something moved, and she lunged toward the kittens, her injured body draping over the two. One of the intruding bobcats sprang toward her, grabbing her tail and digging claws into her outstretched body. The other bobcat grasped Spot by the neck and pulled her from under Amara. Amara let out a fierce cat scream and hissed as her injured hind leg ripped open in another gaping tear. She whipped her head toward the offending bobcat and tore into his neck with sharp teeth, drawing a gush of blood. Milo burst forward, pulling the frightened male kitten out from under Amara. Her wounded hind leg froze, unable to leap toward Milo. She had lost both kittens. Her scream this time was one of pain and horror.

Above the agony of her wounds and loss of the cubs in the faint distance, she heard the cry. It was a howl, the sound blasting across the wet soggy desert. The rain stopped, and thick clouds covered the sky. A smug sense of victory hovered over the challenging bobcats. Then, from nearby brush, close to Milo and Amara's injured body, emerged four coyotes, growling in a fierce, deadly warning. High on the rock above, Magnus the Great stood alongside a large foreboding coyote, staring directly into Stripe's glaring yellow eyes.

"Milo," hissed Magnus," Stop your attack immediately or the coyotes, and I will make sure Stripe, you and your disgusting friends never leave here tonight."

"It is you that must stand down, Magnus or your mate will be dead before you have mated," Milo answered in defiance.

"Why are you doing this, Milo? We were like brothers. I have shared this land with you since we were young." Magnus inched silently closer to Stripe.

"You stole this territory, Magnus," Stripe hissed. "Milo was destined to claim this territory. My father had it all arranged. He was to rule, and I was to have part of his territory. You thwarted it all, Magnus."

"Your father killed Amara's parents, Stripe. He was never to have the territory. I was being groomed for inheritance. Your father tried to steal it from my destiny."

"Stripe is right, "Milo said, stepping forward below. "Her father had promised to claim this territory for me. So all these years, I have had to live silently in your shadow, knowing you had prevented that from happening." His voice was low and vengeful.

Stripe leaped from the rock ledge onto the ground and tore into Amara. With speed-matching lightning, Magnus and the Coyote lunged toward the attacking female. Stripe, Milo, and the two intruding bobcats were subdued within seconds, the four coyotes pinning the bobcats to the ground. Magnus carefully picked up Amara in his strong jaw, careful not to crush her with his teeth, and moved her toward shelter. The two small bobcats limped slowly past the chaos to follow Magnus. He gently laid Amara on the ground.

"Snuggle close to keep her warm while I finish what needs to be done," he said to the kittens, "but be gentle. She is injured," Magnus warned. Cautiously, the two moved close to Amara and laid their cold, exhausted bodies beside her. They nestled even closer when they sensed a slight purr coming from her wounded body.

Milo and Stripe, with the two intruders, were pushed into a pile surrounded by the coyotes. The Coyote leader held back his clan, preventing them from tearing into the bobcats for prey. The pack members moved back and forth in front of the bobcats, head down and eager to attack. The alpha held firm on his command.

"Let me introduce you to the leader of this pack. He is called the "Boss." You may have heard of him. He is ruthless and unforgetting." Magnus strolled over to the four attackers. He looked deep into each of their eyes, his brows squinting with fury.

"He has agreed to free the four of you this time." Barks and growls came from the guarding coyotes.

"The dogs have your scent. If you ever trespass in this territory again, the coyotes will hunt you down and show no mercy. After that, you will be fair game for any of us. Is this understood?"

The two intruders were first to bolt away. Milo turned and leaped from the captors, not looking back at his lifelong friend.

Stripe stood facing Magnus. Her eyes were filled with hate and rage. She looked at the coyotes, heard their growl, and looked back toward the bobcat.

She opened her mouth in a slow hiss but then abruptly turned and ran away.

Magnus felt sure all of the four bobcats would never be back. Again, he faced The Boss, bent in a silent bow, and as swiftly as they had appeared, the pack of coyotes was gone, in a different direction than the bobcats.

Magnus ran to Amara, gently displacing the kittens, and lay beside the injured female. He surveyed her wounds and listened to her breathing. She opened her eyes and began to purr.

"I knew you would come," Amara said in a low murmur.

"I'm here, " Magnus answered, relieved at hearing her speak.

"We're here, too!" exclaimed the cubs in unison, snuggling closer.

"The others?" she asked.

"Gone. Hopefully forever." Magnus replied.

Amara laid her head back down, closed her eyes, and sighed. The smell of the wet desert filtered into her nostrils, along with the scent of the mud-soaked kittens and Magnus the Great. She would heal from her injuries and be strong again, she vowed. Sounds of purring surrounded her and helped her fall soundly asleep.

# The Desert Saga

## Chapter Fifteen

Avery and Caelan jumped on top of Spot and Kicker, prompting clawless swipes from Kicker. The two recently born kittens rolled onto the ground with a playful meow, licking all over Spot, who patiently indulged their playfulness. Amara lounged nearby, not bothering to interfere with the activity before her. Kicker hissed when Caelan bit down hard on his ear, almost drawing blood. Amara called her young kittens to her, sensing the two older juvenile bobcats were becoming annoyed.

The day's sun was slowly setting behind the western mountains, and dusk heralded the time to hunt for prey. Magnus emerged from the nearby brush to enter the den where the new kittens had safely been tucked since birth.

"It's time," he said to Amara. "I must make my rounds. I will take Spot and Kicker with me."

Amara stood up and rubbed her neck against Magnus, releasing a gentle purr and leaning against his sleek body. Magnus lowered his head and breathed in Amara's scent. He began grooming Amara with his tongue, licking her face and neck, realizing it would be a while before he saw her again.

"I'll keep our borders free of intruders," he playfully whispered in her ear as he snuggled next to her warm body. The new offspring rushed into the den. Magnus snorted, unsure he wanted to share his mate with the kittens.

"It will be the new one's time to follow me when I return," Magnus said, reluctantly allowing the young creatures to burrow into their mother's warm furry body, ready to drink her milk.

"While you're away, I'll show the kittens how to hunt, forage and stay safe," Amara replied. "And every day, I will be reminded of you as I watch their boundless energy and see the coloring of their coat, which is exactly like yours!"

Magnus called to Spot and Kicker, who were lounging in the sun outside the den. Magnus motioned to them to pile in with Amara and the little kittens for one last time before the three left, traveling the long trek around Magnus' expansive dominion. They would re-mark the perimeter with their scent to deter any intruders. Amara also would travel around her territory with her new kittens when they were a little older, defining her smaller perimeter. It would be many sunrises and sunsets before they would rejoin each other.

The lives of this family of bobcats would continue with routines, challenges, prey, and predators, but they would always be bound by their ties to the land and experiences together.

Donna Krutka

# THE MOUNTAIN LION

# PART ONE

# PROSPERITY

## Chapter One

Sakari slowly ducked under the small opening of her clay-packed pit house. She looked back and saw that her younger sister was still sleeping and didn't awaken as she usually did when Sakari got up in the morning. The darkness of the night was her favorite time of the day. She breathed in the crisp desert air and looked at the bright morning star above the horizon. It would only be a short time before the sun would rise above the horizon, and she hurried across the short, sandy pathway that took her to her beloved boulder lookout. She climbed the granite outcropping and sat in her usual morning perch, staring at the mountains. They were her mountains, she thought. Her eyes traced the outline of the peaks, every up and down familiar. She listened as a Gila woodpecker on her right called to one on her left, greeting each other across the open terrain. She took a deep breath and sighed, grateful for this pre-dawn time. When the sun came up, the busy day began, and it wouldn't be until the next morning before she could sit quietly and think all her favorite thoughts.

Her eyes caught sight of the mountain lion on his early rounds. He strolled leisurely and freely, she thought, probably encountering great adventures.

However, her attention flew from these thoughts as she heard the great horned owls call from a distance. His night of hunting would close when the sun came up. She squinted and saw the owl take off, his large wingspan making a monstrous shadow against the dawning sky.

The rustle of leaves and the sounds of footfall made her smile. Liseli crawled up alongside her, a slight pant in her breathing.

"You left without me," Liseli said to her older sister.

"You were sleeping soundly, and I dared not awaken you." She kissed her sister on the cheek. She wrapped her arm around the petite girl, feeling the chill in her arms.

"Have you seen him yet?" Ask Liseli, her eyes scanning the terrain in front of her.

"He has already passed. I almost felt like he looked up and saw you weren't here, so he went on his way."

Liseli lifted her chest, and a smile formed on her lips. She loved the mountain lion, speaking of him as if it was her pet. She watched it from afar, attaching an illusional bond to their relationship. Sakari teased her about how Liseli thought the two were friends, reminding her that the cougar was aloof and wild and would never befriend a human.

"If you would have awakened with me, you would have seen him. Now you will have to wait for a whole day." Sakari snickered and gave her sister an affectionate hug, standing up to climb down the boulder face.

The Desert Saga

"We must hurry back to the pit house before Father hears us. We mustn't let him take away our special time in the morning." Sakari slithered down the outcropping with the ease of falling rain, Liseli following her. She had to run to stay up with her sister, glancing around again to catch a glimpse of the mountain lion.

# Donna Krutka

## Chapter Two

Sakari pulled the root vegetable out of the ground. She carefully placed it on top of the others in her basket, stuffing it downward, satisfied that none would fall, as she lifted the basket to her head and stood upright. She twisted slightly from side to side from her waist, trying to ease the ache in her back, a product of the long day of planting and harvesting. A silky, brown strand of hair fell across her face, and she brushed it from her eyes. Sweat beaded on her forehead. She readjusted her brimmed hat to a more sun-shading angle. She would prepare a dinner tonight that would please her father. She pulled her body with the heavy basket to a more erect position and headed toward her family's pit house.

She passed a series of small earthen mounds sprouting an abundance of plants, including beans and squash. Water flowed freely down the irrigation canals, and she watched as the builders reinforced the walls of one of the tributaries that came off the permanent village stream. Fields of corn and cotton glistened in the afternoon sun.

She glanced across the field, and her eyes scanned the horizon. A warmth of emotion filled her. She would go to the foothills tomorrow to collect fruit from the saguaro, cholla, prickly pear, and barrel cactus. Finally, finally, she would be near her mountains. Her mountains! She looked around for the other villagers that would accompany her. Collecting, drying, and cooking the plant took place at the campsite. Her mother had taught her to slowly remove the needles and bake the cholla buds and prickly pear pads in a pit. Next, she would boil the saguaro fruit into syrup, making cakes from the dried seeds and wine from the syrup.

In the distance, she saw her father approaching her, his arms boasting a fresh catch of rabbit meat hanging from a mesquite spear. Nodin walked beside her father, a sizable batch of animal carcasses over his shoulder. She frowned when she saw him look at her, a sense of nausea rushing through her stomach as he smirked a smile. She quickly turned away, not wanting to greet her father and then be forced to speak to Nodin, so she rushed toward the open ramada where her mother and sister were already preparing the food for dinner meal. She dared not glance back to see if her father and Nodin would come in her direction, hoping they would go straight to the open fire to cook the meat the hunters had captured.

"Sakari," she heard her father call out in front of everyone. "Put your basket down and come and help us with our catch. Your place is here with Nodin. We need you to help prepare the meat."

Sakari looked at her sister and then to the ground. Her breathing quickened, and her eyes filled with a look of fury. It took everything she had to answer her father, wanting to run away from the sight of the meat and her father's choice for her as a bride.

"I must finish cleaning today's collection of vegetables, Father, and then I will join you." She hoped her voice was convincing and did not reveal her feeling of disgust. She wanted only to eat the crops that the land grew. She was not a hunter. She hated killing animals. She believed in living off the plants and crops grown by the carefully engineered agriculture advancement.

Her father shrugged and headed toward the open fire pit, Nodin reluctantly following. Sakari let out a deep sigh and headed into the shade of the ramada, a wisp of the breeze brushing against her warm cheeks, feeling cool and welcome after being out in the open sun. The ramada was an open-sided roofed structure made of posts of the mesquite tree and covered with the spines of the giant saguaro. Brush draped over the top to provide shade. It was large enough to allow four women to work comfortably. Sakari unloaded her basket filled with squash, corn, and beans. She sorted the different-sized corn ears. The leaves were bright green with no hint of brown from insect invasion. Her hands worked swiftly to peel away the outer leaves. She grabbed the silky tassel at the top and pulled from top to bottom with one motion. She repeated the motion until all of the silk and leaves were lying in a pile, and the stripped ear of corn showed plump juicy kernels.

Liseli grabbed the leaves and moved toward the sun, out from under the ramada, carefully placing them on the ground one by one to allow drying. She smiled at her sister, happy to be working alongside her. She was five years younger than Sakari, going to great lengths to emulate her older sister. Her eyes followed Sakari's movements as she meticulously cleaned her collected vegetables.

"Tell me a story," Liseli said to her sister. "Tell me about the great Jaguar."

Sakari smiled, gently brushing her hand across Liseli's cheek. Her heart warmed when she worked with her sister. Liseli's eyes glistened affectionately, and Sakari settled into a gentle calm.

"Again, Liseli? You want to hear it again?" She used a sharp stone to cut the corn kernels away from the husk and took care that none fell on the dirt ground, piling them in a big heap ready for cooking. She handed the husk to Liseli, who ran to place it in the sun next to the drying leaves.

"It's my favorite story. Tell me again," Liseli said in anticipation, hurrying back to Sakari.

Sakari glanced toward the fire pit, watching her father and Nodin unload their morning hunting catch. She was happy to prolong her eventual encounter with the two of them.

"The story begins when there is nothing but void." Sakari moved closer to Liseli to speak in a hushed voice.

"A man-god drifts through the void and creates the earth, sun, moon, and stars over time. He then decided to make humans roam freely on Earth. The man-god spent his time both on the Earth and in the underworld. Peering out from the underworld, he spotted a beautiful girl roaming the land. The longer he watched, the more he fell in love with her and wanted to take her as his wife. But the beautiful girl fell in love with a young warrior boy and pledged her love to him. Her rebuff made the man-god very angry. He ascended to Earth, took the form of a jaguar, kidnapped the beautiful girl, and took her back to the underworld. He then turned the boy warrior into a mountain lion, proclaiming that he was to roam the earth for the rest of time, never to take a mate. The

# The Desert Saga

mountain lion vowed he would invade the underworld to recapture his love and found a way to gather all the animals he could to help him. He traveled deep into the center of the underworld, where he found the jaguar, who had the young girl tethered to his side. The mountain lion tricked the jaguar into coming to the earth's surface with the girl, where the sun baked the land, and a great wind blew. When the jaguar emerged, his eyes became blinded by the wind and fiercely blowing sand, and the mountain lion was able to steal the beautiful girl away from the jaguar. He took her to a cave high in the mountains to hide her from the jaguar. It is there that she remains today. The jaguar swore he would roam the earth for centuries to look for the girl and to try to find and kill the mountain lion. He pledged that the sun would bake the Earth and the wind would never stop blowing, destroying the ground until he found the girl. The girl looked down from the mountain onto the sunbaked earth and saw that it was burning up, and she started crying, sending rain tears upon the land. Her tears saved the land and thwarted the attempt of the jaguar to destroy the world. To this day, when the wind blows and the sun beats down without remorse, it is the jaguar's revenge for his stolen love. When this happens, the mountain lion secretly travels to the mountain cave to avoid detection by the jaguar and pleads to the young girl to save the earth. Grateful for the mountain lion's love and bravery, she sends her tears to the land to save it.
"

Liseli had been leaning elbows on her knees, listening to her sister tell the story. Then, finally, her eyes locked on Sakari, and a small tear slowly moved down her cheek.

"Does he still roam our desert?" Liseli whispered to her sister.

She turned to scan the horizon as if searching for the mountain lion. She slowed her breathing, allowing her heartbeat to settle after hearing the story. Her reaction to the story was always the same. She held back her tears and felt anger and joy all at the same time.

"The story goes that he still roams the land," said Sakari.

"And is that him that we see in the morning light?" asked Liseli, hopeful that her sister would say it was.

"I don't know, little one. What do you think?" Sakari nudged Liseli gently and stood up to walk away. A loud voice called to Sakari from the fire pit, and she turned toward her father and Nodin. A scowl came over Sakari's face, and she obediently walked toward her father, eyes hardened with resistance as she walked to join him in cleaning the animals.

Liseli followed her sister's movement with her eyes. Sakari's dark hair flowed down to her waist, blowing in the light wind. A cotton apron, moistened with the day's sweat, clung tightly to her body, and a leather thong wrapped around her neck. She walked with an exaggerated straight back, her appearance obstinately compliant.

Liseli then turned to watch her father and Nodin. They had hunted for hours and showed no sign of fatigue as they prepared their catch. Their hands swiftly pulled the rabbit pellet from the animal's muscular body. Nodin gutted the animal and collected the inedible parts into a bowl made of pottery. The meat was placed on pieces of large stone and set out in the sun for several hours before it was ready for roasting in a stone oven. Sakari watched patiently, ready for any command she received.

"Take the meat collections to the nearby clans, Sakari." her father instructed. "When you finish, return, and we will have others ready. Have Liseli help you."

Liseli jumped up and joined her sister. They took turns wrapping the pieces of meat in the drying leaves of corn that they had separated earlier. Sakari refused to meet the gaze of Nodin, and the two girls followed their father's orders.

## Chapter Three

Liseli stayed close by Sakari, listening to her sister sing a slow melody as they walked. They walked beside the rock terraces built along the hill slopes designed to catch rainfall runoff. The broad, shallow river lay ahead of them. Workers reinforced the canals, rerouting some existing trenches to flow toward a series of small earthen mounds growing crops of beans and squash. Liseli noticed their pace slowing and saw a tall, dark-haired young man standing along the pathway. He held a wooden stick with a rock slab carefully attached at its base used for digging. His sweat-covered muscular body glistened in the sunlight.

Sakari lowered her eyes, a faint smile wrapping over her lips. She clutched the wrapping of meat closer to her body to keep from dropping them.

"Is this your sister?" He said, glancing up at Sakari and then toward Liseli as he asked his question, then quickly turning his eyes back toward Sakari.

Sakari nodded, grabbed her sister's arm, and then turned toward the young man's gaze.

"We are taking today's hunting catch to the nearby clans." Her voice almost sounded embarrassed when she mentioned the meat. She shifted and looked out over the system of canals, surveying the complexity of his creation. A squeal of excitement passed her lips as she watched the water slowly move down the ditches toward hundreds of planted crops. Several dams blocked some of the trenches to make a pool of water that bathed a field of cotton.

"It has been a while since I have seen your work, Calien. It looks magical!" Sakari felt her face blush as she complimented the builder. Maybe she had said too much, she thought.

"Come," Calien said, "You too, little sister. I will show you our new project."

He led the two girls to a large rock wall where water flowed over the top. Sunlight illuminated the cascade of water, and a mixture of high- and low-pitched melodic sounds serenaded the surrounding area. As if pulled by an unspoken invitation, Sakari sat down next to the water and placed her hand into the stream, water flowing against her outstretched hand. Tiny splatters of sparkling droplets landed on Sakari's cheek as she bent down to taste the cool water. Delight filled her eyes as she turned back to Calien.

"I have never seen anything as beautiful. It is wonderful." A smile infused with joy filled her countenance. Liseli had never seen her sister look so radiant and happy. The three sat alongside the stream, time going in and out with the clouds as they giggled and threw water on each other, speaking about the dry weather, the growing crops, the building of a terrace, and anything else that they could think of in the warmth of the midday sun.

Liseli was the first to break the spell of the magical waterfall and reminded Sakari that they needed to carry out their father's orders. Sakari obediently stood up and turned to the canal builder to take her leave. Meeting his eyes, a sudden rush of warmth flowed across her cheeks. She moved too quickly to step toward the desert path and stumbled. Calien reached out to keep her from falling onto the rocky terrain.

Again, as their arms touched, Sakari blushed, turned, and walked away, afraid to look at the young man's face.

"Goodbye, canal builder. Nice to meet you," Liseli said and quickly turned to catch up with her sister. The girls walked in silence as they distributed the wrapped meat to the nearby clans.

"He is very nice," Liseli eventually told Sakari as they returned to their pit house.

"You can't tell our father about Calien." Sakari blurted out abruptly, stopping and pulling Liseli to a stop. "You must be silent. Our father or mother would not approve of my talking to someone other than Nodin. Calien is not a hunter."

"I won't. I won't," countered Liseli, surprised at Sakari's reaction, pulling her arm away from her sister. "But it is not like you care what father or mother thinks. You were just talking to him."

The two began walking again. This time, Sakari slowed the pace. Liseli sensed that Sakari wanted to talk and sat down on a rock off the path where they were walking. Sakari sat down beside her.

"He is different from Nodin. He thinks up amazing ideas and then builds them. Can you believe the flow of water over the rocks? I loved it." Sakari bent her knees, clasped her arms around her legs, and rested her head on her knees. Liseli listened to her sister talk about the builder, her heart pumping with joy that Sakari would trust her with her feelings. Even though she realized that her parents would reject any attempt for Calien to be with Sakari, Liseli knew that would be her sister's choice. As they continued to talk, the sun slid behind the mountains. "Sakari," a loud, deep voice rang out. The girls were startled and saw their father standing in front of them. He scowled and let out a huff.

"Where have you been? What have you been doing?" Sakari abruptly stood up, sending a warning glare to Liseli, and recounted how many of the villagers wanted to ask questions of the girls and delayed their return. Their father pivoted quickly, and the girls followed closely, glancing at each other with a smile.

## Chapter Four

The sun baked the land, crops wilting in the heat. Calien stood over his intricate canal system, the wind blowing dust and sand into his face. He looked up at the cloudless sky, shielded his eyes, and then to the horizon for possible rain. He sighed in frustration. His people would starve without crops. The drinking water storage was desperately low.

Behind him, he heard a commotion. A group of men approached and grabbed Calien by the arms, leading him to the community gathering place. He remained silent as they pushed him along a path into a group of loud-speaking councilmen. The voices quieted as the council leader stepped forward. Calien recognized Sakari's father, Malo. He spoke with authority in a stern tone.

"The crops are dying," Malo said. He glared at Calien. "It is time for the festival of the rain. The council has chosen you to represent the people at the festival."

Calien stifled a gasp, understanding the meaning.

"You have been chosen as a sacrificial offering to the god TEZ to end the drought," Malo continued. "You will be dressed in clothing befitting the god and expensive jewelry adorning your neck. The people will exalt you and worship you before your ritualistic sacrifice in honor of the god Tez, symbolized as a Jaguar."

Calien held his head high and remained motionless. He surmised he was chosen because they blamed him for the lack of water available to the community. However, the council members did not acknowledge the drought. It was Calien's failing.

He lowered his eyes and tried to comprehend all that was happening. Then, a familiar voice suddenly rang out into the crowd around him.

"I volunteer. I will be the chosen one at the festival." Calien gasped as he turned and saw Sakari standing in front of him. Her lips were tight, and her face showed resolve.

"It is a tradition that if someone volunteers for the one chosen by the council," Sakari pronounced," this must be respected. I volunteer."

"No, Sakari," Calien yelled out. "What are you doing? You must take that back."

"Once a volunteer has come forth, no one can change it," Sakari whispered as she moved closer to Calien. "It is now set into the law of the gods."

Malo rushed to his daughter, horrified as to what she had done. He grabbed Sakari and shook her forcefully. "What have you done?" he yelled at her.

Sakari stood alone and proud, and the council members pulled her into the center of the crowd, proclaiming her the new festival sacrifice. Calien tried to reach for her, but a tall hunter blocked him.

"You have done this, builder," said Nodin. "You have doomed her. This is your fault."

A group of warriors shoved Calien to the ground, stomping and spitting. The rest of the crowd rushed to Sakari, stroking her hair and giving her flowers. Her mother looked on in terror, holding the weeping Liseli close to her chest.

Calien remained face down in the sand, unwilling to look up. It was only Liseli who moved to his side.

Donna Krutka

She carefully wiped the sand from his eyes and cleared away the blood oozing from the areas abraded by the warrior's blows. Calien moved his gaze toward Liseli and muffled his sobs.

## Chapter Five

Liseli lay at the feet of Yarseli, her eyes swollen with tears. She had spent what felt like a long-time pleading, or more like begging, she thought to herself.

"You are a great medicine lady. You must be able to help us." Liseli's voice trembled with exhaustion.

The old lady continued grinding the fragrant weeds in the stone vessel. She leaned over to smell her mixture and added a calculated amount of spittle into the clay pot. She stirred it with her fingers until she was satisfied with the consistency.

The girl was not going to leave without her answering, so Yarseli slowly moved alongside Liseli and squatted comfortably. She ran her crooked fingers through the girl's-tear-matted hair. She remembered watching Liseli play in the field with her friend, Mojag. The girl was intelligent and curious, much like the old lady had been when she was little. She struggled with her decision to proceed, but she began to speak.

"You must listen carefully and must not repeat what I tell you. You may die, but there is a way to save her. "And the old lady Yarseli spoke softly and cautiously into Liseli's ear.

## PART TWO

## TOCHO

## Chapter One

He sat in the tree, serene and attentive. His tan furry body blended with the bark, camouflaged. He was hungry, but his prey was abundant, and he could be choosy. A weasel ran by below him, chased by a skunk. He refused to even bother with the skunk. He had early on developed an aversion to its smell. Instead, he preferred larger animals, like the deer and the elk. He put his head onto his paws, relinquishing hunger to restraint. After all, he thought, a mountain lion could choose his meal if he was patient.

A thundering roar came from the distance behind him. He raised his head and turned to look. A large bull elk flew across the field, opening close to the mountain's base. Saliva flung in all directions as the black bear chased the elk, rapidly closing the distance to the prey.

# The Desert Saga

Tocho sprang to attention. His ears coupled together, sensing how hard the bear was working. He knew the bear. They often shared the same prey. The bear was cocky and overindulgent, and Tocho knew he could outrun this predator. The bear, however, was twice his size, and with one miscalculation, the bear could better him.

His sharp claws grabbed the side of the tree, and he slowly descended, dropping silently to the ground. His eyes followed the scene before him. Then, in a sudden leap of confidence, he joined the hunt. Tocho edged toward the elk's line of escape. The animal's breathing pattern was fast and labored. It was tiring as the pursuing bear closed in. Tocho patiently allowed the elk to come within striking distance, and then he bounded into the open and felled the large mammal with one movement. His sharp claws pierced the elk and pulled him to the ground. His forceful jaw landed on the back of its neck, snapping its spine. It was over in seconds with such precision that the bear did not see the elk fall. Tall prairie grass surrounded the kill, shielding the carcass. Tocho lay utterly still, his sleek body canvased over the elk, protecting his prey. The bear roared to a complete stop, angry and confused. He flung his head from side to side, gasping, uncertain which way to turn. He paced around the area, sniffing and snorting, exhausted from the attempt, and overwhelmed with hunger. Finally, the bear slowly turned away, heading back toward the mountains where he had begun his chase.

# The Desert Saga

It had been a while since Tocho had eaten so well. Finding a large elk in the area was rare. He feasted for hours, then pulled the remaining carcass off to the side of the prairie to save for later. Finally, his hunger was satisfied, and he returned to the tree of his previous perch and laid his head on his paws to rest. He would resume his usual tour of his territory at dusk, sleeping most of the warm day digesting his recent meal. His region was large, and he spent most of his time roaming the border of his territory. He marked its edge with his scat, gouging the trees with his sharp claws or urinating on the boundaries. There was clarity as to whose domain other animals were crossing.

The night was warm when he began his rounds. He wandered along a slow-moving stream, drinking slowly, happy to refresh his dry palate. Then, unexpectedly, he heard a sound off to his left and raised his pointed ears. Investigating, he crept forward, staying hidden in tall grass. His keen eyes could see a dark shadow, not moving, and he heard moaning and gasps coming from the figure. Smells of wet fur and blood filled the air. Tocho focused and recognized the form of an enormous bear in distress. It was the bear who had chased the elk into his territory.

Tocho heard another sound coming from bushes further away. He looked up in time to see another set of yellow eyes peer out toward the bear, then disappear. The mountain lion stayed alert to see if the yellow eyes reappeared but soon decided the animal was gone.

Tocho looked back at the bear, then slowly moved toward the creature. A heavy, branched tree trunk rested on the lower half of the bear, pinning him to the ground. There were markings on the ground where the bear had tried to escape. Blood oozed from a wound in his hind leg, and significant gaping scratches were over his eyes and throat. Tocho continued to approach, carefully ensuring the bear heard him coming, not to frighten the bear.

The bear looked toward Tocho. His eyes were glassy, which matched his shallow breathing. As he acknowledged the cougar's arrival, a small whimper of a growl came from his massive fallen body. Slowly, Tocho moved around the branch, evaluating how to help. He saw that the ground below the bear was soft and grassy. The bear was trapped and helpless.

"I am here to help, "he finally told the bear. "My name is Tocho."

"The entire land knows your name. I have heard it since I was a cub." the bear whispered. "I'm Ravage, son of Ultima."

Tocho paused and squinted at the bear. Bile erupted into his throat, and he choked with anger. No, not anger, revulsion. He backed off slightly, trying to decide his next move.

"Your father is the keeper of the mountain?" But, of course, Tocho was not asking a question. Instead, he was merely trying to process how he could justify saving the son of the creature who killed his father.

Ravage did not answer. He gasped and paused between breaths. Tocho closed his eyes, trying to think. He and the bear were equal in the forest. They had no predators other than the other. His father and the bear's father, named Ultima, had met in a battle to the death, both not wanting to give up their role as king. His father, the mountain lion, had lost.

"I'm not my father," Tocho hissed, watching the bear struggle to breathe. "I will help you."

The mountain lion began digging under the trapped hind legs of the bear. Mounds of dirt rose off to the side. Slowly, a slight depression under the bear formed. Ravages' injured limbs could move slightly, allowing the blood flow to return to the hind quarter. But bleeding returned after removing the compression, eventually slowing and stopping. Tocho resumed digging until he created a sizable crevasse under the bear.

"Bear," he hissed. "It is your turn to work. First, you must pull your body from under the tree. You must do this to live." Tocho was stern with his command, but the bear did not move. Finally, exhaustion overwhelmed the mountain lion, and he fell onto the ground next to Ravage. He cautiously scanned the area around before closing his eyes in sleep.

Donna Krutka

## Chapter Two

Rain gently began to fall in the early morning. Tocho blinked away the droplets forming on his eyelids. He sprang to attention, forgetting where he was, alarmed at his negligence. Then, he regained equilibrium and looked at the bear lying beside him. The bear's breathing was steady, but he still had not moved from his position from the night before.

Tocho spotted fresh, green leaves from nearby trees and bushes. He left the bear to gather as much brush as he could carry in his jaws and returned to deposit it around the head of the bear. Droplets of rain began to settle onto the leaves and pool around the bear's nostrils and mouth, causing Ravage to snort and sneeze. Water flowed over the eyes and snout of the bear. He instinctively licked the droplets and swallowed them into his parched mouth. Tocho stood back, his eyes following the bear as he began to arouse and eagerly lap the water with his long tongue. The rain picked up in intensity, softening the ditch Tocho had dug the night before, allowing less resistance for Ravage's bulky limbs to move in the mud around him. He aroused seeing Tocho standing beside him.

"You are there," Ravage exclaimed, his eyes attempting to focus. He squinted, directing his gaze at the mountain lion. "What happened to me?" he asked Tocho.

"A large tree branch fell on you, and you were trapped. You're injured." Tocho strolled closer, listening as the bear whispered. "When ready, you can move out from under the branch. There is room to pull yourself forward."

Ravage turned his head to peer at his hind limbs but cried out in pain as a sharp bolt of electricity shot down his spine.

"Slowly," Tocho warned. "You are cut wide open. You must move slowly."

Ravage scowled at the cat, and then again, with gentle movement, he looked at his legs and the branch that had landed on his back and hind quarters. Then, with great effort, he pulled forward only inches before collapsing in pain and exhaustion. Then, with Tocho's encouragement, he tried again, and after many repeated tries, his body slithered out from under the massive tree branch entrapment. Light rain continued to fall, washing along Ravage's injured legs, stinging yet thankfully cleansing his bloodied wounds.

"Rest now, bear. I will be back. You need rest." Tocho moved away with his usual stealth quickness, and Ravage fell into a fitful sleep, the still-falling rain cooling his fever-ravaged body.

Tocho sprinted to where he had hidden the remaining elk meat. He pulled huge chunks from the carcass and ran back to the sleeping bear. He placed the meat in front of the bear and made repeated trips until enough food awaited the injured bear. For days he stayed by the bear's side, and slowly, Ravage moved from his immobile position until he could cautiously stand up into a four-point stance.

"You have helped me, Cat. Why?" the bear finally asked Tocho. A long slow silence lingered between the two animals. "My father killed your father. You should hate me."

"Helping you doesn't mean I don't hate you," Tocho said harshly.

Ravage looked straight ahead, his ears perched as if listening to the Cat's inner thoughts. Silence encased the two. Eventually, Ravage spoke again.

"I owe you my life. I will have to repay the debt." Ravage turned his head to watch Tocho's reaction.

"You owe me nothing. I don't want anything from you. When you are ready to go on your own, we will part. The law of the forest will take over again." Tocho sat outstretched on all fours and casually laid his head on his forepaws. He frowned, not sure why he was helping the bear. They were enemies. Something prompted Tocho to help the bear. It felt forced, he thought, and he didn't like that. On top of the food chain, he had always been in control, not having to look out for any animal but himself.

"I am ready to go alone, on my own," Ravage spouted at the mountain lion. Tocho detected a pout.

"Ok, so we'll go our way tomorrow," said Tocho, speaking with such certainty that Ravage almost wanted to feel offended. Ravage sat back on the ground, pain causing him to wince as he settled into a resting position. The two would part in the morning, he thought. That would be the end of it. A smug growl came from his snout, and both soon fell into a quiet sleep.

## Chapter Three

Tocho awoke, the smell of smoke meeting his nostrils and causing him to choke. He looked over at the bear, still soundly sleeping.

"Fire," he screamed, astounded that the bear had not been the first to awaken.

Ravage slowly lifted his head, confusion settling in his eyes.

"Fire!" again hissed Tocho. "The forest is on fire. Get up. We have to move."

Billows of smoke surrounded Ravage's massive body. Then, finally, his senses cleared, and he slowly attempted to stand. The night before, he had resolved to travel by himself. But now, spasms shot through his wounded hip. He tried to move faster but couldn't.

"Go ahead. I will follow." Ravage said, growling at Tocho. The mountain lion scowled at the struggling bear. He turned his head toward an escape route, preferring to let the bear go on alone. Something tugged at Tocho from inside. He turned back to the bear and hissed.

"I have no idea why I am doing this," hissed Tocho," but we'll go as fast as you can travel. Stay behind me as close as you can." Tocho moved cautiously, choosing an easy path for the bear to maneuver, the opposite direction from the fire. Clouds of smoke and hot flames swirled around the animals faster than Tocho had calculated. Ravage started to wheeze and cough as he labored to travel.

Tocho abruptly stopped. His eyes looked in all directions. They were trapped. Off to the right, the path stopped, and a drop-off was apparent.

"To get away, we must slide down this cliff." yelled out Tocho." It will take us to the river below. We will be safer by water. It will be difficult for you, but it's our only way out."

Ravage looked into the eyes of the mountain lion. He had never had a friend before. He was a solitary creature, as was the cougar. The cougar had been there to save him from the fallen tree. He had nursed him back to life and now was willing to save them both from the peril of the fire. He looked over the steep, rocky cliffside and then at the fire chasing them.

"Are you coming?' Tocho yelled, looking over the cliff, then at the bear.

Ravage peered over the side of the cliff.

"It's survival or death, bear!" the mountain lion shouted. "You can do this."

Ravage nodded to Tocho, and the two approached the edge and, one by one ventured over the side of the cliff.

"I'm trusting you, Cat. This better work!" Ravage, though depleted of energy, started the descent with pure resolve.

Tocho slid gymnastically along the loose rocks. He often stopped to look behind to see Ravage's huge body haphazardly tumble down the cliff with no control.

Sounds of growls and snorts belched from the bear, awkwardly balancing along the narrow path, fearing to look down. Finally, he landed clumsily at the base of the cliff, Tocho hissing in approval. Both turned in unison to see a rapidly flowing river before them.

"The river," Tocho said, staring into the water. "It's moving fast."

"It's the rain. It's higher because of the rain," answered Ravage. "Can you swim?" he asked Tocho, who stared at the river.

"Of course, I can swim," Tocho spat at the bear. He indignantly walked back and forth along the bank.

"I just like to avoid water, that's all." Tocho scanned up and down the river.

"I prefer taking the long way around the water, finding higher ground. I look for natural bridges. You know, fallen trees, inlets I can jump across." His eyes met Ravage's gaze.

"I don't see any," the bear called out, waiting for Tocho's next move.

"How's your swimming?" Tocho asked, still staring blankly into the river.

"Bears are known for their swimming. I've gone downstream on many rivers looking for new hunting areas. It's my favorite way to travel!"

Ravage could sense Tocho's hesitancy. Finally, the bear growled and called out to the cat.

"Get on my back, Cat. I will take us downstream." Ravage moved closer to Tocho.

"What?" hissed Tocho." No! I'm not riding on your back on that river." So he moved away from the bear and the river.

"You can stay here and be engulfed by fire," Ravage countered. "Or you can jump into the river and swim by yourself. But my offer stands. Get on my back, and I'll take us down the river." Ravage was amused to be taunting the Cat. "We'll consider this payback."

Tocho hissed again, then apprehensively moved toward the bear.

"I don't need payback," he smugly cried to the bear. "You better be telling the truth that you can swim."

With an easy jump, Tocho landed on the bear's back, and Ravage entered the water. The cold water rushed about the bear's arms and legs, relieving his injuries' pain. His hindlegs moved forward, grabbing the water with smooth, graceful strokes. Tocho sunk his claws into the bear's back, afraid of falling into the freezing water. The smoke-filled sky and air soon were replaced with a crisp, cool breeze, and both animals relaxed, leaving the danger of the fire.

Ravage sighed, feeling the cat's claws retract. It had been a while since Ravage swam in a river. His body relaxed, and each stroke felt more powerful.

Up ahead, Ravage saw large boulders in the middle of the river. The water swirled around the boulders, and the bear could hear the river's roar as it dropped off beyond the boulders.

"Cat, hold on tight. The river speed has picked up. Dig your claws tightly into my coat and try to stay balanced. If you fall off, swim to the shore." Tocho obeyed, clutching onto the bear in terror.

"I can't control our direction." Then, excitedly, Ravage yelled, "We're going to hit the boulders."

Ravage's body slammed back and forth between the rocks, water rushing into his face to blind his vision.

The river plunged downward, sharp rocks gouging Ravage from all sides. Finally, Tocho's hold on the bear ripped away, and he was gone. Ravage tumbled, swirled in the water, and fought to aim his hindquarter downriver. Up ahead, Tocho's head bobbled in and out of the water. He tried to grab onto anything he could find. Instead, he bashed against rocks and then did not resurface.

Ravage reached the drowning cat, grabbed him with his sharp jaws, and flung him onto the hard-packed sandy beach. Finally, the bear launched his own body onto the sand and landed in a heap next to Tocho. Tocho slowly opened his eyes, coughing and spitting out water, and looked over to see Ravage snorting the water from his nostrils and shaking his thick coat.

"You're alive, Cat. We made it. We're away from the fire." The bear chuckled and growled.

Both animals calmed their breathing and waited until their racing heart rate slowed.

"Well, that went well." Tocho finally muttered, and the two animals roared and hissed simultaneously.

## Chapter Four

Tocho and Ravage camped along the river, content to stay where they were. They took turns finding food and hunting in the area close by. As they continued traveling, the tall evergreen trees became sparser and ultimately disappeared. The sky was a deep blue with little clouds shielding the sun. Up ahead, the river flowed into an open valley peppered with tall, green columns of trees. The plants had ribbed spines acting as their skeleton, arms coming off their sides.

"Those trees look like protective guardians looming over this vast open region. The land here is different. It appeals to me." Ravage rolled back and forth in the dry sand as the two lounged alongside the slower-moving river, and Tocho exposed his underbelly to the warming sun.

"Do you see those birds with huge wingspans flying overhead?" Tocho said. "They are catching the wind drafts and playing a game of chase." Ravage gazed up to the sky and followed the towering figures with fascination.

Tocho rolled over to be upright and gazed downriver, taking in the scene before him.

"It is different. Minimal high grass and different plants. Interesting." Tocho's eyes scanned from east to west, assessing the prey. "I do not see elk! So, our meals may be less abundant." He paused and then added, "Let's stay here."

As if a similar urge had sprung up in both animals simultaneously, they rose to their feet and began walking. They followed the river for miles, taking in the smells of what had become desert and delightfully feeding off the abundant wildlife that laced their pathway.

The hot sun had initially felt welcoming but then turned hostile, unsettling them both. They learned they had to take shelter and sleep by day and hunt by night. Ravage's thick fur began to shed, yet he enjoyed how the sun made him sweat, which naturally cooled his body. Tocho climbed the significant boulder outcroppings, looking out over the expansive territory. In the forest, he realized trees had hemmed him in. Here, he could see for miles, quickly spotting the movement of prey with his adept vision. The vast openness of the land thrilled his senses, and his body moved with renewed quickness and alertness.

"You seem happy," Ravage said one early morning as they were about to settle into sleep for the day.

Tocho turned his head and gazed at the bear. "What do you mean?"

"You like this land. It has given you energy, as well as peace." Ravage lay his head on the ground and looked out at the desert. "You seem to belong here."

The mountain lion began purring. Ravage remembered that once before, he had heard Tocho purr. It had been when Ravage was injured and lay helplessly under the large branch that had trapped him near death. Then, the mountain lion lay by his side, purring through the night, sending calm messages to help the bear survive. Ravage hadn't heard him purr since then.

"My father knew your father," Ravage said after the two had been silent for a while.

"Your father killed my father," Tocho said in a hissing voice. Ravage took a long time to reply.

"That's the story that has circulated over time. But that is not the truth. My father did not kill yours. On the contrary, your father died saving me." Ravage spoke with a whisper.

Tocho turned his head suddenly in the bear's direction. Rage erupted inside him, and he spat on the ground before Ravage.

"Don't provoke me, bear. I am in no mood to tolerate jest. The whole forest and entire territory know that is not true. Your father killed my father." Tocho's reply was angry and indignant. He growled, staring directly into Ravage's eyes.

The bear stood up and paced slowly back and forth. Ravage's head hung down, and his sizeable black body glistened in the sunlight. Streaks of red feathered through his sleek coat.

He came closer to Tocho to begin his story. He spoke in a hushed, reverent tone.

"The night was dark and still. The temperature of the day had fallen. My father had spent the day showing me how to hunt. We had settled down after devouring our catch of deer, sleep easily overtaking my father. However, I was not yet ready for sleep. I was restless. My belly full of food made me feel more energetic rather than sleepy. So, I wandered around the forest close to where we had settled. Unfortunately, I wasn't paying attention and was lost before I knew it. Panic and carelessness caused me to go in the opposite direction from where my father lay sleeping. I'm not sure how long I wandered through the woods when I found myself staring into the eyes of the most giant cat I had ever seen. Even in the moonlight, I could see the color of his coat was tannish orange with dark hollow black spots dotting his body. Huge protruding teeth jutted out of his tight jaw, and his yellow eyes focused straight on me, halting me in absolute terror. He swung his long tail back and forth, and I thought I saw him grin.

I can barely remember his roar as he leaped into the air on top of me. Pain ripped through my torso as I tried to move out from under his heavy body. His claws ripped into me, and teeth slashed across my face. I tried to wriggle out from under his attack, but his grip was so tight I couldn't move. Then I heard a loud hissing scream, a sound I had never heard. Another monstrous cat flung aside the beast on top of me, and the grip on my trunk released, allowing me to roll to my side to shield my neck. The two cats fought ferociously, screaming and hissing. That was the last thing I remembered. I drifted unconscious, and the rest of the story was told to me by my father."

Ravage looked over at Tocho, both eyes locked onto the other.

"My father had heard the roar of the jaguar," Ravage continued, "and then heard the scream of your father. He bolted through the forest. He came upon the scene where the jaguar held down your father. He flew himself against the jaguar and freed your father from his grip. Joining together, they thwarted the attacker, the jaguar turning and running back into the forest.

Both of our fathers ran to my side. I was barely breathing. My father stood helpless. Then, your father lay his entire body over mine and breathed deeply into me. My father didn't understand it all then, but your father gave me his gift of life, a ritual passed down for eons. He whispered something into my ear, and then he was gone. Slowly, my eyes opened, and I gulped air. I was alive, and your father was not. "

He paused for a long moment and then began again.

"I owe my life to your father," Ravage whispered, his voice solemn with reverence. "My father had to ensure no one knew the mountain lion had saved me. When your father spared my life, he transferred the ceremonial gift of life to me. If the jaguar had known what happened, he would return to kill me to take the gift. The gift must pass freely. But the Jaguar is the "Night Sun" and ruler of the underworld. He can trick an animal into giving him powers that are not his. That is what my father fears could happen."

Tocho listened, sitting motionless and barely breathing as the bear told his story. He had heard of the god known as the "Night-Sun," who would take the shape of a jaguar cat when he roamed the earth, emerging from his journey through the underworld. As a tiny kitten, before he had left his mother's den, she had told Tocho the stories of the "Night Sun," sometimes called the Night god. She had warned him of his elusive powers and ability to transform into a cat. But she had also told him how a bear had killed his father, besting him in a tragic fight to the death.

Tocho looked away from Ravage, a scowl marking his brow long and deep. His head lifted suddenly, pulling him from a trance-like state as the bear continued.

"There is more." Ravage continued. "High in the desert mountains is a cave where the goddess of the rain lives. The Night-Sun has trapped her in the cave for many ages. The story goes that the Night god prevents the rain goddess from showering the earth with her tears until human life is sacrificed. When that occurs, he allows the earth to have rain. In the past, the humans tried to refuse, but the Night god punished them by not sending rain for several years. Once, the rivers ran abundantly with the flow of water and teamed with fish. But now, they have dried up and flow only at his whim. So, he forces her to rapidly deluge the land with rain, causing flooding and little time to store the water to drink and sustain the crops. The Jaguar and his guards protect the entrance to the cave day and night. Any creature that gets close to the cave is never seen again. But my father swore he would find the goddess of rain and release her. He wanted to do this in honor of your father."

"Where is your father now?" asked Tocho after a long silence.

"It has been many moons since I last saw him. I fear he is dead. Perhaps killed by the Night god."

The two lay on the ground, feeling drunk with thoughts of rage, grief, fear, and uncertain expectations. Then, finally, they fell asleep and slept in the shade of the outcropping where they had settled, and both awoke as the sun was setting and the cooler desert temperatures pushed aside the warmth of the day's heat.

## Chapter Five

Ravage growled, stretching his legs and opening his mouth wide to let out a bellow of a yawn. He rolled over onto his back, moving back and forth on the sandy, rocky ground, moaning in pleasure as he scratched. Sudden alertness brought him abruptly to all fours as he heard a cacophony of howls bouncing off the wash before them. He stood motionless, defining the sounds.

"Coyotes," said Tocho, attentive to the sounds of the night desert. "There are probably six or more in their pack, from the sounds of their howls."

"I have never hunted coyotes." the bear replied, sounding a little cautious about the mention of a pack.

"Probably best. Coyotes are skillful hunters. I have seen them take down a bear as big as you. How old are you, bear? Tocho asked, sure he saw Ravage stand taller and push out his chest.

"I am still considered a cub by the forest because I have only lived through two winters."

"It's a wonder you have made it this long. Coyotes generally steer clear from bears, but it's the young inexperienced bear cub they sense they can outsmart." Tocho continued lounging on the ground, watching Ravage walk back and forth, swinging his head like a branch blown by a stiff wind.

Ravage looked out into the terrain ahead, his eyes trying to focus on the area from where the howling was still erupting.

"Will you teach me?" he said, not looking at the mountain lion but staring ahead.

"Teach you what?" asked Tocho, perplexed at the question.

"To hunt. To not be taken down by coyotes." he turned his head back toward Tocho and watched closely for his reaction.

"I can't teach a bear how to hunt!" the mountain lion hissed, disgust mixed with amusement in his reply. "I don't know anything about being a bear!"

"But you are a skilled hunter. Soon after the jaguar attacked me, I was separated from my father and mother. They wandered high into the forest, and I could no longer find their scent. So, I have had to learn on my own. You could help me."

"We are enemies, bear. I can only teach you the way of the mountain lion." Tocho suppressed the urge to get up and walk away from this discussion. "It has been strange enough that we have traveled together this far. I have thought that we need to go our way."

Ravage turned away and lowered his head. He knew it was true. They should have been enemies, he thought. But he didn't feel that way around Tocho. They had been through a lot with each other. The mountain lion had saved his life. A pounding in his chest made him look again at Tocho and ask bravely once more.

"If you teach me how to hunt, I will go my own way, and you won't ever have to see me again. But I'll have a better chance if you teach me how to hunt."

Tocho felt a tug on his heart and realized he liked this bear. If Ravage knew better how to hunt, he could survive the harshness of the land.

"I'll show you some of my ways, but remember, bear, we are not the same. My instinct may be different." Tocho sat quietly, then turned to the bear. "OK, I'll try to help you."

Ravage followed Tocho as he led the two out into the rocky desert. Ravage's pace was quicker than usual, and Tocho noted the bear strutting. The plants were hostile, and both needed to avoid the sharp needles protruding from the thick skin of the plants, which were impossible to remove.

Within a short time, Tocho looked back and saw Ravage digging in the ground beside a fallen, black-barked mesquite tree. Pieces of bark flew up in all directions, and Ravage's snout was soon covered in massive amounts of dirt.

"What are you doing?" called Tocho, annoyed at the bear's distraction. He felt impatient, realizing the futility of teaching a bear how to hunt. "What Ravage are you doing?" he repeated, this time almost shouting!

"Ants. I found Ants!" Ravage swung his claws in every direction, destroying a giant ant hill, ants scattering in pandemonium, and he tongued the escaping insects as fast as they exited the mound. Tocho watched in disgust, unable to take his eyes off the bear as he flung dirt into the air and sucked the ants into his mouth, enormously pleased.

"Ravage," Tocho yelled, pulling away from the spectacle before him, "Do you want to learn how to hunt? It doesn't look like you need any help destroying ant hills." The mountain lion gave a frustrated hiss and lumbered away, slowly creeping into the darkness of the night.

Ravage came galloping from behind, obviously conflicted about leaving his great find of ants behind but determined to learn from the mountain lion.

"I usually just eat ants and larvae, Tocho. Maybe I can find berries. If I am lucky, I can catch a fish in a stream. I have been unable to catch a large meal. Once, not too long ago, I was chasing an elk, and I nearly caught him. It was going to be my first large animal meal. I was in the open grassy valley and had no idea what had happened. He just disappeared. I waited and watched for almost a day longer, but he never reappeared. I need help hunting."

Tocho was silent, hesitant to tell the bear why the elk had disappeared. He turned his head toward Ravage, slowed his pace, and was conflicted about telling Ravage the truth. "No need," he muttered and continued moving forward. "The bear doesn't need to know."

Tocho suddenly stopped and squatted under a low-lying cluster of trees. He looked back to the bear and was satisfied Ravage had been paying attention, taking cover, and crouching on all fours. Up ahead, a group of three deer was lounging in high grass. The deer preferred grazing in the day and had settled into a slightly exposed nest of grass as dusk settled on the terrain.

"Ravage, this is our chance. We are going to hunt one of these deer." Tocho eyed the movement up ahead. He surveyed the deer's possibility of exit and spotted the more alert animal than the others. He glanced at the bear, who stared at the scene with a look of horror.

"Ravage, do you understand? Here is your chance to hunt." The cat hissed a low-sounding growl, and Ravage responded by nodding his head, eyes calming, more alert.

Tocho continued. "The first thing is the element of surprise. Watch the animals for some time before you attack. Notice if they are attentive or distracted. If they are watching what is going on around them, the element of surprise may be difficult. If they appear to be sleeping or distracted, it's worth trying to attack. Remember, you don't want to choose just any situation. It must be the right one. The chase could be dangerous, engaging you in a pursuit that could take you into their territory and terrain. There can be obstacles such as cliffs or ravines. You don't want to take on the challenge and lose the prey. "

"When I decide to go after the animal, I will start creeping toward them, then pick up speed—most of the time, I can catch almost any animal. But you," Tocho hesitated slightly," you must practice your top speed. I'm not sure what you can do. "

Tocho danced on his four legs, moving slowly forward. He signaled to the bear to follow.

"When you reach your prey, you will grab him by the neck or back and strike him with your paw. It must be quick and forceful." The mountain lion studied the bear's reaction to his words, uncertain if he understood. "Are you ready for this?"

Ravage's thoughts flew to somewhere in his past when he had heard those words. His eyes glazed over.

"Are you ready for this?" Ravage's father had asked him long ago as the cub frolicked in a lush field of evergreen shrubs gulping their small, shiny red berries as fast as he could manage. His snout dripped juice from the berries, and the cub would reach his long tongue to lick off the sweet-tasting liquid. The little cub's father slung his front claw in Ravage's direction, resulting in deep scratches on the cub's face, prompting immediate alertness. Ravage ran to his father's side and stayed close as the older bear hunted a large animal. Ravage remembered how he trembled with terror, wishing he would never have to engage in a similar experience again. And now, here he was. He lingered with the old memory for only a second, then brought his attention back to the Mountain Lion. "I am ready."

Tocho began creeping toward the deer, his low-lying belly soundless as it scraped against the ground. Bear tried a similar posture, feeling awkward and ungainly compared to Tocho. He squinted his eyes, realizing he had difficulty seeing the prey ahead. He put his snout into the air, and immediately the scent of the deer bathed his nostrils. He could tell there were three different scents and discern how close they were to where he was. Watching Tocho, he lowered his head, reading for the attack.

Ravage felt his heart pounding. His mouth became dry, and his limbs trembled. A surge of hesitancy pulsed through his muscles, creating confusion about what he was doing and how he would do it. Nevertheless, he focused on the Mountain lion, whose next move was to launch into the deer.

High-pitched terrifying growls and barks came from behind the deer, sending a call of alarm to the entire valley. The deer were slow to get to their feet as a herd of six coyotes stormed at them, speed and precision catching the deer off guard as the pack slammed mercilessly into the larger mammals. Screams and howls shot out in every direction. The bear stopped in his tracks, his coat immediately moist with sweat pouring over his body, adrenaline rushing. His mouth gaped in horror as the coyotes tore the animals apart, each deer overwhelmed by two coyotes working together.

Tocho crept up alongside Ravage, equally mesmerized by the spectacle before them. They both looked at the other and, in unison, turned away to seek shelter away from the feeding frenzy. Ravage continued to shake, unfamiliar with this feeling of alarm that reverberated through his body. He felt both pity and disgust at what he had just witnessed. It became clear that he did not want to engage in such violent attacks. He had no desire to kill another animal so raw and vilely. He would tell Tocho that he preferred to eat berries and ants and larvae rather than attack in the fashion of the coyotes. And as for defending himself against the coyotes, he had no answer. He supposed he would probably not survive, he said to himself. He didn't want to be that kind of bear for whatever reason.

The two traveled in silence. Then, at last, deep grunts and growls came from the bear.

"You are silent," Tocho said to Ravage.

The bear slowly went past the grand saguaros, glancing up and recognizing the magnificence of the tall cactus. The disintegrated granite that lined their path seeped in between his toes. He could smell the sweat on the mountain lion, realizing he, too, had been rattled by what they saw.

"I have decided I don't want you to train me. I will take my chances that coyotes don't attack me, and if they do, I know now that I won't have a chance of survival." A large gulp of saliva seemed to get stuck in his throat, and he swallowed a second time.

"I couldn't do it, Tocho." Ravage almost whispered. "Despite my being one of the biggest animals around and knowing other animals should be frightened by me, I can't make myself hunt in that fashion. My father was always ashamed that I did not want to hunt. He would growl at the top of his lungs, telling me to do as he did, but I never could." Ravage slumped down under a thick, branched, tangled mesquite tree. Branches scratched his back, not caring if he couldn't get comfortable.

Tocho peered at the bear, seeing him differently than before. Instinct had driven Tocho to hunt and feed on many different animals. It was routine, and he had never analyzed the whole process. However, this bear was different from what he was. Tocho watched the bear as his saddened eyes blinked in confusion, not understanding his feelings.

"It's ok, bear. We're different, and hunting is part of our difference. Please don't beat yourself up because you can't hunt deer, elk, or even a mountain lion like me. This makes us not enemies. That's good, don't you think?" Ravage pivoted his head in the mountain lion's direction and almost smiled. Instead, ripples moved across the bear's forehead, careful to contemplate what Tocho had said.

"So, we can then be friends?" the bear asked, his voice more upbeat than moments before.

"Ok, bear. We can be friends." Tocho said, unfamiliar gladness in his answer.

The two fell silent, exhausted. Then, finally, they found shelter, settled down, lay their head down on their paws, and drifted off to sleep faster than expected.

## Chapter Six

A crash of thunder woke the two animals simultaneously as the water fell from the sky in sheets. Streams of water started pouring down the sloped hill around them, puddling in the area where they had been sleeping. They bolted upright, and both looked around at their surroundings.

"We need to go up the hill," said Tocho, Ravage frowning as he surveyed the steep hill ahead. The mountain lion ducked his head and started climbing the slippery rock before them. Ravage took several steps then slipped, sliding backward on several tries before he landed a sure paw into a crevice to pull himself upward. The two had to shake the falling rain out of their eyes often to see where they were going. Talking was not an option. Voices were not audible above the noise of the deluge. The steepness of the path increased, and Tocho looked up, thinking he had spotted the top through the drenching rain. A wide gap in the mountain wall stood before them, and each animal pulled toward the cave entrance, limbs shaking from the challenging climb.

Tocho glanced back at the bear, nodding as Ravage put one paw in front of the other, a short distance behind. Lightning struck ahead of them, illuminating a larger-than-life image of a spotted cat guarding the cave's opening. Beside the Jaguar, they visualized an outline of a female with outstretched arms. A flowing dress draped her wet body, and her face spoke of radiance and sorrow. The Jaguar stood upright, a fierce gaze staring down at Tocho. The mountain lion stopped his ascent, and Ravage took the cue and looked upward.

It was the rain goddess with outstretched arms soaking the land with her tears—the torrents of water poured out of her eyes. The travelers stood mesmerized, a sight unbelievable to them both. Then, a piercing scream and hiss roared out into the rain-drenched valley, warning Tocho and Ravage to stay away. Tocho lifted his paw to move closer. The Jaguar sprung at Tocho, surprising the mountain lion. Sharp claws nicked the side of Tocho's neck, but he rolled slightly left, missing the thrust of Jaguar's attack. The Jaguar's breath felt hot and foul on Tocho's face as he lunged forward, sinking his teeth into the attacker's ear. He twisted violently, getting back onto all fours. The bear roared at the top of his lungs and plowed into the fight, clawing and battering the jaguar like a plundering boulder. The jaguar fell back, grabbing the rain goddess and pulling her into the open cavern. Heavy rocks cascaded into the opening, quickly blocking the entrance into the cave. Tocho and Ravage stood panting, eyes still holding a warrior's gaze as they looked with disbelief at the blocked cave. The stillness of the air stood in sharp contrast to the blowing rain that had suddenly stopped. Both turned to the other and hastily sat on the ground to recover from the attack.

Tocho licked at his wounds and wiped the blood from his eyes. He looked at Ravage hard and long and hissed, which almost sounded like a laugh to Ravage.

"For an animal that wants to eat ants and berries, I say you attacked that monster with quite a punch. Thanks. You just may have saved my life."

"That may make us even, right, Tocho?" Ravage watched to see if he was getting the mountain lion's approval.

Tocho waited for a long moment, then nodded. To Ravage, he seemed to be thinking about some distant thought. Ravage almost jumped when the mountain lion suddenly turned to the bear and shouted.

"The Jaguar lured us up here because he was going to try to take the Ancient Gift of Life. Only he thought it was mine. That's why he wanted to kill me." Tocho's eyes were wild and alert, confident of his conclusion.

"But the gift has to be given freely." retorted Ravage.

"Maybe he doesn't know that. Or maybe he was going to try to torture me to get it. Anyway, we must never let him know that it is not mine. No matter what, he cannot know.!"

"Do I have to die to transfer it?" Ravage whispered as if the jaguar was able to hear their conversation.

"We have no idea. Maybe my father died because you were dying, and he took death from you. We don't know why the Jaguar wants it, but we must be careful. We must not speak any more about this here. But we will speak about it later." So, the two slowly descended the mountain, glad the path was easier without rain complicating their footing. The descent was smooth and uneventful, Ravage grazing on berries and seeds on the way down, Tocho grabbing small rodents to eat as the two traveled silently.

## PART THREE

## THE AWAKENING

## Chapter One

Something wet was sloshing all over her face. She tried moving her head back and forth, escaping the irritating wetness, but her hair was caught, trapping her. She tried moving her arms, but they wouldn't budge either. Finally, her fingers searched around and touched a hard surface encasing her. She blinked; the sloshing stopped momentarily and then started again. She wrinkled her nose when the wetness worked across her nostrils, prompting her to sneeze. Once again, she blinked her eyes and stared. She was looking into the eyes of a mountain lion. He had been licking her face with his long, scratchy tongue.

The mountain lion moved away from her line of sight, and she felt the hardness release from her left arm. She lifted her freed arm, stiffness pulsing through the limb as she opened and closed her fingers. She reached around her head, and her hand landed on an immovable object pinning down her hair. Slowly and carefully, something pushed away the rock, allowing her to lift her head off the ground. She surveyed her surroundings, assessing a low ceiling made of stone and chunks of rock piled all around, including on her. She was startled, watching the mountain lion piece by piece push the stones off her trapped body until finally, her limbs and trunk were free of the rubble.

She lifted one leg off the ground, then the other. She flexed her knees and rotated her ankles. Attempting to sit, she fell back, almost hitting the ground. The mountain lion prevented her fall and then pushed her upright. She squealed and reached to pet the cat, pulling it back in haste, worried about the cougar's reaction. She pushed off, trying to stand, but let out a cry as she plopped onto the hard surface when her legs would not hold her weight.

"It will get easier. You will soon be able to stand," a voice sang out.

The girl whirled her head around to look at the Mountain lion. A cougar, she thought.

"Did you talk?" she blurted out in disbelief. "You're a mountain lion!"

"My name is Tocho. I'm called the Interfacer." The cougar spoke with almost a purr. His eyes watched the girl's face startle.

"Your name is Liseli. You may not remember that now, but you eventually will. Now come. We must get out of this place. It's not safe since you have awakened. Follow me. At first, you will find it hard to stay close, but soon your limbs will work better, and you will keep up."

"How come we can talk? How did you know my name? Where am I?"

The girl again attempted to stand. This time her legs didn't wobble, and she took two steps.

Tocho leaped ahead, taking quick strides and quickly moving around obstacles. Liseli grunted, walking like an injured grasshopper running away from a toad. She took several more steps and climbed over the rubble without tripping.

"How come I can't remember anything?" she shouted. "What do you mean when you say I will eventually? Where am I, and what is happening?'

She squinted and frowned, huffing when she could no longer see the cougar. She moved forward until she saw a blocked passageway, then turned her head and saw the light shining through an opening. She picked up each foot as if walking on glass and exited the cave, stunned by the bright light that momentarily blinded her vision. She raised her hand to block out the warm sun, which caused her eyes to water and clouded her vision. She gaped at the terrain in front of her. Large boulders populated the landscape, and colors of brown, tan, and fading- green haphazardly smeared the terrain. She smiled as the wind blew across her face, and she licked her lips, tasting the dust in the air.

Not too far off, she saw the tall tree-like green cactus with multiple arms shooting off its ribbed skeleton. She knew this tall cactus. Its green spiny body looked sunken, as if in drought conditions. Tall tree cacti stretched out over the terrain as far as her eyes could travel. She had never seen so many.

A hiss from close by made her look ahead to the boulders above, and she spotted the shadow of the mountain lion blocking the sun's blinding image.

"You need to climb these rocks. You must get away as far as you can from the cave. It is not safe," Tocho said, again repeating his warning.

## Chapter Two

The rocks were dry and crumbly, making it hard for Liseli to get a sound footing. Her hands smarted as the granite under her fingers scraped against her palms and shoeless soles. She slipped, but caught herself, then looked up toward the mountain lion. He scowled with intolerance.

"Patience, cat," she said. "I'm doing the best I can," and continued to climb.

Reaching the pinnacle of the boulders, she gasped, seeing the vastness of the desert terrain. Somehow, she was familiar with what she saw, and a wave of ecstasy pulsed through her body.

"Where are we going?" she said softly and almost muted. "Where are you taking me?'

Tocho stood beside her, looking out over the desert toward the next set of high mountains, then back to Liseli.

"We must travel to the east side of the desert basin, toward the closest set of mountains. It is there that you will find where you will deliver your plea. The path is rugged and will take some time, but you don't have much time. That's why we must hurry." He leaped ahead before Liseli could reply, and she released a grunt of exasperation, slowly moving forward to try to stay up.

The sun was high in the sky, brightly glowing with intensity. Her body began to warm, and she took deep, awakening breaths, igniting a sleeping spirit. Memory flashes surfaced as she trudged the desert path following the mountain lion. Her eyes closed momentarily, and she saw running water, a large ball court, and a smiling face. Then, the memory faded, and her eyes bolted open as she turned her head in all directions to look for the elusive mountain lion.

A fierce scream came from ahead; Liseli fell to her knees, her head low. She spotted a cluster of bramble bushes off to her right and quickly pulled her exposed body toward the bushes. Another high-pitched scream terrorized from above. Liseli pulled her trembling arms up over her head and held her breath. She slowly looked up as a hiss and growl came from a different direction. Tocho stood tall and unconcerned, staring into the eyes of an animal twice his size, black spots splotched in a rosette pattern over his tan-coated furry body.

"The girl is mine, Tocho. Let me pass. I mean, you no harm." the animal growled.

"It is not time yet," Tocho hissed. His eyes continued to stare into those of the Jaguar. "She is still mine." Tocho angled his muscular body in a threatening stance and squinted his eyes.

The enormous animal turned his head toward Liseli and growled deep and long. His eyes met hers, oozing terror. He slowly moved toward the girl, but Tocho stepped in front of him and blocked his approach.

"It is not time," Tocho repeated," You must leave her to me. Now go," The predator stood still hesitantly, which alarmed Liseli. Liseli knew the mountain lion was mighty in the wild, but this animal seemed able to overpower Tocho. Then, in a breathless second, his body turned, and he leaped away, no more words spoken.

Liseli slowly stood up. Her trembling body chattered uncontrollably.

"Who...who was that? What did he want? What did you mean?" She looked up at the mountain lion, searching for answers.

"You only need to know that you must hurry. You don't have much time." Tocho turned away from Liseli, continuing ahead. Liseli ran toward him and grabbed his long tail.

"STOP!" she screamed. "I need to rest." Sobs exploded from her tiny body as she flung herself on the ground, tears and gasps heaving from her chest. Tocho stopped and stared at the girl, uncertain how to react. He slowly approached this broken creature, walking back and forth, then around her in circles, before he finally sat down next to her, allowing her sobs to reside slowly and her breathing to become more regular.

"That animal was a jaguar," he said. He paused, eyes squinting and looking at Liseli.

"The jaguar is the personification of the god Tezcatlipoca. He is the god of providence, associated with the Night sky, the night winds."

A startled gasp came from Liseli. Tocho was afraid she would start crying again and moved a little closer to try to provide reassurance.

"What does he want? How come I can see him?" Liseli's voice again sounded muted. She shivered, remembering the stories of the god of the night sky. He was a demanding god. He wanted strict obedience and had no tolerance for resistance to his directives.

Haziness surrounded more memories, and she returned to the mountain lion awaiting his answer.

"He wants you. You are here to carry out a mission, and he wants you to fail. So, he will watch us both, making sure you fail. I am here to protect you as long as I am able."

"A mission? What does that mean?" she wiped her tears as she looked at the mountain lion.

"You will eventually remember. I can tell you no more." He shut his eyes, preventing any more questions. Liseli was too exhausted to ask any more questions. She, too, shut her eyes and tried to rest. Closing her eyes brought another round of flashbacks, each vision confusing and unsettling. There was a girl, a boy, and a lady with missing teeth and crooked fingers. Water was pouring in all directions, and then it suddenly stopped, and the sun baked the ground all around. She fell still and must have slept because the next thing she knew, she was being nudged awake by a small creature whispering loudly in her ear.

## Chapter Three

"Wake up, wake up!" the little prairie dog loudly whispered in her ear. "They are coming for you; you must get out of their path!" He stood up on his hind legs with his forelegs going back and forth as if he were wringing his hands. Liseli pulled herself to a sitting position. She blinked and looked around, trying to remember where she was. The sun filtered in through the spiny bushes surrounding her, and she blinked, seeing the outline of the creature talking to her.

"You are talking!" she exclaimed, forgetting she could hear animals talk.

"Of course, I can talk. I talk very well, but that doesn't mean you shouldn't hurry before being eaten alive!" The little prairie dog tried to nudge her again, not moving her.

"What should I be afraid of?" Liseli replied, her eyes searching for the mountain lion or anything that might appear alarming.

"You are about to be attacked by an army of scorpions! Look down on the ground toward the opening of the brush. You have been sleeping in their territory, and they consider you fair game. So first, they will sting you everywhere, then bit by bit, they will feed on you. So, hurry if you don't want such rude and unwelcome treatment!" The prairie dog jumped up and down as he spoke.

Liseli looked down and spotted a large army of scorpions marching toward her, tails arched high behind them. She leaped from her resting spot, backed into the brush, and saw no escape from the horde of insects.

"What do I do?" she screamed at the prairie dog, her eyes flashing in panic.

"This way," he said, ducking under a snarly bush opposite the entrance of Liseli's encampment. The girl hesitated, then dove under the spiked bush, letting out a cry as sharp thorns embedded in her back as she exited.

The desert morning was cool, and a soft wind blew off the mountains ahead. Liseli shivered thinking about the nest of scorpions and turned to the prairie dog to thank him.

"My name is Jabberrunner. You are certainly big and rather odd looking." He spoke with a high-pitched voice, quickly rambling so that it was hard for Liseli to follow what he was saying.

"My name is Liseli, and I am a girl. I am a human," she corrected, "But I have never been able to talk to animals. I'm not sure how it is possible." Then, again, she looked around as if she was trying to find the answer to her questions somewhere around her.

"We can talk, just like you can. We have no time to discuss this now. We must hurry. Tocho told me to wake you up while he was hunting. He needed food and had been on a hunt most of the night. I was supposed to ensure you were okay, and I almost messed up. I can't believe I almost let scorpions attack you!" He ran ahead, looking back to ensure Liseli followed, mumbling and chattering while carefully picking a pathway easy for Liseli to travel.

"Where are we going?" She yelled at Jabberrunner. "I have been following the mountain lion, and he hasn't told me anything."

"Don't you remember anything? It will make no sense until you do." The prairie dog stopped, letting the girl catch up. "You must hurry faster. I told Tocho I would make you go faster." He then took off ahead, scampering at almost an uncatchable speed.

"You both tell me to go faster!" she exclaimed, raising her arm to her eyes, shielding the sun as she glanced around. A lightning pulse shot through her head as another flashback interrupted her thoughts.

"I remember a girl and an old lady with missing teeth," she said, slowing her pace and squinting to visualize the image.

"I don't think I liked the old lady because I get frightened when I see her face. But, of course, I also get frightened when I see the girl's face, but it's different." She put her head down and mumbled almost in a whisper. "It's hard to explain...."

She looked up and could not see the prairie dog. She quickened her pace. "Hey, wait up!" she yelled, tripping on a rock in her path but checking herself from falling.

"OW," she exclaimed, watching the ground more carefully to avoid rocks and spiky plants with sharp barbs. She reached her arm over her shoulder to try to brush the cactus spikes off her back, only to drive them in deeper.

An extensive mountain range with jagged peaks loomed ahead. Liseli turned her attention in that direction. The terrain became steeper, and the sun's intensity increased. She sat down on a nearby rock to rub her aching feet. A broad-leafed yucca plant was within arm's reach, and she pulled off enough leaves to craft a protective covering for her feet. Peering around in all directions, she stood up and saw no sign of the mountain lion or the prairie dog. She moved ahead to try her new sandals when one shifted on her foot—slipping, falling, and gashing her knee. Tears flowed from her eyes, and she stopped herself from crying.

"Which way should I turn? Where are you?" she called out, feeling alone and desperate. From behind her came a sound of brush crunching. She swirled around but saw nothing. Then, up ahead of her, she heard low-pitched growling. Liseli squatted onto the ground, nimbly hiding behind a collection of bramble bushes. In front of her stood a pack of six coyotes, staring at her and blocking her path. She stood up and boldly faced the group.

"I am Liseli. I travel with the Mountain lion. We are going to the far mountain. You must let me pass." She stood tall and brave when she spoke to these animals.

"You have no place in this land." Their leader growled back at her. Then, several coyotes crept toward her, their head and body low, eyes forward, ready to attack.

A sudden hiss came from behind, and the mountain lion jumped into the coyotes' path, sounding a terrorizing scream. The six coyotes stopped, and their leader strolled forward.

"Tocho, is it true? Is this human with you?" The voice of the alpha coyote was slow and doubtful.

"She is with me. Let us pass." Tocho moved closer to Liseli and nudged her forward. The two slowly advanced past the pack, cautious of sudden movements. Snarls and growls erupted as they proceeded. Liseli stayed so close to the cougar that she could feel his breath on her neck. Tocho began picking up speed and distancing the two from the hostiles.

"Would they have attacked?" she asked the mountain lion when she finally could speak.

"It is hungry times," he replied. "I'm unsure what they would have done sensing you were alone." He continued choosing a path more accessible for Liseli to travel.

"Where did you go? I felt alone." Her voice spoke with emotion.

"I sent the prairie dog to tell you I would come back. So where did he go?" Tocho looked around in annoyance.

"Of course, I am here, sir Tocho." Jabberrunner squealed, coming out from hiding behind a group of rocks. "Those were coyotes, and they love eating prairie dogs. I was hiding. It never occurred to me that they would attack the human. Oh me, oh my!" he exclaimed, following close behind the two.

Tocho let out a hiss and spat, and continued. Liseli sighed.

"Where are we going?" she managed to ask.

Again, the mountain lion did not respond and continued, chased by the prairie dog. Within seconds, Liseli could not see the mountain lion. His mysterious, elusive behavior baffled her. He was insistent that she hurry to a specific location. Once again, now, she was heading on a path without direction. She couldn't see the prairie dog either. He was staying very close to the mountain lion for protection from predators.

The wind began to pick up, blowing sand into her face and stinging her cheeks. She blinked rapidly to clear her vision. Raising her hand to shield her eyes, she tripped into a cactus bush, barbs sticking into her leg, and cried out in pain. Determined to go forward, she picked up one foot and put it in front of the other, sensing she was pushing against a solid wall. Her mind flashed a vision of the girl she had seen before. She was taller than Liseli, with long black hair reaching to her waist. She had a sleek, muscular body capable of working hard, yet a feminine air. She stood proud and obstinate in Liseli's visions, a scolding frown on her face. A rush of the same previous emotion coursed through Liseli's body, filling her with calm and terror. "I know this girl," she thought. "I feel like I know her well!"

The sand pelted her face, and goosebumps erupted as she ducked her head to soften the sting. She squatted down, trying to get low enough to block the wind, but it swirled, coming at her from all directions. Noises of footfalls sounded around her; maybe someone was following her, she thought. She shrugged, deciding it was noise from the storm, and paid no more notice. The sand plugged her nostrils and filled her ear canals. She dared not swallow for fear that a mouthful of sand would clog her throat. Breathing became more complicated and little by little, she sank farther to the ground, pulling her legs up close to her trunk and burying her face between her knees. The desert temperature dropped, and cold enveloped her body. Then, from out of nowhere, a blanket of warmth encapsulated her as she felt a fur coat surrounding her. The mountain lion gently pulled his body beside hers, shielding her from the blowing sand and cold temperature.

It must have been hours that she stayed in this protected cocoon. Then, finally, she awoke no longer covered by the mountain lion, the wind and sand calm.

Putting her stiffened arms to the ground, she pushed her hesitant body to a standing position. She extended her arms outward to get her balance, almost toppling over from her wobbly legs. Again, she was alone.

Her eyes traced the terrain. Tall mountains stood before her, a landscape emboldened by the sandstorm. Colors sharply defined with hues of green, amber, yellow, and brown danced in the sunlight. A smile laced her lips, and her eyes sparkled with wonder and joy as she realized she loved this place. She had encountered insects, cold, sand, and prickly plants but loved it all. She somehow felt this was home.

She began walking toward the mountains. A low moan rumbled from somewhere around her. Her head pivoted in all directions, grasping for clues as to the source of the moan. The moan was intermittent and waxed and waned in its intensity. She looked to her right, taking the chance and approaching the area under a thick collection of bramble brush. She picked up a small dead branch of a black-barked mesquite tree and parted the brush. Her arm moved slowly, bracing for anything that might jump at her. A dark-haired boy lay curled up on the ground before her, sand covered and shivering. She swallowed apprehensively, trying to determine if he was alive, keeping her distance. He moaned again, and Liseli jumped in a startle. She gently poked him with her stick, afraid to get any closer. He moved after being prodded, opened his eyes, and stared into Liseli's widened eyes. He gasped, and the boy slightly raised his head, sand falling from his hair. Struggling with cold and exhaustion, he attempted to sit up, and his upper trunk fell back onto the hard-packed desert floor. Liseli instinctively moved to help him, reaching for his shoulders to help pull him upright. The boy sneezed and choked the more he moved, trying to free the sand from his nostrils and open his mouth.

"Who are you?" Liseli managed to say to him between his intermittent breaths. "Have you been following me? What are you doing out here alone? How long have you been here?" She paused for a moment to let him answer. Then, when he didn't, she began again. "I can't believe you survived that horrible storm."

The boy stared at Liseli for a long time, then frowned in disbelief. He closed his eyes. Liseli could tell he was frightened and confused. His skin whelped from the blowing sand, and his knees and legs were peppered with abrasions.

"I'm ..., My name is......." Talking prompted a violent bout of coughing then he vomited a mixture of mucous and sand.

Liseli sat down next to him and pounded him on his back. The boy raised his hand, acknowledging her help, and she stopped pounding.

"What's your name?" she asked, hoping he wouldn't have a coughing fit this time.

Again the boy shot a bewildered look at Liseli. He swallowed with difficulty, taking his time to answer.

"My name is Mojag." his voice steadier. "You're right. It was a horrible storm."

Liseli looked at the boy in more detail. He appeared to be about her age, with approximately twelve earth rotations, with no hair on his upper lip. He had dark eyes and similarly colored shoulder-length hair. His upturned nose and small ears seemed familiar to her. She felt heartened by his friendly face, and warmth about this boy rushed through her.

"I am going to the mountains. The ones up ahead." She wasn't sure why she told him this. She didn't know her heading. "Where are you going?" she asked. Liseli watched as the boy scanned the horizon for the mountains.

"I am going with you, Liseli," said Mojag.

Again, his voice spoke of familiarity. Liseli cocked her head to one side, surprised at his reply. "How did you know my name? Do I know you?"

"Of course, I know you. You are following the mountain lion. I'm coming with you. We'll go to the mountains together." He observed her face, hoping to see some form of recognition.

Donna Krutka

A hiss and high-pitched growl rang out behind the pair, and Liseli and the boy turned to face the mountain lion's narrow eyes and upturned his lip. Then, hissing, he stared at the boy.

"You have been following us since we left the cave, haven't you?" The mountain lion growled, ears laid back and crouching low. "How did you manage to get free?"

"When you awoke Liseli, you also awoke me. I looked around and saw you take her out of the cave. But I am confused. I remember who I am and why I am here. So why doesn't she?" Mojag looked over at Liseli, his eyes searching for an answer.

Again, the mountain lion came closer to the boy. Mojag felt a hot breath on his face. He shrank back in terror.

"I should let you wander forever in this land. Who invited you here? If you interfere, all is lost." He hissed again at Mojag, eyes wide with anger.

"Leave him alone!" Liseli screamed and quickly moved between the boy and the mountain lion. "Don't harm him! He is going with us." she grabbed the boy and pulled him behind her, surprised at her boldness. She dared to stare at Tocho, uncertain of his response.

Tocho raised his ears, his slow hissing persisting. He backed away a short distance and let out an eerie growl. "I'll allow you to come, but you're never to reveal to her anything about who she is or why she is here. She must find that out on her own." His voice was deep, and his eyes locked on Mojag. Chills visibly ran through Mojag's frightened body. He nodded in agreement and then moved even closer to Liseli.

The mountain lion turned away and began moving along the rocky path. The trail took an immediate upward turn. Liseli and Mojag followed, wanting to stay close as the pace quickened. Again, the little prairie dog emerged, hiding in the brush.

"You have to do what he says," Jabberrunner warned, speaking to Liseli and Mojag. "Follow closely and don't get behind. It's dangerous out here." Then, distressed and impatient, he signaled for the two to go ahead of him.

The trail challenged the young followers. But first, they needed to maneuver over large boulders and thick cacti. Liseli's footing slipped as she climbed, and Mojag grabbed her arm as she lost her balance, almost tumbling off a high outcropping. Terror filled her eyes when they looked down over the abutment to the ground far below.

"Thanks," Liseli managed to say to Mojag, her heart still pounding from the near fall.

"I keep seeing terrifying flashes when I close my eyes." Liseli cautiously began. "I know I'm supposed to figure this out by myself, but I can't get the feeling of horror out of my head."

Picking his words with a watchful tongue, Mojag asked, "What do you remember so far?"

"I keep seeing an image of a girl with long dark hair. She is standing tall in front of a group of warriors. I feel terrified when I see this image as if she is in some danger, and I feel helpless." Liseli closed her eyes to think harder, but the images faded. Eventually, she opened her eyes in time to see the mountain lion turn the corner ahead and get to her feet in haste.

Mojag stood up to follow her. He glanced down at his feet and saw the little prairie dog beside him.

"Who are you?" he asked the little creature, hanging back somewhat from Liseli to avoid hearing him speak. "Why are you along?"

Jabberrunner smiled and pushed out his chest as if being asked an important question. "I am called the keeper of time. Tocho named me that himself. He wanted to make sure Liseli did not slow down or falter. I am going to try to make sure she doesn't fail."

"Fail? Fail at what?" Mojag kept his voice low.

"I can't tell you anything, Mojag," Jabberrunner answered, slightly increasing his speed.

"Wait, little prairie dog. I've known Liseli all of my life. I followed her into the cave to protect her. She can't even remember who I am."

"Liseli must figure it all out by herself." He started to move awake quickly, then saw Mojag's sad eyes. Jabberrunner stopped and whispered to the boy. "She will figure it out soon. If she does not, Tocho will help her. He's like that." The little prairie dog ran ahead as Mojag caught up to Liseli.

## Chapter Four

The four travelers camped overnight huddled together. The mountain lion positioned the boy and girl toward the back wall of a shallow cave. Jabber and Tocho scavenged for roots and berries for the hungry, young humans. After eating, Liseli and Mojag quickly fell asleep, exhaustion wiping out any resolve to continue.

Liseli awoke with a start. She and the boy were alone in the cave. She squinted to get a better look at Mojag. His hair was black and slightly curly, a lock falling onto his forehead. Again, she thought he looked about her age, with high cheekbones and a soft lip line appearing to want to smile easily. His skin was darker than hers, as if he had spent much of the day in the sun. He had long legs, was taller than her, and his arms were no longer like a young boy's. Slight bulges in his upper extremities showed muscle development. She watched him for some time before he opened his eyes and saw her staring at him.

"Do I know you? I mean...before, did I know you?" She waited carefully to hear him answer, but she feared he shouldn't tell her. Finally, she decided his silence was helpful. She realized it was an affirmation of her question.

"If I tell you what I remember, then it won't be breaking the Mountain Lion's orders, don't you think?" Liseli turned her head in every direction, trying to see if Tocho was around them.

"I guess not" Mojag looked around to ensure they were alone. "OK, go ahead."

"I remember a girl with long black hair. She is standing in front of a group of men. The men yell at her, and she stands tall and proud." Liseli watched closely for Mojag's reaction. She thought she saw a slight glint in Mojag's eyes and maybe a smile on his lips.

"Go on," Mojag encouraged. "What else?"

"I remember an old lady with teeth missing. She seems to be frantically telling me something and pointing. I think she is pointing to a cave." Liseli licked her lips and put her hand to her temple. "I think she points back to the other girl. I feel like the girl is my sister. My mind and body shake with apprehension when I see these visions as if something bad is about to happen."

Mojag turned and nodded. He was careful not to say anything else, but his eyes met Liseli, and she knew she was right.

Liseli's head pounded with a thunderous jolt, sending pain throughout her body. She fell back against the cave wall, both hands shooting to her forehead, trying to keep her head from cracking open. Mojang grabbed her arm in alarm, terror laced over his panicking face. Beads of sweat erupted on her forehead, and her breathing was deep and gasping. Then, slowly, her furrowed brow relaxed, and she opened her eyes.

Liseli said, breathing deepening. "I saw a bright green and red light flash before my eyes, and my head pounded like it was going to explode," Liseli said, breathing in an irregular pattern. "Then, it all disappeared, and I can see and remember more clearly."

"You are Mojag," she said, turning toward the boy in sudden recognition. She thrust her arms around him, holding him, her rapidly beating heart slowing. Of course! You are my best friend." The two held tight to each other until Liseli pulled back to continue talking.

"The council had sentenced my sister Sakari to die in sacrifice to the God of the Night." Liseli put her head into her hands, trying to focus.

"Wait, why was she going to be sacrificed?" Liseli closed her eyes, brow curling. "We were in the middle of a drought, and the Night god who roams the earth as a Jaguar required a human sacrifice to bring rain." Liseli stood up and strode back and forth.

"A man, the builder, was chosen for the sacrifice." Liseli gasped as she recalled the rest." My sister volunteered in his place. I remember, now, that if someone volunteers in place of the original choice of the elders, it is final."

"Is this right, Mojag?" Liseli's voice was high-pitched and rapid. Mojag did not answer. He sat on the ground, his eyes fixed on Liseli and barely breathing.

"The lady without teeth in my vision is named Yarseli, which she told me means "water lady." So, I went to her to beg for help."

Liseli became quiet and then started turning in small circles.

"She wouldn't help me initially, but I begged and begged her."

"She told me there was a way to save my sister, but it was nearly impossible. She told me I had to go to the mountains." She ran toward the cave opening where the two had been sleeping. She pointed frantically. "Those mountains." Standing motionless, she took in a deep breath and sighed. She returned and sat down by Mojag, a frown on her forehead and her head slightly bent toward her chest.

"That's all I remember." Then, finally, she turned toward Mojag and asked with insistence.

"Can't you tell me if I'm right? It's unfair that you can't tell me what I need to know." Her voice sounded angry and frustrated.

Mojag observed her, trying to be encouraging as well as cautious.

"The truth is that I don't know any more than what you just said. I watched you talk to the older woman and saw you heading toward the cave, and I decided to follow. I remember our parents telling us never to go into those caves because when someone ever did, they never came out. I was terrified you were going into them. So, I followed you in case you needed me."

They sat quietly, wanting to get up and get going. But instead, Liseli gently rested her hand on Mojag's arm, a sense of calm pulsing through her body.

Almost in unison, they stood up and headed out of the cave. The bright sun greeted them with force, and the day's heat felt good compared to the cave's cool. Liseli waited for her eyes to adjust, then picked a path angling toward the mountain, and Mojag followed. They both looked around, trying to spot the Mountain lion. Up ahead, the tiny figure of a prairie dog stood beside a path, ensuring they saw him before continuing.

They traveled up and over boulders, facing steep climbs, which slowed progress. However, the temperature dropped as they ascended the mountain, providing a welcome break from the hot desert sun. The sound of tiny feet scampering behind them made them giggle, realizing a prairie dog was following them.

Like the night before, as the sun began to set, Tocho waited beside an opening ahead of the two travelers and turned his head toward another protected outcropping. A freshly hunted rabbit lay at the entrance of their night-time resting place. Jabberrunner motioned to a pile of berries and blossoms he had collected for dinner.

"It is important to eat," Tocho said to Liseli and Mojag. "Hunger will slow you down."

"I can make a fire," Mojag spouted, sure he and Liseli would not want to eat raw rabbit meat. He immediately gathered pieces of desert plants and sticks, and within a short time, he had a fire carefully placed with the rabbit meat slowly cooking on a well-constructed roasting mount. He made certain Liseli waited for it to sizzle before he let her taste it.

"My father taught me to make sure meat is well cooked, or it could get me sick," mused Mojag, pleased with his contribution to the meal.

Tocho sat in the middle of the gathering, watching the young boy prepare the meal. Liseli ate most of the berries and flower blossoms the prairie dog had collected. She watched the fire and cooking meat closely, her eyes wide with hunger.

"I heard you tell the boy what you remembered," Tocho said to Liseli. "Have you remembered anything more?" His eyes squinted as he peered into Liseli's.

Liseli looked from the cooking rabbit to the Mountain lion, surprised that he had heard her exchange with Mojag.

Liseli looked deep into the mountain lion's yellow eyes, a pulsing connection occurring that hadn't happened before.

"I know you said I had to figure out who I am and my mission, but can you help me? I need your help to understand."

Tocho lowered his head in a nod, and Liseli began speaking.

Donna Krutka

## Chapter Five

Deep into the night, they talked. Tocho purred and occasionally growled as Liseli told him every detail she could remember.

A long silence descended on the two as Liseli's voice cracked with exhaustion. Her throat was dry, and her swallowing became difficult.

"I need water," she said, wishing for a cascade of water flowing nearby.

Jabber was soon at her side, offering her berries to quench her thirst. Liseli quickly gobbled the berries, petting the prairie dog's head affectionately.

"I will tell you why you have come to this side of the mountain," Tocho said. "The goddess of rain lives in the high cavern found at the pinnacle of this mountain. She is trapped there by the Night god who guards her during the day. At night he is forced to go to the underworld, where he must travel during the night hours to stay alive and to rule over the underworld. He has guards from the underworld to watch the cave entrance. He only releases the rain princess allowing her tears to bathe the earth when your people give him a human sacrifice. Besides the jaguar, only two creatures know the way to the cave and have seen the rain goddess. I am one of them. Suppose you can survive the journey, Liseli, to the cave, arriving at night. In that case, you may be able to plead to the rain goddess to release her tears, and your sister will not have to sacrifice her life. Unfortunately, the goddess is sealed inside the cave, making it nearly impossible to approach her.

Liseli sat quietly. She put her hand to her temple, listening intently. Rain goddess, Night god, surviving the journey, extremely difficult! All this ran through her head.

"I must do it. I don't have a choice. My sister will die." Her little voice sounded meek and innocent. The mountain lion looked at her, realizing she knew nothing of what she would encounter. "You must take me!" she demanded of the mountain lion, desperate and pleading.

"I'm the only one who can," Tocho whispered in a hushed tone. "That is why I'm here!"

Liseli drew in a deep breath and exhaled slowly. Her eyes drooped from exhaustion, and her head fell back against the boulder behind her, landing so forcefully that she cried and rubbed the back of her head. But within a short time, Tocho watched as her head fell slightly forward, and she was asleep. He laid his head on his paws and closed his eyes. It took no time for him to sleep.

## Chapter Six

Liseli awoke with gentle persuasion, early morning light rising over the top of the mountain. She slowly sat up, looking for the mountain lion, who was nowhere in sight. Then, off to her left, she saw the figure of her friend Mojag sleeping. He stirred and then sat upright when Liseli got to a standing position.

"Are we going now?" said Mojag, much more awake than Liseli felt.

"You heard us talking?" Liseli said, not really too surprised.

"Yes," Mojag said.

"How much did you hear?' Liseli frowned.

"All of it. I'm going with you."

"It is very dangerous. We might die." countered Liseli.

"If you die, I die." Mojag sounded too casual. "Why do you think I followed you in the first place? You need me, and I intend to stick with you. So, let's get moving."

Liseli sighed and rose, her heart glad Mojag had intended to remain.

"Where is Tocho?" asked Mojag, annoyed and bemused. "Are we just to travel on our own?"

The little prairie dog jumped ahead of them and stopped momentarily.

"Jabber, where did you come from?" asked Liseli. He beckoned them to follow.

The two started walking, following the prairie dog. Desert sounds of coyotes, hawks, and hoots from owls sounded over the desert, provoking comfort and wariness as they climbed higher into the mountain.

Liseli soon had difficulty picking up one foot and putting down another. She frowned with fatigue. Mojag grabbed one of her arms to help pull her forward. They sensed urgency and danger, seeing yellow eyes peering through the bushes and vanishing.

"Something is following us," said Mojag, looking behind them. "I just heard a snap of a twig." Liseli didn't turn toward the noise, either not caring or hearing what Mojag had warned.

"Do you think that's the top?" he asked Liseli in a hushed voice, pointing in the distance. He looked back to see the girl's head bent over as if trying to sleep. Nevertheless, she remained walking, one step mechanically placed before the other.

A hissing noise came from above them, and they looked up in time to see the apparition of a large Jaguar, yellow eyes peering down on the two climbers. The sun was close to setting behind the mountaintop. The hiss and growl intensified. Liseli and Mojag instinctively moved close to each other, Mojag throwing his arms in a protective gesture around Liseli.

A monstrous black shadow passed before Liseli and Mojag, and they huddled together in a tight ball. Both hid their heads in terror as a roar belted into the night. A massive black bear positioned itself between the climbers and the jaguar, who continued maliciously hissing.

"Bear, you are protecting the two children.?" the Night god screamed.

The Jaguar lunged for the bear, hissing as the bear roared. The tearing of flesh and colliding of two ferocious bodies exploded before the frightened pair of climbers. Mojag saw the movement ahead of the dueling animals. He grabbed Liseli's arm, pulled her up from the ground, and pointed toward the mountain lion ahead of them. Tocho stood at the pinnacle of the mountain top next to an opening of the cave. His countenance was fierce and urgent, helping Liseli snap out of her trance-like immobility and begin climbing. Mojag was close behind her. The steepness of the path caused Liseli to slip several times, sending rocks and dirt down behind. Mojag would grab Liseli to keep her from falling backward. Finally, the opening to the cave rose before them, and Mojag thrust her forward and followed when a large boulder fell from above the entrance and blocked where they had entered. Tocho stood before them. The inside of the cave was silent, opposite the screams and roars of the battle outside the cave. They each heard the panting breaths of the other as their eyes adjusted to the darkness.

"How did you do it, Tocho?" asked Liseli, finally able to see his yellow eyes off the side of the cave. "How did you get us in here?"

"And what was happening out there?" Mojag said, still having difficulty calming his breathing. "A bear appeared to help us? Who was he?"

Tocho pushed the two deeper into the cave, urgency in his purpose.

"There is time to tell you about him later." The mountain lion replied. "The bear is buying us time. It is only a matter of time before the Jaguar realizes you two have entered the cave. We must find the Rain Princess. Liseli, you must concentrate on your mission."

Liseli could feel her legs trembling. Her body felt cold and limp. She struggled to swallow; moisture was devoid in her mouth. She took several steps, moving ahead of Mojag. Her heartbeat pounded in her ears. "I am not afraid," she said, trying to convince herself to go forward. "My sister. I must remember my sister."

A rustle of noise came from inside the cave. Liseli moved toward the sounds, expecting to be met by impending terror. Instead, she squinted carefully and saw a figure of a young girl, not much older than she was. She hovered in the corner, a piece of cloth wrapped around her shoulders. Liseli squinted and saw dark hair flowing to the girl's waist. She had tan-

Donna Krutka

colored skin, high cheekbones, and a soft mouth, downturned. Liseli trembled when she stood up and turned. She did not speak.

Liseli fell onto her knees, her head bowed in reverence and gratitude. Time seemed to stand still as Liseli lifted her eyes and slowly addressed the princess.

"I have come to you to ask for your help. Drought has come upon the land. We are dying, but the god of Night, the Jaguar, has told us that if we sacrifice one of our kind to him each year, he will allow rain to bathe the earth, and we will be able to survive for one more year." Liseli swallowed again, this time almost choking from the dryness.

"It is my sister they will sacrifice." Tears would not flow, although Liseli felt them trying to well up in her eyes. She continued. "The medicine lady in our village told me I could climb the mountain and ask for your help. She said that you could save my sister." Liseli lowered her head, ready to say the rest of her request. " I am asking you to save my sister. Please help me. Please," she begged, "take me instead of her. In our culture, it is final if one volunteers their life. She did that. She stepped in front of the builder the tribal council had chosen and volunteered in his place. Now I want to volunteer to take her place." A gush of relief flushed through Liseli's body. She had said what she had come here to say. She had asked for what she needed to ask. It was over. She had climbed the mountain, and now she was here. She took a deep calming breath.

The Desert Saga

The tiny rain goddess stared back at Liseli with a look of sadness in her eyes. She was hiding a secret. She slowly approached Liseli, her tiny feet gliding effortlessly over the rock floor. She stopped and looked back and forth between Mojag, the mountain lion, and the girl. She then addressed all three of the companions.

"I am Princess KaKama, goddess of the rain. The Night God, the Jaguar, trapped me in this cave for centuries. He has promised me every year that he will free me if I shower the land with my tears, and then he will let me go. It has never happened. He continues to keep me prisoner. He has also tricked you and your people over the centuries to make them think a sacrifice is needed to bring rain. The sacrifice has been for naught. He stole the people you gave freely and took them to the underworld, where he goes every night to build his forces to one day invade the earth and defeat the sun god. But I, too, have tricked him and now your people. I have no more tears. They are gone. My tears are dry, and I have no more. There will be no more rain. Your people will all die, and the lands will become harsh and hot, with dust blowing from east to west. I have watched you build canals taming the rivers, bringing water to the planted crops, such as corn, cotton, beans, and squash. I have seen your warriors hunt for game in the surrounding land, your building multiply, and your artistry flourish. Your pottery and baskets are treasures, bringing trade and prosperity to surrounding peoples.

But that is all going to come to an end. The drought will be harsh and encompassing. If you want your people to live, you must leave the land. You must find another place to live, higher in the mountains or by the great water off to the west. Your sister's sacrifice will be for nothing. To save her, you must return to your people and tell them to leave. "

She slumped to the ground, her last store of energy released as she finished her words. Tocho came to her side and lay his head over her slumped body, wishing he could give her strength with his touch. The two stood motionless, and Liseli watched, despair catching in her throat. There was no more for her to do. She had done what she could. She and her people were doomed.

Then, rage surfaced, and her eyes shot to the cave entrance. The Night god was outside, being held off by the bear. It was only a matter of time before he would break into the cave and possibly devour both she and Mojag.

"We need to get out of here," she said, turning toward Mojag. "We have to go warn the people."

"How are they going to believe us? Where will they go? What can we do?" Mojag's voice crackled as he spoke.

"I know a way," said Tocho.

Liseli's eyes slowly turned to the mountain lion. She had trusted Tocho, but now, the mission was hopeless.

"What way?" Liseli said, angry with despair.

"There is a passageway at the end of this cave. I have known about it since I was a kitten. It leads through the mountain to a large valley with trees and rivers. Your people would be able to survive. But they would have to make the difficult journey that you have just made. They would have to believe you enough to follow you."

Liseli sat motionless on the floor of the cave for a quiet moment. "I don't know how I could convince them. And what of the Night god? I'd have to get there before the Jaguar takes my sister."

"You can do this, Liseli," Tocho said slowly. "You've learned much since you began this journey. You're brave and strong. You act with compassion. You will find a way."

Liseli stared at the mountain lion, tears streaming down both cheeks. His dark yellow eyes with swirls of black and purple danced before her. She wished she could have his power and confidence. She stayed slumped and motionless for the longest time, then nodded and pulled herself to her feet. Mojag jumped up and stood next to her.

"Mojag, will you help me convince them?" Liseli's voice cracked with hoarseness.

"I will be by your side at every moment of the day. I will help you." Liseli smiled as her friend puffed out his chest in brave resolve.

Liseli and Mojag started grabbing rocks and dirt to dig a small opening in the barricaded cave entrance. They slipped out into the open as the roaring of the bear and hissing of the Jaguar continued. Both figures were bloodied and limping, neither showing signs of retreating. They took no note of the two humans.

Liseli turned to Tocho and ran to him to hug him. She wrapped her arms around his muscular body as far as they would reach and put her face into his soft fur. He smelled of the desert, mesquite, and sand, and she loved him for all he had done to help her.

"The bear will distract the Night god enough for the two of you to slip past," said Tocho. "Now go; time will not wait." Liseli hesitated, unable to pull away.

"I am still with you, little one," he said, Liseli attempting to smile at his reassurance. "I will be here when you need me. But now, you must go ahead without me. When you reach the cave at the bottom of this mountain, you must look carefully to enter only where we left the cave. Every other entrance will send you back to a different time, and you will not find your people. Once you have entered, you must close your eyes and only proceed with the mystical sense that guides you. You will experience a cooling fog and be bathed in the musky smell of the desert. When that happens, you must sit down and wait. Continue to keep your eyes closed, and the fog will clear. If you do not do this, you will lose all memory of who and where you are. Recall when we first met and how long it took you to remember. It is then that you can exit the opening before you. Again, it will take you back to your time and people. If you do not do as I tell you, the cave may entrap you until the end of time." Tocho stared at the girl and then at the boy, his body tight with authority.

Liseli slowly nodded her head and turned away. She did not want to let the mountain lion see the fear in her eyes. Mojag also nodded and swallowed, his throat feeling a tight constriction.

"I will find a way," Liseli replied. "I will at least bring back as many that listen as possible. I will find a way to save my people."

Their descent down the mountain proved much more manageable than their ascent, and urgency emboldened each step they took. They would slide down the loosened rock and then pop up to regain sure-footedness. It wasn't long before the screams and roars of the dueling animal warriors faded into the background. They slowed their pace to catch their breath.

Mojag was the first to ask Liseli the questions on his tongue.

"What are we going to do, Liseli? What is your plan? We can't just walk into the village and tell them what the rain princess has said. They won't believe us."

"We must find and get through the cave and then to the village. But, first, we "I'll speak with the medicine lady." Liseli mused, almost as if speaking to herself. "Maybe she can help us with a plan."

## Chapter Seven

Liseli and Mojag reached the cave at the base of the mountain. The opening was easy to locate, and they grasped the other's hand before entering.

"Are we ready to do this?" asked Mojag. "He told us to close our eyes. "

"Hold my hand tight," said Liseli, and both took several steps forward.

The air smelled dank and musty, and both coughed while trying to breathe. The darkness felt sticky and thick, and the two obediently kept their eyes closed. Liseli held her arms still to feel the mystical sense of direction Tocho had described. She bumped into a moist rocky wall and had to do all she could to keep from opening her eyes. She could feel Mojag's hand trembling in hers, but then suddenly, their shivering stopped, and a tingly warmth pulsed through her fingertips. Her feet moved ahead without her giving any directions. She walked, pulling Mojag at her side until a thick, muggy fog settled onto her arms and legs, surrounding them. She sat down on the ground as Tocho instructed and quickly pulled down her friend. The mist swirled around her, a soundless wind blowing into her face from every direction. Then, as sudden as it had come, the wind stopped, and the air was calm. Fog no longer tickled her arms and legs, and she knew it was safe to open her eyes.

"It's all over, Mojag. You can open your eyes." Liseli watched as Mojag slowly blinked open his eyes and rubbed them with his fists.

"Look, Liseli, there's an opening," Mojag said, his voice high-pitched.

A visible opening to the cave stood before them, bright light illuminating a path. Liseli glanced around her and searched for landmarks to help her remember this same spot in the future.

Her legs were stiff and awkward as she stood. Mojag stepped gingerly, his joints creaking as he stood. Finally, they reached the opening and peered into the brilliant, sunbaked landscape.

Before them were the pit houses dug into shallow pits. The village looked like it did when they left, which seemed like a long time ago to both. Nevertheless, they had made it back.

Liseli looked around, sure the thumping of her heart would arouse suspicion in the village since it sounded like a tribal drum calling the town to attention. She turned to Mojag, watching his face to see if he could hear her heart. His eyes were wide and blinked quickly, his pupils dark and open. His head turned back and forth, searching for familiar objects or people.

The village was quiet. The usual hustle of the village occupants was missing. The two stepped out from the protection of the rocks and proceeded cautiously forward. They heard muted voices in the distance. They angled toward the sounds, crouching low to avoid being noticed. The ground was dry, and the sand was hot, slightly burning their bare-skinned knees.

"Look, there they are!" Liseli exclaimed. "They are gathered in the ballpark. All of the people. I can't see what they are doing."

Mojag moved ahead to get a better vantage point.

"They are all looking at something or someone. I can't tell what it is," Mojag motioned Liseli to follow him.

The two moved closer to the collection of people. Liseli stopped and gasped. In the middle of the circle stood her sister, Sakari, dressed in a tightly woven wrap, ceremonial colors of red, yellow, and blue patterned throughout the fabric. Desert flowers of purple thistles and yellow sunflowers adorned her silky, dark hair, flowing to her waist. Her eyes cast down toward her feet, which bore sandals sparkling with crystals like Liseli had never seen.

Her face was solemn, yet Liseli could see the same gentle conviction her sister always exhibited. Tears formed in Liseli's eyes, and she blinked to ensure she didn't miss anything happening before her. Her father stood to Sakari's left. His eyes were stern and grim. His mouth was drawn in a tight-lip mannerism, matching the scowl he made as his eyebrows rotated inward. She almost didn't recognize her father. It was as if he were transformed into a creature filled with malice and cruelty.

"That man doesn't look like my father," Liseli said, not realizing she had said her thoughts out loud.

"Shhh!" said Mojag quietly under his breath. "We are too close to speak other than in a whisper." Liseli put her hand to her mouth and nodded.

Liseli's father began to chant. The tribal drums began their rhythmic beating in the background, soft enough so the tribe could hear the chief's chant. The chief danced around the circle, raising the tribal leader's staff high. Initially, a low-pitched chant began to build into a crescendo shouting louder and louder. His voice was hoarse and explosive. Liseli put her hands to her ears, realizing that the chant was the ceremonial sacrifice litany and it was his daughter being sacrificed. Liseli felt panic in her throat. She pictured Sakari pulled toward the high ground where a stone platform stood. Fallen desert tree stumps were piled on top of the granite. She glanced around the crowd to see if anyone would help her. Toward the back of those gathered, she saw the grief-stricken countenance of a familiar face. He looked up and immediately spotted Liseli. The two locked eyes, and he moved in her direction.

"Calien," she whispered as he squatted down on the ground beside Mojag and Liseli. He embraced the girl, and Liseli began to sob.

"Liseli, where have you been?" Calien said. "Sakari has sent messages to me to find you for her, but I never found you. There are tales that you and the boy lay dead in the fields, and the coyotes and the mountain lion consumed your bodies."

Mojag gagged and then let out a slight laugh. "We have been trying to save Sakari and went to the high mountains to find a way." the boy whispered.

"What is happening?" Liseli quickly asked, thinking of nothing else but saving her sister.

"After Sakari volunteered to take my place in sacrifice to the God of Night, Nodin began to torment me. He destroyed the irrigation canals I built and ensured the community considered me disgraced. The people have suffered much from the loss of water to irrigate the crops. He has never forgiven Sakari for not accepting his marriage proposal. Neither has your father forgiven her. Sakari is to be sacrificed tomorrow at first light."

Liseli looked out at the large swatches of land to see the dying plants of maize and squash, remembering the previously lush gardens made possible by the water canals Calien had engineered to capture the rains.

"You stole her heart, and she used to tell me!" Liseli said to the builder. "She would not let you die because of Nodin's jealousy and spite. Nor at the bidding of our father. She truly loved you, Calien."

Calien reached out and gently wrapped his arms around the small girl. Tears flowed from his pain-filled eyes. They stayed motionless for several long minutes until the crowd in front of them began to chant.

"What can we do?" Liseli asked, not expecting an answer. There was no answer, she thought. They were all trapped.

"Liseli," Mojag interrupted, "remember what we are to do. Remember the warning of the Rain Goddess. We must warn the people."

"We cannot get them to listen to us," she said, her head bowing in acknowledgment of defeat. "How can we persuade them?" Liseli quickly told Calien all that had happened over the last few days. Mojag would occasionally add more detail. Calien's eyes grew wider as he listened.

"We must find the medicine lady, Yarseli," Calien said in a hopeful whisper. "She will help us."

The three maneuvered away from the crowd, who were intently focusing on Sakari and her father. The chanting drummed in the background as the three headed toward Yarseli's hut. The sun was soon to set behind the horizon. Liseli looked up in time to see the orange highlights cast on the village surrounding mountains. She gazed at the crest of the high mountain and thought about the mountain lion. Where was the Jaguar? Had he escaped the battle with the bear?

Yarseli was waiting for them as they approached her quarters. She reached out and hugged Liseli.

"You are alive, child!" she exclaimed. Her joyful face quickly turned to concern.

"You must tell me all that has happened to you, girl," she said in a gruff voice to Liseli. "And you, boy," addressing Mojag, "What were you thinking following her?" A small smile crossed her lips, and both Liseli and Mojag knew she was pleased he had been there to help Liseli.

They sat on her floor, Calien silent but carefully listening as Liseli and Mojag told the medicine lady all that had happened. Then, when they came to the part where the mountain lion had sent them back to persuade the people to leave the land, the two stopped and waited for her to respond. She nodded, recognizing that the children had no idea how to proceed.

"And tomorrow, at first light, they will sacrifice Sakari." Liseli gasped, anguish in her voice.

The group of four sat silently inside Yarseli's hut. The chanting had long stopped, and the night resounded with darkness and uncertainty. The medicine lady rose from the floor and walked back and forth around the hut, softly muttering to herself.

She sat back onto the floor, her face stern and emotionless.

"I can understand why the mountain lion made you hurry. He is aware of all that I am going to tell you. I have had a sense of dread for days. Before the first light, there will be a lightning storm. It will be like one you have never seen. There will be no rain, but the lightning will start a fire inside the village. The dryness of our land will cause a burning wave of destruction. The villagers will act quickly to protect the village and the huts. The warriors and hunters must also respond by protecting the people and our resources. When this is all happening, it is then that you, Calien, must go to find Sakari and rescue her from the guards. She will be heavily protected, so you must be prepared to fight to the death to get her from those surrounding her. Can you do that?"

Calien sat up to a new height, and his eyes grew wide and alert. A sudden fierceness came over him. "I can do that. Before I was appointed to be the chief builder, I was a warrior. My father taught me to fight when I was a small child, younger than you, Mojag."

"I will fight next to you, Calien!" shouted Mojag, his voice louder than he had intended. Calien nodded and patted Mojag on his head with black curls.

"And you, Liseli," Yarseli said," must call the mountain lion. "He will hear you and will lead us out of the valley. We will have to leave because, following the lightning storm, numerous fractures along the mountain's base will open up and swallow up the valley. We will not have much time, so we must be prepared. "

"How do you know all of this, Yarseli?" asked Liseli, standing next to her, their eyes intently focused on the medicine lady.

"What are you saying, medicine lady? All of the people will die? How will this come about?" Calien blurted out the question, the other two unable to understand the meaning of her prediction.

"The stars and wind have been sounding this prophecy for me to decipher for some time. The mountain lion revealed that when a young woman saves the life of her treasured love, the end is coming. He foretold that the Night god would trick our people into believing he would shower us with rain. But that was not going to happen. Unless the people leave the area and follow him to the high mountain, the earth will open up and swallow them at its base."

The entire group fell silent, each looking with terror at the other.

"I will talk to the village tonight to tell them what will happen. I'll give them the Rain goddess's prophecy and warning. I hope some may listen, so our people will not become extinct. The mountain lion will be our guide out of the valley. Those that choose to stay will die. Those that follow have the chance of making the journey to safety. It will be their choice." Yarseli's head lowered, and her voice became muted. "I fear not many will listen to me. It is too hard to believe." she added.

Again, the four were silent. It was Liseli who first spoke. "How am I to call the mountain lion? How do I know what to do?"

The medicine lady looked at the girl and gently smiled. "He listens to you. You will know when he has heard you. You could summon him from the beginning." Liseli peered into the tearing eyes of the old lady and opened her mouth to speak, but Yarseli held up her hand and cut her off.

"Now go, all three of you. There is much to prepare. Gather food for the journey and any source of protection you can carry. Stay hidden, all three of you. No one must suspect what we are planning." The old woman stood abruptly, turned, and waved the three visitors out of her hut, closing the door behind them.

## Chapter Eight

Yarseli climbed on top of the pile of boulders in the village center, where the chief and his counsel gathered the people. Word had traveled quickly through the village that the medicine woman had a prophecy to announce. Many came, curious and respectful, to hear her. Her diminutive figure did not lessen the magnitude of her importance to the village. When she spoke, few argued with what she had to say. Time after time, her predictions of the future had saved a child from death, warned the village of danger, or told of a foreboding. She was revered and often unquestioned. But she knew this was going to be different. She was going to tell the people something complicated to understand.

All was quiet as she raised her right hand above the crowd.

"My people," she began, "I come to tell of terrible times ahead." Yarseli paused and lowered her head, glancing at the sand below the boulders where she was standing.

"The rains will not come despite our offering to the God of night. The Night god has tricked us, and he intends to wipe us from the face of the earth." A loud murmur moved across the people. Yarseli looked straight into the eyes of those around her.

"We must leave this land. We must go up the mountain to a passageway that will take us to another land. There we will find water and survival. We must go tonight before it's too late. Tomorrow is too late. You must take only the clothes on your back and as much food as you can carry. You must heed my warning."

Liseli and Mojag huddled together behind dense spiny bushes, watching the medicine lady speak. Fireflies flew around Liseli's head, and she batted them away, concerned they might draw attention to her and Mojag.

Shouts of questions came from the crowd. Angry voices bantered back and forth until a loud male cry resonated over the others.

"How do you come by this information, old lady?" roared Nodin. "Why should we believe you this time?"

"The mountain has revealed this information to me. It will be confirmed tonight when a lightning storm hits our village. There will be no rain, only lightning which will bring fire. If you choose not to believe me and do not flee up the mountain, you will face the consequences tomorrow when the earth at the base of the mountain will open up and swallow those that remain here. But if you follow us up the path to the top of the mountain, an opening to the other side will be revealed, and our people will be saved."

"She is a liar," said Nodin. "We should not believe the old woman!" He turned and shouted at the crowd standing in front of Yarseli. "I am the tribal leader's chief warrior, and the chief knows nothing about all this. Are we going to leave our village on such quick notice just because of the words of this old woman?"

Others mumbled agreement, and a roar of dissent came from the crowd.

"Be as it may, I have told you the prophecy. Those who believe me should follow. Gather your food and meet at the mouth of the junction of the two washes at sundown. Be prepared for a difficult journey." Yarseli quickly vanished as the villagers quarreled and bickered over the medicine woman's announcement. Finally, some who had listened and decided to heed the old woman's word left the gathering and went to their huts, quickly packing food and water into carrying pouches.

Donna Krutka

## Chapter Nine

The night was dark after the sun sank below the horizon. The moon was late to come over the mountain, providing only a sliver of light onto the wash where a small number of people gathered.
"There are so few," muttered Liseli as she emerged from the shadows. She looked around for Mojag, then remembered he was with Calien. A shudder went through her body as she pictured her sister preparing to be sacrificed at first light. Calien and Mojag had to free Sakari. Up ahead of her, she could see Tocho's outline waiting alongside the path. Somehow, she had done as Yarseli told her to do. She had summoned the mountain lion with her thoughts, and within a short time, he was standing beside her.

"I told you I would be here," he said." I will lead your people up to the hidden cave."

Liseli sighed, lowered her shoulders, relaxed her frown, and sat beside him. She took slow, deep breaths for the first time since she and Mojag had returned to the village.

"I am glad you are here," she whispered to Tocho. She could feel him purring as he brushed against her trembling body.

A crash of thunder sounded, and lightning lit up the entire valley. Those around Liseli let out startled cries. The lightning and thunder continued. Tocho raised his nose toward the sky, then abruptly leaped to all fours, his ears pointed backward, and his head lifted.

"I must go now. I am needed elsewhere, but I will return. Stay focused, Liseli. Keep the gathering group closely around you. Remember, I am with you." Tocho sprang from Liseli's side and was gone. The girl stood tall, taking deep breaths to remain calm.

It was happening just as the medicine woman had predicted. The people ran haphazardly in circles of panic. Calien and Mojag watched the chaos. They made their way toward the village's outer boundary, searching for where Sakari was held captive. Mojag spotted two warriors standing side by side in front of an opening to a hut, swords crossed and legs in an overlapping stance. He motioned to Calien and pointed, Calien nodding in agreement. They both realized Sakari was inside the hut.

Calien remained crouched low on the ground.

"We need a plan to distract the guards," he whispered to Mojag.

Lightning struck a nearby tree, and a loud clap of thunder startled the warriors. One of the guards ran from his post in terror, heading toward the village. Another bolt of lightning shot through the sky, and thunder boomed overhead. The remaining guard screamed orders for the other to return as another bolt of lightning streaked across the sky. Continued lightning and thunder unnerved the remaining guard, who danced back and forth in agitation. Finally, a nearby hut exploded into flames. The lone guard jumped in panic and headed toward the fire to rescue those inside the hut.

Calien's steps were quick and purposeful. Mojag stopped at the hut's entrance, standing guard, as Calien silently entered inside. He waited for his eyes to focus and adjust to the darkness. At the back of the hut, he could make out a dim shadow, then recognized

Sakari kneeling. Her hands rested with palms together upright as if praying to the gods. Her eyes were shut, and her head bowed. She looked up, blinking several times, then gasped as she recognized Calien standing before her. She jumped to her feet and grasped him around the neck. Tears flooded down her cheeks, and she began to sob violently. Calien steadied his breath as he held her tightly against his chest. Another loud lightning bolt cracked the air next to their hut, and Sakari pulled away from Calien, wiping her wet cheeks with her sleeve. Fear turned her eyes black with panic.

"What are you doing here?" She asked. "They will kill you if they find you here."

"We have come to take you to safety," Calien replied, gently wiping a tear from her cheek. "I can answer your questions as we go along, but we must go now."

He grabbed her hand, and she pulled away, not allowing him to pull her into the night, even though the pleading in his voice prompted her to want to obey.

"Calien, if I leave, they will find and kill you. I can't let that happen." Sakari stood tall and rigid. Her eyes focused sharply on his face.

Calien approached Sakari and cupped his hands softly alongside her face. He slowly pulled her toward him and gently kissed her lips. Hesitant at first, she relinquished, her kiss dissipating the horror and despair she had been feeling.

"The medicine woman has foretold a prophecy that will destroy our people if we don't leave here, now!" Calien's cheek continued touching Sakari's." You must trust me," he whispered into her ear, not wanting to pull away.

Sakari's heartbeat slowed, and she broke Calien's embrace. She stood erect, peering into his eyes. His countenance spoke of urgency and truth, so she reached her hand out, and Calien grasped it tightly.

Mojag signaled as they emerged from the hut that all was clear. The three moved silently away from the hut, skirting the village's perimeter to make their way toward the wash.

"Stop!" yelled out a voice behind them. "Stop! Now!" Nodin rushed toward them, holding a spear in his right hand.

Without warning, a large, dark shadow burst atop a boulder and crashed into the warrior, knocking him backward. Cries of pain erupted as he hit his head against a rock. Tocho stood atop the warrior, making sure he did not get up. Nodin did not move, his breathing shallow and his eyes tightly closed. The mountain lion hesitated momentarily, then turned and signaled to Sakari and Calien to follow. Mojag ran ahead as fast as he could to tell Liseli they were coming.

The fire rapidly moved through the village as lightning relentlessly streaked across the sky. Repeated snaps of thunder muted the screams erupting from the people of the village. Smells of burnt thatch and rock filtered into the air. A group of terrorized villagers gathered at the junction of the two washes. Yarseli stood on a boulder and spoke.

"Our journey is long and dangerous. There may be those who won't survive. But if you stay behind, you will certainly die. You do have a choice. Only come if you are willing to undergo the perils and hardship to make this journey safe. We have no idea what lies ahead. We only know what lies behind us. It will be strange, but this mountain lion will be our guide." She pointed her crooked fingers at Tocho. "The builder, Calien, will interpret his orders. Follow his directions explicitly. Do not listen to any other commands. Others will lead you to peril."

Yarseli stepped down from the boulder, pointing to the others to move forward. She then sat down and huddled in the sand.

"What are you doing, Yarseli," questioned Liseli as the old lady made no effort to move.

"I am going to stay here," she said to the girl. "I am too old to make that journey. I did it in my youth and almost died at that time. However, I will stay back and try to help those left behind, as a medicine woman should do. If they try to follow, I will also try to delay anyone chasing you, Sakari, and the group. You must go now, girl. You have been brave and compassionate. Your people would not have had a chance without your help. Now go, girl, before it is too late. "

Liseli hugged the old woman, not wanting to let go of her embrace. Yarseli looked up into Liseli's face and gave her a toothless smile as big as the crescent moon. She untied her beaded necklace and wrapped it around Liseli's neck.

"This necklace will guide you when you are lost. It has powers you may not understand. Keep it safe and away from the Jaguar. If it gets into his hands, he can wreak havoc. Now go, little one. Listen carefully to the mountain lion." Liseli kissed Yarseli on the cheek, and she turned toward the others, trying not to look back. She put her hands on her chest, trying to push the heaviness away. Tears flowed down her face as she caught up with the others.

Donna Krutka

## Chapter Ten

Tocho remained visible to the climbers, though as elusive as he had been when Liseli had met him on her first journey up the mountain. Calien and Sakari walked at the head of the group. "Tell me how you got to me, Calien," asked Sakari. "Where are we going? What are we doing?"

"It was your sister, Liseli, who first met the mountain lion and climbed to the highest part of the mountain. The old woman, Yarseli, had told her that it was there that she would find the rain goddess and plead for your life. But instead, the Rain goddess told Liseli there would be no rain. The Night god, whose earthly form is the Jaguar, had captured the rain goddess and stolen her rain. He planned to take our people into the underworld, where we would serve him for all of eternity. Your sacrifice would have been wasted. Our people would still be plagued by drought and would eventually die. "He also told her of Yarseli's prophecy about the destruction of their village and, ultimately extinction of their people. The two whispered, Sakari often interrupting for clarification. She grabbed Calien's hand, and he felt the trembling in her grasp.

Liseli walked next to Mojag, picking up each foot slowly and carefully placing it back onto the ground. She stumbled and fell against Mojag, who caught her from falling to the ground.

"You're tired," said Mojag, helping her steady her gait.

"Aren't you?" she replied. "We haven't slept for the longest time."

"We need to rest. How far do you think the mountain lion will make us go?" Mojag's eyes squinted to try to see Tocho up ahead.

"We must get as far up the mountain as possible before the medicine woman's prediction happens." A streak of lightning shot across the sky overhead, and Liseli put her hands to her ears to ward off the loudness of the thunder. The lightning and thunder had not let up since they had started their climb.

Mojag looked back and saw the climbers following each other one by one. He squinted his eyes and concentrated on each face that followed.

"Our fathers and mothers did not come," Mojag said, his voice soft and saddened.

Liseli walked silently, not responding to Mojag.

"My father had promised my sister to Nodin," Liseli replied after a lengthy period. "When Sakari volunteered in the place of Calien, I saw my father turn quickly toward her, his fist clenched and his eyes filled with fury. My mother would forever be beside my father, no matter what he did. I knew they wouldn't come." Liseli looked straight ahead with no change in her pace or gait.

As they walked, Liseli shielded her eyes from the wind that blew sand and debris into her face. She often blinked furiously to retrieve her vision.

"There is a cave up ahead where the mountain lion is entering," yelled Calien to Mojag. "A dust storm is starting to form up ahead. Get the people behind you to follow."

Mojag circled back behind him and gave Calien's orders to the others. The followers stumbled over the larger rocks, dodging between dense spiky plants. They entered the mouth of the cave and quickly huddled together, heads down and eyes closed. They could make out gusts of wind roaring outside the cave entrance, uplifting loose sand and rocks. Mojag made his way to where Liseli crouched with her hands cupped over her ears. They couldn't speak over the loud noise of the wind.

Up ahead, Calien was motioning for them to continue. One by one, the followers stood slightly upright, staying low not to hit their heads on the cave ceiling. The further they got from the entrance, the less they heard the sound of the fury outside.

"Where is Yarseli?" asked Mojag, looking around for the old woman.

"She didn't come. She gave me this." Liseli held out the beaded necklace the medicine woman had draped around her neck. "She is staying back with the others. She said it is her place to be with them." Mojag's eyes widened, and he took the necklace between his fingers and rubbed the beads. His eyes filled with moisture, and he looked back at Liseli and gave her a nod. Then, carefully and reverently, he positioned it correctly around her neck.

"She was wise and good. I will miss her." Mojag hugged Liseli for the longest time as if staying in this position would bring back the medicine woman.

The group continued to make their way through the cave like a slow-moving parade of ants leaving an ant hill. Liseli's skin tingled, tiny pinpricks rolling over her arms and face. The scent of the musty desert hit her nostrils. A cooling fog settled over the group, and Liseli recognized this as the cave she had traveled through on the way back down the mountain. Calien had yelled for everyone to sit on the ground and tightly close their eyes. Almost in unison, they slumped to the cave floor, grabbing and holding onto anyone around them, obediently closing their eyes.

Time stood still as they sat blinded while thickened air smothered their nostrils. Some remained calm and breathed easily, others choked and snorted, some coughing violently. Then as suddenly as it had descended on them, the fog lifted, and Calien's voice could be heard instructing everyone to move forward. The group stood, blinked their eyes, and staggered forward in confusion, exiting the cave through a portal that had materialized before them.

Liseli took a deep breath after exiting the cave, grateful to be away from the mustiness and fog. Mojag rubbed his eyes and blinked multiple times. They stood at the base of a steep rocky cliff that towered before them.

"Where are our leaders? Who is guiding us?" mumbled some in the group. The darkness was so prevailing that many struggled to keep up with the group ahead. Uncertainty and fear settled over the climbers.

A scream came from the front of the group, and Calien yelled for everyone to stop. Prolonged, low hissing sounded all around the group. Then, before them, they saw a gigantic triangular head connected to a slimy black body splattered with colors of pink and yellow, a swaying tail attached to the monster's body moving back and forth. A sleek, thin forked tongue extended from its mouth as it hissed again, shooting steam and snot violently from its nostrils.

Calien fell backward into the group, his body trembling with adrenaline.

"Tocho, where are you?" he called out to the mountain lion." What do we do?" Calien slowly got to his feet, holding his arms out to block anyone from going forward.

Another hiss sounded above them as a similar creature stuck his monstrous head over a ledge, slowly moving forward.

"Stay together," yelled Calien. "Huddle closely. Make us look as large as we can in a tight knot." Then, without hesitation, the group melted into a layer forming a human shield, bodies trembling and hearts beating like rapid-sounding drums. Thick, foul-smelling saliva dripped from above and landed on the group below, screaming in disgust.

The creature above crept toward the cliff's edge, with long fleshy legs flying into the air. Screams emerged in unison from the group. Calien tightly closed his eyes and lifted his arms to protect his head from the creature's impact. None came as the leaping lizard flew over his head and onto the back of the lower lizard. Oozing contact sounds erupted as the two creatures rolled over in combat, back arching and bodies twisting. They were scratching and hissing as long claws dug into their opponent's body, each attempting to gain a dominant hold. A malodorous stench came from the dueling creatures, the climbers gasping and choking, throwing their hands up to their faces to block the smell. The lizards rolled off into the desert's thick spiny brush, away from the path the group was traveling. Calien frantically motioned to the others to follow, leading them around the fighting reptiles. None looked back, rushing forward, only slowing when the sounds of the dueling lizards dropped into the distant background. Sweat peppered their foreheads, and gradually, their breathing slowed to a regular rhythm.

The path came to a junction, and Tocho stood tall and erect in front of the group. He swiveled his head in the direction he wanted Calien to continue, and the group easily followed. Calien herded Sakari, Liseli, and Mojag behind him, grabbed Sakari's hand, and moved forward.

Donna Krutka

## Chapter Eleven

The three warriors moved up the path toward the fleeing group of villagers. Lightning struck their path countless times, forcing them to fall back and take cover. Nodin's eyes were angry and crazed. He motioned to his two companions to move ahead. The crooked hand of the old lady again emerged from the hidden outcropping and pointed at the followers. A lightning bolt landed in front of the pursuer, and they crouched in horror. Each lightning strike she called upon drained her more and more until she fell into a crumpled heap, unable to lift her arm. She watched helplessly as the three warriors were finally able to move up the path and out of her line of vision. She hoped she had given the group enough lead to escape the warriors.

Nodin's agile body bounded over the rocky terrain, not paying attention to the scrapes and gouges made by the native plants. His heart raced with fury, and the two other warriors fell behind his fast pace. Finally, he came to an entrance of a cave and waited for the two other pursuers to catch him.

"They must have entered this cave." His eyes raged with ferocity. "We must follow."

The other two warriors held back, not moving.

"She is gone, Nodin." one shouted. "She is not going to come back. She was to be sacrificed, and you would already have lost your promised mate. So it is foolish to follow."

"How dare you question my command!" Nodin spits out back to the two. His eyes were dark with malice." You are never to question me!"

"The cave has spirits, Nodin," the other warrior called out. "We have been warned our whole life never to enter this cave. It belongs to the Night God. So he has forbidden us to enter."

"They have taken Sakari with them," screamed Nodin. "I must get her back."

"Our village is burning. We are not going with you: our people, Nodin. We must go back. "

The two frightened warriors remained stationary. They watched as Nodin entered the cave and pivoted to look at them. His eyes were dark and determined, and he beckoned them to follow. His face turned like stone as the other two raised their spears, then turned and ran back toward the burning village. Nodin let out a warrior's cry. He stood alert and uncertain before the mouth of the cave and then turned and plunged forward into the cave, not looking back at his village.

The cave smelled dank and foul. Nodin shook his head to evade the smell and frowned as his hand slid along the slimy wall of the cave to steady his gait. His eyes wouldn't focus on seeing his surroundings. Slowly, he crept forward, uncertain of each step. He squinted, hearing voices up ahead of him. He quickened his steps, closing in on the voices, when thick, suffocating fog settled around him, causing him to fall to the ground, violently choking and unconscious.

## Chapter Twelve

Liseli struggled to pick up one foot and put it one step ahead. Then, she shifted her weight and tried to pick up the other foot but crumpled onto the ground. Her head hit the hard sand, and she let out a cry.

"Liseli, are you all right?" screamed Mojag, quick to be at her side. Liseli moaned, pushing with both arms to get her body upright.

"Wait, Liseli. Don't get up yet. You are exhausted and need to stay here for a bit. We both need a rest." Mojag scooted up next to his friend and pulled her upper body to rest on his lap. Other group members walked by, feet shuffling in a trance-like state. Liseli kept her eyes closed as she pulled her hand up toward the bump on her head.

"We'll be left behind." Liseli managed to whisper, words being slow to form.

"First, a short rest." Mojag's voice was assertive.

The little prairie dog came alongside the two. It sniffed and circled the two, carefully assessing Liseli.

"She can continue. She is tired but not injured.' Jabberrunner stood on his hind feet, standing tall and continuing to sniff the air. "Liseli, you need to get up and hurry up!"

Liseli opened her eyes with a slight whimper and began to stand up. She grabbed Mojag's shoulder and steadied her swirling head to get her balance. The smell of dampness mixed with mountain rock filtered through the air.

"Do you remember, Mojag, when we raced each other? You used to try to beat me, but most of the days, you never could." Liseli's eyes widened, and her face softened. She moved forward, still leaning on Mojag.

"Then, one day, we started to run, and I noticed you had thick corn husks wrapped around your feet. We had always run barefoot, but this day was different. You were able to cover the distance at a much faster speed. Was it the corn husks, do you think?"

Mojag let out a laugh. Liseli continued to allow Mojag to help her move forward.

"If you remember, Liseli, we had not raced for several moons before that day. Over that time, I felt different. I was taller and had started noticing I could throw the spear farther. It seemed easier to climb the outcroppings in our village. My voice was crackly and sometimes squeaky. My body was changing. I was embarrassed and afraid to come around you. But when I saw you on the high outcroppings surrounding the village, you called me and asked when we would race again. You continued to ask and ask. So, I let you set up our next race. That next time we raced, I beat you. I never thought I ever could." His eyes watched Liseli to see how she reacted. She remained silent, thinking about what he had told her. He decided to continue.

"That is why I am not as tired as you are now. I somehow am stronger and can endure more climbing than you." Mojag's heart skipped as Liseli frowned. He thought she would pull away. But, instead, a gush of relief ran through him when she continued to lean on him.

"But you still are the fastest girl I have ever seen. And the strongest." A half snort mixed with a scowl came from Liseli as she moved forward.

"Sakari said that one day this would happen. I never stopped bragging to her about how I could beat you running to the boulders. She told me you would someday be stronger than me and would be able to jump higher and farther. I never believed her. But..." Liseli's voice faded away.

"We will race again, Liseli," Mojag said quickly. "When you are rested and feeling stronger. You will see that you still are fast, and I will have difficulty beating you." His words were soft and tender. Liseli looked at him, and he recognized a slight smile on her lips. Then she looked straight ahead, no more words exchanged, and they continued the exhausting climb upward toward the mountain top.

## Chapter Thirteen

Calien gently guided Sakari to a place of rest, positioning her protected from the blowing wind and the abundant spiky desert plants along their pathway. She breathed in deep breaths, and her stare was blank with emotion. She had not complained at all, Calien had thought, and he knew she never would. She sat with her back against the granite stone, and he sat beside her. She took his hand as he reached for hers.

"How much further do we have to climb?' Sakari asked subtle exhaustion in her voice.

"We are close to the summit' he said, wiping a strand of hair from her eyes. "The last part of the climb is steep and rocky. But the mountain lion will help us make it to the top." Calien leaned his head back against the stone.

"Have you ever seen the Jaguar?" Sakari asked Calien.

"The Night god?" he asked. "No, but I have heard the stories. The tales speak of his strength, fierceness, and demand to get his way."

"Do you believe we can outrun him?" Sakari's asked, hoping to be reassured.

"Maybe not outrun him, but Tocho can outsmart him. I have come to believe in the mountain lion. Liseli, Mojag, and the medicine woman convinced me he could save us. I want to believe he can defeat the Night god's purpose." Calien was silent for a while and then began again.

"I am a builder of canals. I had seen the waters diminish since the first days when I started building.

Back then, the waters flowed freely and abundantly. The crops flourished and fed the village. We had food for the entire year and even enough to store. But then, slowly, the waters hesitated, and the crops began to diminish in amount. Even though some years we had early, harder rains, the later, shorter rains that were more important for growing crops didn't come. The hunters were making more unsuccessful trips to the wilderness to find wildlife. They tried to keep that secret, of course. The Night god demanded a yearly sacrifice, and your father always supplied him with one. Despite the sacrifices, the waters did not come, and the crops continued to diminish. I told your father over and over that the waters were not coming. He always told me the Night god would provide, and all I needed was to dig deeper into the soil to find the water. He said I was to build canals, and the Night god would supply the water. We argued often. Your father was always very angry with me."

Sakari closed her eyes and listened to the thunder that rumbled in the background. Then, she turned to Calien and softly laid her head on his shoulder.

"My sister and I watched the mountain lion make his way around the perimeter of our village almost every morning. It was as if he were there to protect us. Liseli especially said that often." Sakari laughed, then added, "She felt like he was her personal friend. Sakari smiled; thoughts of how often she and Liseli had talked about the great animal surfaced from her memories.

"I trust him as much as I trust anything." She said with reverence. "He has seemed to always be there for us. If anyone is to protect us from the wrath of the Night god, it would be the mountain lion." Sakari let out a long sigh and then took a slow breath.

A slow rolling hiss followed by a guttural growl came from the boulders above. Calien felt Sakari's hand tighten in his, and her body leaned toward him. In the darkness, yellow eyes peered out, piercing the night with precision. The hissing continued, and foul breath churned toward the two huddling together. Tocho jumped from the opposite direction and stood between the jaguar and Calien and Sakari. Both gasped in horror and peered around Tocho's massive muscular body to catch the fierce eyes of the Night god staring directly at them.

"You will not get by me," droned the Jaguar, his voice dripping with a threat. "None of you will live, Tocho. You know you can't get by me. So, a fight between us will always end with my victory."

Sakari stared at the strong jaw of the Jaguar, saliva dripping from his panting mouth. She shivered in fear as she assessed the difference between the two animals. Tocho's large front paws were more prominent than the Jaguar's, ready to grasp Jaguar's neck and inflict a suffocating neck bite. But she felt like the Jaguar was the strongest of the two cats, even though Tocho could jump higher, making it easier for him to escape.

"It is you that cannot get past me, Jaguar," quipped the mountain lion. "I have waited to thwart you for a long time. I am the protector of this mountain. Only those whom I allow can climb to the top."

"And I am the protector of the rain goddess. Only I can allow others to enter the cave where she abodes.

Unfortunately, it appears you intend to enter that cave." the Jaguar stared maliciously at the humans around him." You forget who I am, Tocho, and what I can do."

The sudden attack surprised even the Night god as the mountain lion lunged toward the Jaguar. His tawny-colored body slammed into the Jaguar, and the two rolled over and over together, both attempting to grab and tear at the other's neck. Tocho maneuvered his hindlegs to help him spring forward when the Jaguar came toward him. Tocho sunk his teeth into his opponent's back, and the jaguar twisted his upper trunk to sink his jaw into the attacker's shoulder, missing his grab at the neck. Calien and Sakari could hear the hiss of the Jaguar while it almost sounded that Tocho was purring.

"The Jaguar is killing Tocho," screamed Liseli, who had heard the hissing and ran to where the fight erupted. She huddled next to her sister, Mojag, close on her heels.

"What can we do?" she yelled, horror and terror filling the air. Blood poured off the back of the mountain lion, marks of open gashes seen along his round head. A slit in his right ear made that part of his upright ear lie backward.

The Jaguar readied to take his final plunge toward Tocho's neck when the mountain lion twisted violently onto his back and raised his claws upward to meet Jaguar's dive. A slicing scream rose into the sky as sharp blades gauged into the eyes of the attacking cat, talons tearing his eye sockets—blood and fluid pouring from both eyes of the Jaguar. The Night god fell backward, rolling onto his belly before he could leap away from the Mountain lion. He frantically swiped his paws over his face and smothered his head in the loose dirt nearby. He hissed and screamed. Then, disoriented and confused, he rolled into the desert bushes, stumbled over boulders, and out into the night.

Liseli was the first to reach Tocho. His breathing was shallow but steady, and his eyes moved in all directions to look for the Jaguar. Panic appeared on his face as he recognized Liseli.

"Get away, girl. He could kill you!" He attempted to move his body as if to protect her from assault.

"Stay quiet, Tocho. He has left. The Jaguar is gone. He is not dead, but you bested him. I think you blinded him." Liseli hugged the Mountain lion, not caring if his oozing wounds covered her in his blood.

Sakari and Calien rushed forward, calling for water and cloth to help the mountain lion with his bleeding flesh. The surviving group huddled close to their leader. Calien stood upright and tried to steady his voice.

"We are all right. Try to help each other remain calm. We are near the summit but will camp here for the night. Stay close to one another. Be on the lookout for anything strange. Stay together,"

Calien turned back to Sakari and Liseli, and Mojag. "Is he doing ok? Will he live? Will he be able to lead us to the summit?"

Liseli stroked the sweat-drenched coat of the mountain lion. He could hear a soft purr coming from the great creature.

"He will be ok," whispered Liseli. "He will be able to take us the rest of the way. But he now needs to rest."

Donna Krutka

She once again laid her head on Tocho. The mountain lion closed his eyes and let sleep settle into his injured body.

## Chapter Fourteen

Yarseli hovered by the passageway to the cave to see if any more of the villagers would come this way. Screams from the town erupted over the entire valley. The lightning and thunder remained relentless, and fires engulfed for miles. Something off to her right rustled in the dead branches of the desert floor, and she turned her head in alarm toward the sound. The two warriors following Nodin up the mountain rushed past her. They held their swords high in their hands. They focused on returning to the village and failed to see the old woman crouched alongside the path. Yarseli waited for Nodin behind the other two, but he never came. She slowly stood, her knees cracking and her back hunched with tightness. She moved toward the village, still determining her next move. She wanted to help her people, but they had proved stubborn. If Nodin was not in the village, there might still be time to convince the others to go to safety.

The smell of burning thatch slammed into her nostrils, and she coughed violently. A large assembly of people had gathered in the center of the village, drums beating out a rhythm calling for the people to gather around. Many raised their hands, invoking the protection of the Night god, as fire and lightning continued to engulf their surroundings. Yarseli approached the people, trying to find a place to stand high enough to talk to those that would listen.

"There might still be time to leave," she screamed. "You can still climb the mountain. You can still go to the other side of the mountain. But you must go now."

No one seemed to hear her above the drums, the screams, and the invoked prayers. Yarseli stood on her perch, saying the same plea over and over. She finally climbed down, her muscles shaking in exhaustion, and walked away toward the mountain. She turned her head to look back at her people for one last time.

She made her way to the cave's opening, her breathing tight and her chest pounding. She sat down beside the entrance and leaned back toward the rock wall. She began to chant in a low voice, looking over the valley of her ancestors. Her mind flashed to the stories of her people coming north from a land populated by different peoples many years before. There were hunters, warriors, and others who had learned to grow foods such as maize, beans, tomato, avocado, squash, and chile. Their society had been rich with religious tradition, and they had developed a practice of ball playing. They had crafted pottery and jewelry and learned to weave yarn into beautifully colored fabrics. Tears flowed down her cheeks as she looked upon the burning town. As she cried, her tears turned to terror as the ground began to rumble beneath her.

"I loved my people. I loved the valley." Her eyes turned upward toward the summit of the mountain. "Hurry, Liseli. Save the seed of our people." She closed her eyes and took a deep breath.

The boulders behind her started to split, and she shielded her head as rock particles fell all around her. Within a short time, the ground opened up and fell precipitously, swallowing up the fiery village and all those remaining.

## Chapter Fifteen

Screams of panic erupted from the climbers as the ground began to shake and rocks bolted down the mountainside. Tocho opened his eyes and tried to stand. Deep gouges oozed blood from his hindlegs and torso, and his upper eyelids were swollen, obstructing his vision.

"The mountain is unfolding. It's as prophesized," said Tocho, "We must get to the summit before the opening to the other side collapses. We must hurry." The mountain lion rose to his hind legs and slumped back onto the ground. His breathing was rapid, and Liseli could hear his heart pounding.

"He can't get up," yelled Liseli. "We must help him!" Calien turned and called out to others of the tribe.

"Help the mountain lion. Come now!" Calien's voice screamed out above the noise of the falling rocks.

A group of five men gathered around Tocho. Two lifted his hind legs, and two his forelegs, and the fifth steadied his head. Then, slowly and carefully, they put one foot in front of the other to make their way to the summit.

"It is not far. Work together," instructed Calien, both Liseli and Sakari supervising the path the group was to traverse. The earth underneath them continued to shift, and they evaluated each step.

The crescent of the mountain was before them. The darkness of the night made it difficult for all to see.

"There!" exclaimed Mojag. "The cave is there!" He pointed to an opening at the top of the rocky crest.

Sakari let out a gasp looking up to the cave entrance. Besides the opening, a tall warrior with a long spear stood blocking the cave entrance.

"Nodin," exclaimed Sakari. "How did he get there?"

Calien scowled, anger and disbelief in his voice. "He must have been following us."

"Give me Sakari, Calien!" Nodin hissed. "This would not be happening if it were not you that thwarted her sacrifice to the Night god."

"What's happening here and now would not have been changed by sacrificing Sakari, Nodin. The medicine lady, Yarseli, foretold the prophecy. The Night god has been tricking our people. The drought and the destruction of our lands were prophesied."

"No, Calien, you caused this. We can still save our people. First, we must appease the Night god. Hand over Sakari!"

"You would sacrifice the girl you were to marry?" Calien stepped closer to the entrance.

"No builder, you are right. It is you that should have been sacrificed. You were the original choice the council made. Therefore, it is you that must die. It is the only way to stop all of this." Nodin moved forward toward the group.

"Stay back, Nodin. We are going into the cave." Calien screamed, stepping closer to the entrance.

Lightening flashed, and thunder roared, frightening the entire group around them. The earth shifted violently under their footing. The five bearers of the mountain lion lost their hold, and Tocho slammed onto the hard rock beneath him, a scream coming from his wounded body.

Calien took the disarming moment to lunge for Nodin. He knocked the warrior off his feet, grabbed the sword from his hand, and held it to his throat.

"We are going into the cave. We have little time left. You have the choice to come with us or to stay here and die. It is your choice."

From up ahead, a hiss and high-pitched scream came from inside the cave entrance. The jaguar emerged, eyes bleeding, sightlessly roaring with malice. Screams from those around erupted as a large aperture opened up in front of the cave entrance. Only a narrow earth band connected the group to the cave entrance. Fire and steam shot into the air from the abyss below.

Tocho lay on the ground, attempts at getting up failing. Liseli stayed close but moved away as she saw the Jaguar come closer.

"Tocho, get up. Tocho, you must get up!" yelled Liseli. "He is here." She looked around to see if others were there to help. Bodies were knocked to the ground, unable to balance on the rolling earth.

The jaguar leaped into the air, sniffing at the surrounding area, his keen sense of smell angling him toward the mountain lion. Tocho sensed the attack and pulled his head upward, thwarting the Jaguar's intended aim of plunging his teeth into the mountain lion's neck.

Behind the two cats, sounds of fury exploded when two black figures rushed forward, one knocking full force into the jaguar's body, causing him to roll forward away from Tocho. A roar came from the first figure, and Tocho looked up to see a massive black bear sinking his teeth into the Jaguar and ripping at its neck. Blood and muscle flew through the air. The jaguar became limp and dropped his head onto the ground. The bear stood up on his hind legs, holding the trunk of the jaguar between his teeth, swinging it back and forth. The second black figure rushed to Tocho's side. He, too, let out a roar, those close by cowering in terror.

"Ravage, "Tocho said in a muffled voice. "You are here." The bear gently lay beside the near-dead mountain lion, sounds of sniffling coming from his snout.

"Who is with you?" Tocho was able to ask weakly.

"It is my father, Ultima," Bear answered, tears forming.

"He is alive?" whispered Tocho.

"He has been waiting and watching the cave entrance for an unspoken number of days, Tocho, waiting to best the Night god. I found him here when I came searching for you."

"And you, Ravage, I have watched for you. I have longed to see you." Tocho's voice was weak and fading.

"I am here, Tocho." Ravage tucked his head next to the mountain lion.

"The Jaguar? Remember, he must not know, Ravage." Tocho's breath was unsteady. "You are in danger, Ravage, if he knows about you!"

"Hush, Tocho. My father, Ultima, has taken care of the jaguar. It is you that needs me now. "Ravage attempted to lick the blood from his friend's eyes; He wanted to look one more time into the soul of this brave mountain lion. Then, Ravage whispered into the mountain lion's ear and blew a forceful, steady breath into Tocho's nostrils.

"No Ravage, no! " Tocho cried out with the last effort he had left inside him.

The earth shifted and roared, steam coming from the chasm before the cave opening.

Calien screamed to the group to continue toward the opening. Several climbers lost their footing and almost fell into the abyss before being clasped by someone nearby. Calien grabbed Sakari's hand and pulled her forward, shoving her toward the mountain as rocks and dirt fell around the climbers. One by one, the climbers jumped across the crevasse.

"Liseli," Mojag screamed. The roar of the mountain deafened his cry. Panic squirted into his throat as he looked around to find his friend. Mojag's foot slipped from under him as Calien caught Mojag's arm and pulled him across the gap. Molten rock bubbled below them, and fire and steam continued to build.

Tocho opened his eyes. His friend, Ravage, lay beside him, lifeless. Tocho got to his feet, his strength and mobility once again returning. He shook his head and lifted his hindlegs and forepaws.

"Ravage," he screamed at the bear, his cry almost inaudible from the sounds of the mountain around him. "What have you done?' Tocho continued to yell. "What did you do?"

The jaguar lay dead not far from the bear, the huge Ultima standing dazed and uncertain.

"What happened?" screamed Tocho. "Why is Ravage dead?"

Ultima came slowly to the side of his son. He leaned over and pushed at his head and chest, with no movement occurring. He looked back at Tocho and lowered his head. He slumped onto the ground beside his son, a soft sound of growl audible above the roar of the mountain behind them.

"He gave you his gift, Tocho. He gave you the gift of life as your father gave him. He gave it freely." Tears streamed down the face of the massive bear. Tocho and Ultima remained motionless until the crashing of rock and eruption of fire made it impossible to stay.

"Go, Mountain lion! Finish your journey. You must take his gift and pass it on.'

"What of you?" Tocho asked, his eyes looking deep into the anguished face of the bear.

"I stay with my son. We perish together." Ultima moved closer toward his son, sheltering his body from being hit by falling rocks.

Tocho turned and looked toward the cave. All were gone save a tiny girl, paralyzed with fear. He took one last look at his treasured friend, Ravage, and turned toward Liseli.

"Liseli, you must jump." he hissed, and Liseli turned, her eyes trying to focus.

"Tocho, is that you?" her voice was laced with disbelief. "How is this possible? I thought you were dead."

"I am here, and we'll jump together."

"What about Sakari and the others?" Tocho could hear her swallow with fear.

"They have already jumped. So, it is just you and me, Liseli," Tocho coaxed.

"I am too afraid. I can't make it. The gap is too large. I will fall into the fire." She stared at the fire below.

Tocho came up alongside Liseli. Her body trembled in violent spasms.

"Remember when I would roam your land and see you were watching me when each morning you and Sakari sat on the high outcropping? Didn't your sister say that you thought of us as friends?"

A small smile laced Liseli's lip. Her head turned from looking down at the fiery gap toward Tocho. "How did you know that? I wanted us to be best friends. But I never knew you heard us talking." Fear again settled in on her face as she again looked down.

"No, Liseli, look at me, not down. Do you think you would want to ride on my back?" Tocho approached the frightened girl, keeping enough distance to avoid knocking her off balance. A slight rumble and quake stirred the ground beneath them.

"If you get on my back, we can cross the gap together. But, of course, you will have to trust me and hold on. Can we do this together?"

Liseli turned toward Tocho, but she lost her footing and stumbled as she took a step. With a quick response, Tocho leaped into the air and positioned his body underneath the girl. He screamed for her to hold onto his neck as he flung his body across the crevasse, landing on the ledge at the cave entrance. Liseli's body continued to tremble as she released her grip on his neck and fell onto the hard rock surface. She looked back in time to see the earth give way where they had previously been standing.

# Donna Krutka

The two moved into the mouth of the cave before rocks and dirt avalanched over the cave entrance, closing the passageway to the outside of the mountain. Liseli and Tocho huddled in the darkness. Slowly, their heartbeat begins to slow, and their rapid breathing settles.

"You have done it, Liseli," Tocho whispered. "You have saved your people's seed. You also have saved your sister."

Liseli's eyes slowly adjusted to the darkness, and she could see the outline of the mountain lion.

"You have been there for me every step of the way. You have my heart, great mountain lion. It was you that saved our people from total extinction." She was quiet momentarily before asking, "Will anyone know what we both have done?"

"Stories will be told, Liseli. There will be many versions of what happened to your people. None of them will be right, and yet all of them will be in part true."

"What happens to those of us that survive?" asked Liseli.

"They will take what they remember and leave behind what they forget. It will be a new civilization."

"How did you survive?" she asked, so many thoughts filling her mind with questions.

"My great friend Ravage, the bear, gave his life to me. My father died for him, giving him the power of transformation to pass that gift to another freely. He forfeited his own life for me." Tocho took his time to continue. He felt like his heart had broken.

"And now, I will also someday pass on this gift."

Neither spoke for a long while. The inside of the cave remained soundless, shutting out the chaos on the other side of the blocked entrance.

"Sakari and Calien? And Mojag?" Tocho knew she had been holding back the question.

"They made it safely across the gap. They are up ahead." There was a silence before Tocho spoke further. "But they do not know that you have survived."

"What are we to do?" Liseli asked, her voice remaining frightened.

"We will find them, but first, we must rest. The journey to the other side of the mountain is long."

Tocho began to purr, and Liseli laid her head on his chest.

"It's not over?" Liseli said aloud, trying to sound brave.

"We'll go forward together, Liseli," Tocho gently laid his forepaw on the girl reassuringly as they settled against the cool wall of the darkened cave and slowly fell into a deep, exhausted sleep.

The Desert Saga

Donna Krutka

# Acknowledgments

The journey to becoming a writer has so many twists and turns. It may begin in high school when your English teacher gives you the assignment to write something creative. For me, it was Sister Pauline, and to this day, I remember the story I wrote. To my amazement, one of my best schoolmates remembered my story, too. But the urge to write was replaced by years of learning medical scenarios and scientific facts as I attended medical school and a pediatric residency. I practiced medicine and would encourage many patients to reach for the stars, embarking on a lifelong search for adventure and accomplishments. And then, suddenly, when I felt like work was left behind, I became impassioned with a desire to be creative. I never was an artist in the sense of painting pictures or modeling clay. At one time in my youth, I played a musical instrument, but that time was long ago. But I decided I liked to write, and thus began to create stories. It turns out the making of a story is more than just random. It has structure and guidelines and must fit into patterns. I was schooled by my daughter, Natalie, an immensely talented young writer who wrote a book about my father's World War II experience. She was 23 years old at the time, and it launched her career in digital marketing, with page after page of copying and editing being a part of her job. My

The Desert Saga

daughter, Lauren, began working in a media company in Los Angeles and taught me much about building a story. She has written scripts, worked with writers, analyzed stories, and patiently critiqued my work to help me learn how to create and refine my tales.

My husband, Larry, became my biggest fan. He often bragged to our family and friends that he was amazed at my consistent writing schedule: up at 5 am every day to write for no less than two hours. He was eager to read my stories and gave me insightful, constructive criticism and unfailing encouragement to continue writing.

My friend Cindy Gazecki suggested I join Master Class to learn more about writing, which I gladly did. Learning from the greatest in the field was highly beneficial. One of the writers urged his pupils to look around their world to find story ideas. My world is the desert and thus came the inspiration for my stories. My friend Lisa Schilling and Ann Domin read my stories and enthusiastically supported my efforts.

My high school friend Joe Davis has been my most significant helper. He has acted as a reader, researcher, editor, formatter, computer expert, and confidant. With his help, I learned how to correct my Word Document. He also introduced me to my incredibly talented illustrator, Andrew Ellingson. Andrew transformed the text from my stories into visual characters that made them come alive. He was great to work with, and I will forever be grateful for his help with this project.

Donna Krutka

And finally, I must give credit to the desert and the animals I live around.  The desert is a magical world with an ever-changing personality that never fails to surprise and delight its beholder. However, it can also be hostile and unforgiving.  The animals in the desert have had to cope, share, and adapt to the many changes of harshness and intensity.  Survival depends on vigilance, preparation for the elements, successful search for food, and mating.  There may be no right or wrong in the desert, but there is little margin of error.  The inhabitants must stay alert to stay alive. The characters in The Desert Saga have been molded from research on animal traits, patterns, and characteristics.  Learning about each of them has been an incredible journey as I built the story around them.

The area of Tucson and Phoenix in southern Arizona, along the Gila and Salt Rivers, was inhabited by a culture of people referred to as the Hohokam.  Some have translated this term to mean "those that have vanished." The Hohokam were thought to have migrated from Mesoamerica anywhere from 300 BCE to 300 CE.  They inhabited the land and vanished somewhere around 1400 CE.  There is debate as to what happened to them.  Some speculate that drought and sparse rainfall drove them away.  The question of disease and tribal war has been raised.  The Hohokam practiced cremation, so no human remains have been found in Arizona.  They did leave behind stone structures of pit houses, which were shallow pits dug in the ground covered by clay and brush used to smoke and cook game.  Remnants of ballparks, as seen in the Maya culture, can be found in inhabited areas.

The Desert Saga

They built complex irrigation systems with elaborate canals that were used to control flood waters and promoted the cultivation of many crops, including corn, beans, cotton, and squash.  Pottery and jewelry making was also part of the culture.

    Although the question as to why the Hohokam culture vanished, the story of The Desert Saga takes the liberty to postulate how they disappeared.  In reality, the peoples of <u>Pima</u> and <u>Tohono O'odham</u> (Papago) have been considered direct descendants of the Hohokam.

References

Wikipedia; Hohokam culture

Encyclopedia Britannica, Gloria Lotha, editor

Donna Krutka

## About the Author

Donna grew up in Oklahoma City, Oklahoma. She attended Oklahoma State University and medical school at The University of Missouri School of Medicine, Columbia, Missouri. She did her residency in Pediatrics at UCLA Harbor General in Torrance, California. She practiced medicine in Oklahoma City, Oklahoma, and then moved to Tulsa, where she did General Pediatrics for 35 years. She married Larry Krutka, and together they raised six children. She and Larry were triathletes, competing in events worldwide, including many National USA Triathlon Championships and the Hawaii Ironman World Championship. After she retired from her Pediatric Practice, the couple moved to Tucson, Arizona, where she fell in love with the desert and its amazing wildlife. It was in the desert that she began creating her stories and launched her writing career.

**Author: Donna Krutka**

The Desert Saga

## About the Illustrator

Andrew Ellingson is an artist living in Colorado Springs, Colorado, with his wife and four children. He draws his inspiration from nature and its endless forms. His primary focus is painting wildlife around the Rocky Mountains using acrylic on canvas. Andrew strives to imbue each piece with life and energy, embracing the natural way paint moves and striking a harmonious balance between chaotic abstract elements and each subject's organized, realistic aspects. He has been creating art his whole life and working on infinitely complex and varied approaches to his paintings for well over a decade.

Donna Krutka

**Illustrator: Andrew Ellingson**

The Desert Saga

# ILLUSTRATIONS

## THE BOSS

Donna Krutka

# JABBERRUNNER

The Desert Saga

# LENNY

Donna Krutka

# DREAD, THE RED-TAILED HAWK

The Desert Saga

## THE DESERT BOBCATS

Donna Krutka

# THE MOUNTAIN LION

Made in the USA
Las Vegas, NV
06 October 2023

78684755R00233